In Fine Feathers

IN FINE FEATHERS

CHARLES GARVICE

WILIDSDE PRESS

Originally published in 1924.
Published by Wildside Press, LLC.
Visit us online at wildsidepress.com.

CHAPTER I

Lord Northbridge sat in the dining-room, alone and pensive. The cloth had been removed; the glittering épergnes holding hot-house fruits, the old English glass, the antique silver, were reflected in the highly polished table. The servants had finished waiting, and had left the room. The hush that prevailed was intense, an almost "tingling silentness." Even the grandfather clock, in its honoured place beside the Chippendale bookcase, seemed to tick with a muffled sound, as if it knew that upstairs someone was battling with death. Many a child had been born in that house, many a life had passed away; the old clock could have told some strange, romantic stories; but it ticked on, marking the seconds which lead from birth to death; and Lord Northbridge, as he listened half unconscious, felt as though it were mechanically murmuring, like the voice of Fate:

"She is dying! She is dying!"

With a resentful movement of his head, he fought against the impression. He told himself that his natural anxiety was getting on his nerves; that, after all, what was happening upstairs was a common thing; that all would be well. But in his ears the clock still seemed to tick the words:

"She is dying! She is dying!"

He got up and took a step or two towards the clock, with the half-formed intention of stopping it; but, with a shamefaced gesture, he went back to the table; then, passed his hand over the fast-silvering hair, as though to brush away the thoughts that lay in the throbbing brain. The suspense was making him nervous. Once he thought he caught the sound of a cry; but after listening intently for a moment, and finding it was not repeated, he tried to think he had been mistaken.

He poured himself out a glass of wine, and had scarcely done so when the door opened to admit the old butler, whose usually impassive face was covered with smiles. In spite of the fact that there was no one else in the room, the man's voice barely rose above a whisper as he bent down and said something to the master.

"Eh, what?" said the earl, bending towards him, while a bright flush lit up his face. "What's that you say?"

Once more the butler spoke, rubbing his hands together with a smile of satisfaction.

A look of quiet happiness came into the eyes of the Earl of Northbridge, and as the old servant turned to leave the room, he said:

"Thompson, I—er—hope you and your fellow-servants will drink the health of Lady Northbridge and—and—Lord Raymond."

"Most willingly, my lord," smiled the old man.

Left to himself, Lord Northbridge rose to his feet, glass in hand, and if anyone had been listening, they would have heard him say, half aloud:

"To my son and heir—God bless him!"

It was a very long time since those words had been uttered in connection with Northbridge Hall. The last three inheritors had either been childless, or bachelors; and it was feared that the property would once more pass into the hands of a distant relative, instead of to a direct descendant; for Lord Northbridge was unmarried, and there seemed no desire on his part to change his state.

Then one day he had brought home a sweet young wife to the Hall, upon whom his whole heart seemed centred. He loved her with the deep, passionate affection of a man whose life has been empty for many years, and who has never learnt to know all that love signifies. People often said that if anything should happen to Lady Northbridge the shock would be almost more than he could bear.

It is a terrible thing to love too intensely; it is apt to incur the jealous anger of the gods, and then they do not spare in their wrathful chastisement. But now it seemed that they were careless of earthly things, for the happiness and love of the Earl of Northbridge had just been crowned by the birth of a son; and he felt he could desire no other treasure from life, if his wife were but granted a complete recovery.

Lord Northbridge pushed back his chair upon the polished boards. He would go up and enquire after his wife; perhaps they might even let him see her. He was so anxious; but he was very happy, too, now that he knew that all was over.

Outside his wife's door he paused, not daring to knock, lest the slightest noise should be prejudicial to her welfare.

"Lucy!" he whispered, hoping she might feel his presence. "Lucy!"

It seemed almost as if they had heard the murmur of his wife's name within the room, for the door opened, and a nurse came out. She did not appear in the least surprised to see him there, and motioned him to follow her along the corridor, so that they might speak without the possibility of the sound reaching the invalid.

"I am glad to be able to tell you that the boy is a fine, strapping little fellow," began the nurse, "and——"

"Yes, yes, nurse; but my wife?" he interrupted, with impatience.

"She is naturally very weak—very weak indeed; but I don't think there is any need for anxiety."

"Can I—can I see her?" asked Lord Northbridge.

"In about half an hour, I think you may. I want to keep her quite quiet for a while; it will hasten her recovery," was the reply.

"Then I will wait as long as ever you wish," he said, eagerly.

"Oh, you may see her in half an hour's time, Lord Northbridge. Please don't be too anxious!"

With that the nurse turned and left him. For a moment Lord Northbridge stood looking after her with a curious, jealous feeling, as he thought that a stranger was allowed to be near his wife, while he who loved her was excluded. Then, with a sigh, he made his way down the wide staircase, to wait, with as much patience as he could summon, until the happy moment when he might see his wife again, after the long hours of anxiety through which he had been passing.

In the great oak bed upstairs, in which Queen Elizabeth was supposed to have slept, on the occasion upon which she visited the Hall during one of her many progresses, lay Lady Northbridge.

She seemed very pale and fragile; but there was that same look of deep happiness upon her face, which had come into her husband's eyes when the old butler had brought him the news of the birth of his son.

By the bedside knelt a healthy-looking country woman, stroking in silent sympathy the white hand that lay outside the counterpane. Presently Lady Northbridge broke the silence.

"Marion," she said, in a faint voice, "I—I want to see my baby."

Instantly the nurse came forward, holding a tiny bundle in her arms, which Marion took from her and placed upon the bed beside its mother. Lady Northbridge drew aside the warm enveloping shawl, and smiled as she looked down upon the tiny pink face within.

"What a quaint little bundle of humanity!" she murmured.

"He's a fine little fellow," answered Marion. "You should be very proud of him, my lady. He's much bigger than my boy, already."

"Oh, I am proud of him—I am indeed," replied Lady Northbridge. "But I was forgetting your baby, Marion. You've been away from him too long; you must go to him; and Marion, has—has my husband been told yet?"

"Yes, my lady," said Marion, with a smile; "and Thompson said he looked as proud and happy as a king; and his lordship told him to ask all the servants to drink the health of your ladyship and the son and heir."

"The son and heir," repeated Lady Northbridge, musingly. "I wonder if I shall live to see him grow up, Marion? Do you know, I feel as if I had dropped out of life altogether, somehow—as if I were just looking on. I—I can't say how it is exactly—I don't know——"

"Hush, my lady, hush!" interrupted Marion, as she saw that Lady Northbridge was beginning to ramble. "You mustn't give way like that. Think of his lordship, my lady, and the little Lord Raymond. You must try and get better quickly, for both their sakes."

"Oh, I know—I know. But if I shouldn't get better, there's no one to look after my boy. There's absolutely no one, I tell you. I'm his mother, you see—I'm his mother."

Lady Northbridge had grown excited, and Marion had great difficulty in soothing her.

"My lady, you know I should look after him like my own, if anything—but nothing *is* going to happen. You're going to get well very quickly now."

The doctor, too, came forward with a word of warning; and when the young mother had grown quieter, he said:

"Lady Northbridge, I should advise you to give your little son to Mrs. Smeaton to be nursed. You are hardly strong enough yourself, and she has professed herself most willing to undertake the charge."

"That is very kind of you, Marion. But, oh, I did want to have my baby all to myself," replied Lady Northbridge, sadly.

"I will take the greatest possible care of him, my lady," answered Marion, quickly.

"Oh, I don't doubt you for a moment, Marion. I trust you implicitly, and I am sure that my baby could be in no better hands."

The door opened, and Lord Northbridge entered the room on tiptoe. He was much older than his wife; but the lines and furrows in his face seemed to have been smoothed away by happiness. Marion and the doctor tactfully withdrew to the other end of the room, leaving husband and wife together.

"Dearest," said Lord Northbridge, tenderly, as he bent down to kiss his wife's fragile hand, "I am so glad—so very glad you are better. I—I want to see my boy."

With a proud smile. Lady Northbridge drew the bed-clothes from the little face; and, gently lifting the tiny morsel from the bed, the earl kissed it tenderly upon the little pink forehead. When he gave it back to its mother, his eyes were glistening suspiciously. "My boy!" was all he said; and then he bent and kissed his young wife, too.

"I am so glad you are pleased, Arthur," she whispered; then, glancing at Marion, she added aloud:

"Marion says he is as big as her baby; and he is a month old, you know."

Lord Northbridge turned with a kind smile, as Marion came to the bedside.

"Ah, Marion, I had forgotten your little son. He is going on well, I hope?"

"The children are to be foster-brothers, Arthur," said Lady Northbridge.

For the fraction of a moment a shadow seemed to creep into her husband's face. Then the doctor crossed the room to his side.

"Lady Northbridge is hardly strong enough, my lord, to have charge of the child."

"I see, I see," replied the earl. "We must, of course, consider Lady Northbridge in every possible way."

He bent once more to kiss his wife's hand, and as his eyes met hers they were full of ineffable love and tenderness. "I am glad to see you better, dearest," he said. "I have missed you so much."

Lady Northbridge looked very pale, now that the excitement of her husband's coming had passed away.

"Take me in your arms, Arthur," she whispered. "I feel I could sleep there."

The doctor motioned Lord Northbridge to do as his wife desired; and Marion took up the child from the bed, so that it should not disturb its mother's rest. She crept into the dressing-room adjoining, and, as she did so, she heard Lady Northbridge murmur:

"Arthur dear, I am so tired—so very tired."

A lump came into Marion's throat as she looked down at the bundle she carried in her arms.

"God grant she may live, little one," she prayed silently; for she was fully aware that the doctor was somewhat anxious about the young mother's condition.

The child awoke and began to cry; but Marion managed to soothe it to sleep once more.

After a time she fancied she caught the sound of sudden movements in the next room, followed by a muffled cry. Marion, however, still sat with the sleeping child in her arms thinking they would come and call her if she were wanted, and fearing to intrude, lest she might awaken Lady Northbridge, should she be asleep.

Presently she caught the murmur of voices, and the closing of a door. A few moments later the doctor entered the room, and Marion immediately saw by the look on his face that something was wrong. Before she could question him, however, he said in a low voice:

"I very much regret to tell you, Mrs. Smeaton, that Lady Northbridge died from heart failure a quarter of an hour ago."

A month later, one afternoon after lunch, a car drove up to the Hall, and into it there stepped, dressed in deep black, the Earl of Northbridge. Terribly affected by the death of his wife, he had scarcely shown himself since the day of the funeral, but now urgent business called him up to London. His boy was left in the care of Marion Smeaton, his devoted nurse, but Marion was perturbed at the moment by the ill-health of her own little son. A day or two later he was worse, and as it was expected that the earl would be away for a fortnight at least, and as the staff of servants at the Hall had been greatly reduced, so that there was no one of importance to thwart her, Marion, pretending that leave had been given her, resolved on her own responsibility to take Lord Raymond with her to her own cottage—if it was only for a day or two. And so it came to pass that the son and heir of Lord Northbridge, in the care of his nurse, for the first time quitted his ancestral home.

CHAPTER II

Marion Smeaton's cottage stood on the edge of Metherston Common, a bleak stretch of moorland bordering the woods round Northbridge Hall.

Although the conditions that suited gipsies were constantly diminishing, even in those days, yet the common still afforded, as it had done from time immemorial, a convenient camping-ground for any who chanced to pass through the neighbourhood, and the surrounding property suffered in consequence. So there had naturally been much comment among the villagers when Marion—Lady Northbridge's favourite maid—had married one of their number.

Luke Smeaton was tall, swarthy, and dark-haired, with true gipsy eyes and instincts. He had neither respectability nor prospects; and to all intents and purposes supported himself and Marion by desultory periods of wood-chopping. He did not ill-use his wife, as gossip asserted; but he had intimated early that he expected obedience as well as affection, and that it would be wiser if she did not evince a desire to pry too closely into his personal affairs.

A month after his marriage, Luke Smeaton had built a hut some yards away from his cottage, and a few days later an old woman, supposed to be his mother, had taken possession of it. There she had remained, sustaining existence as best she could, aided in no small measure by Marion's generosity, and the charity of the villagers.

The day after her departure from the Hall, Marion Smeaton was seated at the latticed window of her cottage, nursing her little charge. Every now and then she stepped noiselessly to an inner room, to satisfy herself that her own child was sleeping.

It was early in June; and the setting sun lit up the dark furze bushes on the common with a crimson glow.

Looking dreamily out across the moor, Marion became aware of a small crowd of men and horses making their way towards the cottage. She rose, and wrapping the sleeping child in a shawl, went to the open door, shading her eyes with her hand that she might see more distinctly. As they came nearer, Marion saw once more the sight she knew so well—a gipsy tribe, with its usual crowd of half-naked children and string of caravans.

With an exclamation of disgust she closed the door and reseated herself; for she disliked her husband's connections exceedingly.

Ten minutes passed; and then there came a sharp, but subdued knock at the door.

"Come in," said Marion; and the door opened slowly, admitting a ragged, sunburnt gipsy. He nodded lazily, and glancing round the room, said in a tone of interrogation:

"Luke?"

"He's out," replied Marion, in a low voice.

"Where?" asked the gipsy.

Marion hesitated. She knew well enough, but was afraid to say. "I—I don't know exactly. Do you want him?"

"I don't," he replied; "but Zera does."

"Very well," said Marion, rising; for she knew that Luke would not dare to loiter when so powerful a personage as the gipsy queen required him. "Go back and tell her that my husband will come directly. I'll go and find him."

The man nodded, and, without a word, left the cottage. As the door closed behind him, Marion crept on tiptoe to the adjoining room. Satisfied that her child was likely to sleep some hours, if undisturbed, she drew the shawl closer round the sleeping form in her arms, and, locking the door of the cottage, walked down the path that led to the Northbridge woods.

Looking cautiously round, to ascertain that no one was about, she drew a whistle from the folds of her dress, and blew it softly once or twice. She waited for some few minutes; and then made her way to the hut that Luke had built for old Martha. She knocked at the door, and, without waiting for it to be answered, lifted the latch and entered. The room was almost in darkness; and as Martha rose from a seat in the corner and hobbled towards her, Marion could not help shuddering at the uncanny spectacle.

"Be it ye, Marion?" she croaked.

"Yes; I'm seeking for Luke."

The old woman nodded.

"I've whistled twice, and can't hear his answer," continued Marion, from the doorway. "I think he must be in the hollow among the ferns."

"Most like," said Martha. "Who's a-wanting him?"

"Zera. The tribe have just come on to the common."

"He'd better be after going, then," replied the old woman, with more interest.

"He can't go if he doesn't know she wants him," returned Marion, impatiently. "I think I'll go down to the hollow, and look for him. Oh, but I can't," she added, quickly, as her eyes fell upon the sleeping child in her arms. "I can't take the little lord there. The bushes would very likely scratch his face."

"Give him to me, then," said Martha, sharply.

"To you? Oh no—I'd rather not—I mean I shouldn't like to trouble you."

"Trouble!" sneered the old woman. "Ye're afraid. Ye think as ye're the only one as can nurse an earl's brats. Ye're mighty proud o' yerself, I must say. Ye forgets as I nursed children long before ye were a-thought of. Ye'd better be half give it to me and find Luke."

Marion hesitated a moment; then, with the suddenness of desperation, she laid the child in Martha's arms.

Luke was not in the hollow; and, having come thus far, Marion determined to go up to the village, and enquire for him at the "Blue Peacock." She was half-way there when she heard her name called.

"How's your charge, Mrs. Smeaton?" said a voice; and Marion looked up to find the Northbridge doctor's *locum tenens* at her side. He was a young man, and Marion did not particularly care about him, for he was secretly addicted to drink.

But since Dr. Walton was in charge during his colleague's serious illness, she had to answer to him in the absence of Lord Northbridge and Dr. Simmons for the well-being of the earl's son.

"Little Lord Raymond is very well, thank you. Doctor," she replied; "but my own boy is still ailing. Perhaps you would call in to-morrow?"

Doctor Walton thought a moment. "I may be able to manage it to-night, perhaps. I'll see, anyway."

Marion thanked him; and hastily made her way to the "Blue Peacock." Her husband was there, as she had expected, and, after delivering her message, she returned more leisurely to the hut. As she neared it she fancied she heard the child crying, and quickened her steps. The door was open; and as she stood upon the threshold, Marion's heart stood still with fear. Martha was holding the motionless figure of the child in her lap as Doctor Walton bent over it.

Choking back the hysteria that threatened to overwhelm her, Marion staggered into the room.

"What—what has happened?" she asked, hoarsely.

"It was a fit," said the doctor, gravely. "It was not Martha's fault. Nothing could have prevented it. I passed the place a few minutes after I met you, Mrs. Smeaton, and heard the child cry. It's hard that your child should be taken; but you must be brave, for there's still Lord Northbridge's son to be thought of."

Marion started, and stared at him; but he was bending over the child, and did not notice her. Then her eyes wandered to old Martha's face, with its cunning leer.

"Doctor," Marion said, suddenly, "it is a mis——"

"Misfortune," interrupted the old woman. "Don't be a fool, Marion. Other people have lost their brats beside you, and not made such a fuss about it. It was no fault of mine, nor yours. If the other had gone, he'd 'a' lost a coronet, and a'a broken up the earl altogether. Goodness knows he's had enough to bear, what with the death of his young wife, an' all."

The subtle emphasis she threw into the last words made Marion sick and giddy. If Lord Northbridge knew that his son was dead, the shock might kill him.

Hitherto he had not been able to bear the sight of the child, whose birth had taken from him the wife he had idolized. But what would he say to her if he knew she had been careless enough to leave it with an old gipsy woman, and that it had died whilst in her care? Supposing old Martha had—but no, Doctor Walton had himself said that the child's death was due to natural causes. Yet was Doctor Walton a responsible person? He was scarcely in a fit state to give a sound medical opinion. His hands were trembling, and his eyes were bleared. What should she do?

Sick with fear and uncertainty, Marion could only repeat the question; and, after what seemed like years of agony, she heard Doctor Walton say, somewhat thickly, though his tone was sympathetic:

"My poor girl, I think you'd better take the little one home. Don't fret about it any more than you can help. I should advise you to take your charge up to the Hall, and stay there, as Lord Northbridge will be back in a week at least."

He wrapped the tiny body in an old blanket, and placing it in Marion's arms, supported her down the path to her cottage. There he left her, and, promising to send a certificate of death on the following day, went away.

Marion laid the child in the empty cradle by the window, and, kneeling down, burst into dry, choking sobs. Into the midst of her agony there came from the inner room a peevish cry; and rising hastily to her feet, she went to fetch her son. With a savage tenderness she clasped him to her, and had almost determined to go to the doctor and confess the truth, when the door opened, and her husband entered the cottage.

"Are ye mad?" he said, in his deep, guttural voice.

"Nearly," she replied, bitterly; and with one hand drew him to the cradle.

He muttered an oath, and bent down. "Dead!" he said, sharply. Then he glanced at the child in her arms. "My lady's, isn't it?"

"Yes," replied Marion, avoiding his eye.

"H'm! Hard luck on the old earl. He's not likely to have another child. The Hall 'ull go begging. Ye're in for it now, my girl—they'll say ye did it on purpose. Here, let's look at the kid"; and bending down he took the body of Lord Northbridge's son from the cradle. He carried it to the window, and holding up a small oil lamp that Marion had hastily lighted scanned the tiny features. "The two kids are awfully alike!" he muttered.

Suddenly he started, then threw back his head and laughed. With unsteady fingers he drew the blanket round the motionless form in his arms, and stumbled to the door.

"I be going to take it to Martha's," he said, thickly.

"No, Luke, you're not to. She can't do anything," Marion replied, quickly.

"No matter," said her husband, calmly. "Stop here till I come back."

Before she could prevent his going, he had opened the door of the cottage, and Marion heard his heavy footsteps on the dusty road. An hour later he returned. He was in excellent spirits, and had apparently again visited the "Blue Peacock."

"I've got the stuff for the coffin," he said, somewhat jocularly; "and now I'll give ye a piece of advice."

Marion looked at him fixedly for a moment. "If Martha's been influencing you to hide the truth from Lord Northbridge, you'd better save your breath, Luke, and not tell me what you're going to do. I'm going to find Doctor Walton, and tell him he made a mistake about the children."

Luke stared at her for a moment in amazement.

"Oh, no, ye don't," he said, brutally. "Ye wouldn't like it to be said as Marion Smeaton murdered——"

"You dog!" she said, between her clenched teeth. "You——"

"Here, chuck that," he said, good-humouredly. "It amounts to that; ye weren't with it when it died—they'd say ye neglected it."

Without a word Marion rose from the chair, and going into the inner room laid her child upon the bed, closed the door, and returned to her husband.

"You dare to say that again," she said, with suppressed passion.

"I do," he retorted; and he lit his clay pipe and began to smoke with quiet enjoyment. "And what's more, it would save a deal o' time if ye listened to what I be a-going to tell ye, and not interrupt at every turn. Our child died to-night, d'ye understand? I say our child died to-night," he repeated, in a louder tone; "and if ye dare to say as he didn't, I'll kill ye. D'ye hear?"

All Marion's nerve seemed to be slipping from her; and, clutching hold of the mantelpiece for support, she buried her face in her hands.

"Oh, God!" she moaned.

Luke Smeaton looked at her with contemptuous eyes, and coming up behind her, he said, coolly:

"Old Doctor Simmons died this evening, and the earl's just left London for the Continent, I'm told, and won't be back just yet. The child in the other room is the heir of Northbridge; so now ye know!"

CHAPTER III

In the wide embrasure of a window at Dartworth Manor, one beautiful morning in spring, stood the tall figure of a girl. The lower portion of the window was thrown open, letting in all the glory of light and sweet-breathed air, and the noisy cawing of rooks in the trees close by. The upper portion was immovable, however; and through the stained glass the sunlight fell upon the girl's fair hair and pallid face, so that it looked like the pictured head of a saint—sweet, ineffably tender, hoping all things, believing all things.

There was a rumour that the warm friendship which had existed for so long between the families of the Manor and Northbridge Hall would soon be still further cemented by a marriage between the Hon. Veronica Dartworth and Lord Raymond. But with whatever feelings the parents on either side might have viewed such an arrangement, the young people themselves had as yet given no tangible support to the rumour.

Lord Raymond, it was true, seemed too intent upon himself and his own welfare to give much thought to anyone else. He was exceedingly selfish by nature, and as utterly unlike either his father or his dead mother in temperament as he was in appearance. He was usually silent, sometimes to sullenness, and was so observant of everything and everybody that the intensity of his gaze was often unpleasant to new acquaintances. He was swarthy in appearance, and might have been considered handsome had he not been so much addicted to a life of dissipation. This gave an unhealthy pallor to his skin, and a puffiness about the eyes far from prepossessing.

He had just passed his majority, but looked much older; while Veronica was just twenty, and as yet only dimly conscious of the fact that it was her parents' wish that she should marry the dissolute heir of Northbridge. For Lord and Lady Dartworth it must be said, however, that they were neither of them aware of the true facts of Lord Raymond's life; they only remembered that he was the idolized son of their best and oldest friend.

Veronica was turning from the window with the intention of going to her room to don her habit, preparatory to her morning gallop, when the door opened and Lady Dartworth entered.

"Why, Veronica, I've been looking for you everywhere!" she exclaimed. "Lord Northbridge has asked us to dine there to-night."

Veronica's eyelids drooped, and a slight shade of annoyance, or reserve, passed across her face.

"But, mother, Cousin Judy is coming," she said.

"Yes, Lord Northbridge knows that, for he asks us to bring her with us."

"Do you want to go?" asked Veronica.

"Yes, dear, of course," replied Lady Dartworth. "I think Judy would like it, too. It would be a nice change for her. Besides, your father never can refuse an invitation to Northbridge."

"Then let us go by all means," said Veronica, carelessly, making a movement towards the door.

Lady Dartworth stopped her.

"Where are you going, Veronica? Geoffrey is in the library with your father."

"I don't expect he wants to see me very much, mother. I was just going to get ready for my ride," replied the girl.

"But you will see him before you go, won't you?" asked Lady Dartworth, somewhat surprised.

"No, I don't think so, if you don't mind, mother. I've got a headache, and hardly feel up to visitors this morning."

Lady Dartworth did not quite understand her daughter's avoidance of Lord Raymond, but pretended not to notice it.

"Very well, my dear," she said, with a tender smile. "I'll tell him you've gone riding. Perhaps he'll only stay a very short time."

As Lady Dartworth sat down at a writing-table to reply to Lord Northbridge's invitation, Veronica left the room; and ten minutes later, from the drawing-room window, Lord Raymond saw her graceful figure disappear round a bend in the drive.

"Isn't that Veronica riding down the drive?" he asked.

"Eh?" said Lord Dartworth, moving to the window and peering out, but, of course, seeing no one, since Veronica was by now quite out of sight. "I'm sure I don't know."

"Yes, it is Veronica," replied Lady Dartworth, who had joined her husband. "She has a bad headache, and begged me to give you her kindest remembrances, Geoffrey."

Lord Raymond made no reply, but continued to look out of the window so that the expression of his face was not seen, for it had grown dark at the fancied slight. He bit his lip to control the angry words which came so readily to him, and looked more unprepossessing than usual; although, when he presently turned to Lady Dartworth, his expression was masked by his usual set smile.

"Well, how is it to be about to-night? I hope you're coming. The guv'nor will be terribly cut up if you don't."

"We shall be most happy to come," replied Lady Dartworth. "I've written to Lord Northbridge to say that we shall be glad to bring Miss Slade with us."

"That's all right, then," rejoined Raymond. "Until to-night, Lady Dartworth —good-bye, sir."

With the frown once more scoring deep creases upon his forehead, Lord Raymond left the house, and with something like an oath sprang upon his horse's back. He dug his spurs into the animal's side and, with never a nod or look at the groom, rode away.

"Did ye see 'im?" asked the man, with an air of disgust. "I call it right down low-bred and vicious, I do. Thank Gawd I ain't that 'oss—that's what I ses, and I ses it with all my 'eart." From this it will be seen that Lord Raymond was not a man to be popular with many of the people he met during his walk through life.

On this beautiful morning when God's green earth was sweet with the promise of summer, Lord Raymond seemed utterly out of place. He used his spurs unmercifully, until, panting and fevered, the poor brute at last drew up at Northbridge Hall. A groom came forward and took the horse under his charge; and Lord Raymond slouched up the steps, his face like a thunder-cloud.

"Confound the proud monkey!" he muttered. "I'll teach her how to insult me —dash her impudence!"

Meanwhile, Veronica took her morning ride with deep thankfulness in her heart, which she did not express in words even to herself, because she had escaped an interview with Lord Raymond.

Through the elm-woods of Dartworth ran a bridle-path which Veronica often used, since it was her favourite ride; and usually she met no one, save an occasional keeper; for trespassing was strictly prohibited. This morning, however, was an exception to the rule, and Veronica brought her horse to a standstill, for through the shady arches floated strains of sweet and haunting music. It was as though the Spirit of the Wood had awakened after many years, and was sobbing out its heart—there under the green leaves and low-hung branches—in a harmonious melody that pulled for pity at the very heart-strings.

Veronica sat her horse absolutely spellbound, for the moment thinking she must be dreaming. The music throbbed on, and at the sad, almost barbaric mournfulness, that broke into a shimmer of echoes through the wood, a lump rose in her throat and she felt her eyes grow dim.

Suddenly through the trees she saw the figure of a man approaching, apparently so absorbed in his violin that he did not notice her. His tall figure was swaying to the time of the music that he drew from his instrument, and his face was as wistful as the sweet, throbbing melody.

Veronica hastily brushed her hand across her eyes, for she was angry that a rather shabby stranger should have had the power to move her so. That same moment, almost within a few paces of her, the man looked up, and his eyes met hers. Instantly his music ceased, and he put the violin under his arm, as though fearing that Veronica might have designs upon it.

"Do you know you are trespassing?" asked the girl, coldly.

The stranger raised his cap—of a curious pattern of scarlet cloth—from his head, disclosing a crop of crisp brown hair curling about his ears. His grey eyes looked steadily up into the girl's face as he answered her question; and for a moment she forgot her anger in curiosity, as she saw that he was a well-built, handsome fellow.

"Trespassing!" he repeated, in a voice which, while it bore the hall-mark of education, had a soft "burr" that was far from unpleasing. "Indeed no, lady; I did not know it. I came to find a quiet spot where I could play my music, and, unaware that I was trespassing, I entered these woods."

Veronica's anger had altogether vanished; but she still made a show of it for the sake of appearance.

"You are trespassing. You must have climbed the fence. How else could you have entered the woods?" she asked.

"Why, yes; I had forgotten," replied the man, with something like a start. "There was a low fence, and I jumped over it without thinking. Believe me, I had forgotten the fact, lady."

Veronica was more than ever puzzled and interested by the intruder's manner and educated speech.

"There are plenty of boards on the trees and fences warning trespassers," she said, after a pause.

"I did not see them, lady," was the answer. "But, excuse or no excuse, I am trespassing, and I beg your pardon."

With a polite inclination of the head, he donned his cap, and turned to leave her.

"Wait a minute!" said Veronica, suspiciously. "What is your name?"

"Tazoni," he answered, proudly, his hand resting on his side—apparently an habitual pose. "I live on the common yonder," he added, with a gesture towards the moor.

"You are a gipsy, then?" said Veronica, with surprise and disappointment.

"Yes, lady," he replied, looking up at her as his quick ears caught the curious intonation of her words.

The girl gathered up her bridle, which she had let fall upon her horse's neck while they talked; and there was a resumption of her former anger in her eyes, as she said:

"Well, you cannot plead ignorance of your offence any longer. I hope you won't venture to repeat it. Lord Dartworth dislikes all gipsies. You've done his property a great deal of harm——"

"Pardon, lady," the man interrupted, quietly. "You do us an injustice. The small company over which I am the master has never injured Lord Dartworth's, nor any other man's property. Therefore, having as yet done you no real injury, you have no right to thrust your hatred and contempt in our faces."

Then he turned and left her, and for a moment after he had gone Veronica sat her horse as motionless as a statue. Her pride—of which, without doubt, she possessed a great deal—pride of self and pride of family—had received a set-back by the calmness of a gipsy; and for a moment she felt that she hated this low-born man, who had dared to reprove one of such superior rank and station.

Nevertheless, as she rode slowly homewards, Veronica's thoughts were full of a pair of grey eyes; and she could not help wondering how he, who was no more than a vagabond gipsy, though he spoke like an educated person, could have interested her so much.

CHAPTER IV

"I am so glad you have come!" said Lord Northbridge that evening, as he shook hands with Lady Dartworth and Veronica; "and it was extremely kind of you to come, too, Miss Slade, after such a long and trying journey."

Miss Slade was aptly described by her acquaintances as "the little brown mouse." Whatever clothes she wore, she always seemed to give one the impression of being a study in brown; and she had funny little "ways" which made her rather amusing, since she was clever enough to know just the point at which to drop them. Undoubtedly she was clever, for she always gave the impression of being a soft, harmless creature, while, as a matter of fact, she was a power to be reckoned with, though very few had been sharp enough to find this out.

"I was only too delighted to come," she answered, in her soft voice. "I am not the least bit tired, thank you."

"That's right; I'm glad to hear it," replied her host. Then he turned to speak to Veronica and Lord Dartworth; but chivalrous as he was, and although he had spoken to Miss Slade for no more than a second, he could not help feeling that there was something about her which he did not altogether like, though what it was he could not tell. He put the thought from him instantly, remembering only that he was her host, and that she was a relative of his dearest friends.

Presently the door opened, and Lord Raymond entered the room.

"I'm late, I suppose," he said, going up to Lady Dartworth, but making no apology for the fact he openly confessed. He glanced at Miss Slade while he bent over Lady Dartworth's hand, for during her former visits to the Manor he had been from home. With Veronica he was extremely sullen; but she always made it a rule to ignore his moods entirely.

"Geoffrey, I want to introduce you to my cousin, Miss Slade," said Lady Dartworth; and, as Lord Raymond acknowledged the introduction, he regarded Judy with the fixed stare that disconcerted many. Then he took a seat beside her, as he made up his mind that at any rate she looked interesting. Even if she were not as pretty as her cousin, he argued to himself, at least she would serve his purpose; for he had quickly made up his mind to play off Judy Slade against Veronica, in order to show the girl who had snubbed him on so many occasions that he did not care a fig for her favour.

Judy Slade was quick enough to see his intention, for he did not trouble to hide the glances he threw in Veronica's direction; but Miss Slade had her own cards to play, and fully intended to play them for all that they were worth. At dinner, Lord Raymond paid her special attention, while he almost neglected Veronica, who was seated at his right.

"Have you heard that we've got some gipsies camping up on the common?" asked Lord Northbridge, turning to Veronica, during a pause in the conversation.

The girl, who had been unusually silent, smiled thoughtfully, as she said:

"From your tone it doesn't seem as if you're prepared to give them a hearty welcome, Lord Northbridge."

"Oh, they're the biggest rogues and thieves living; and you can never get the best of them: though, thank goodness, they are dying out of late years."

"Are they all alike?" asked Veronica, curiously interested in the subject.

"Well——" hesitated Lord Northbridge.

But Raymond turned from a remark of Miss Slade's, and broke in upon the conversation in his usual abrupt fashion.

"All alike?" he exclaimed. "Of course they are. Gipsies are vermin; and if I had my way, I'd shoot 'em down like dogs."

A shade of annoyance crossed his father's face.

"That is rather a sweeping condemnation, Geoffrey," he said, in his low, well-bred voice, which formed so great a contrast to the harsh tones of his son. "They're not all alike, if the truth must be told. There are good ones amongst them here and there."

"But they must be rogues to live," answered Lord Raymond, setting down his glass.

"Not necessarily," said Lord Dartworth. "A gipsy is a clever fellow, and often very much sought after."

"Have you ever employed them?" asked Veronica of her father.

"Yes," he replied, "most certainly I have. The park fences were made by a gipsy tribe; and I think you must own that they are very well made, too, Northbridge?"

"Oh, yes, very," replied his host. "But I'm afraid you wouldn't like to tell us how much that act of good-feeling cost you in the shape of poultry and sheep."

"I never lost a sheep or a head of poultry during the whole time they were employed," said Lord Dartworth, emphatically.

In Veronica's shadowy brown eyes there was something more than ordinary interest, as she asked:

"Father, do you remember any of their names?"

"No, my dear," replied her father. "It's a long time now—I expect they've died out, or become scattered."

"Or the whole lot of 'em have been nabbed, and put into gaol for thieving, most likely," broke in Lord Raymond, rudely.

"That I'm sure I couldn't tell you," replied Lord Dartworth, blandly. "To judge from what little I knew of them, I should scarcely imagine such to be the case. By the way," he added to his host, "wasn't Luke Smeaton—Marion's husband—formerly a gipsy?"

Lord Northbridge's face saddened a little, as it always did at the mention of any one or anything connected with his dead wife.

"Yes, Smeaton was a gipsy, I believe. He has been a sad trouble to his wife, anyway, although she hasn't heard from him for over a year. He seems to turn up at odd times, and then disappear in the same sudden way."

"How is Marion now?" asked Lady Dartworth.

"I'm afraid she will never be any better," Lord Northbridge answered, sadly.

"What do they think is really the matter with her?" asked Lord Dartworth.

"Extreme nervous debility," replied Lord Northbridge. "Ever since she lost her child, she has been afflicted by a most extraordinary depression, and the doctors say there is no cure whatever for it."

"It is certainly curious," remarked Lord Dartworth. "I suppose the doctors ought to know their own business best; but one would imagine that something might be done for the poor woman."

"She has had the very best advice, but nothing has seemed to do her any good. Some doctors ordered her change of air; but she always gets worse when she is away from Northbridge."

"I can't stand the woman!" said Lord Raymond, harshly; "she simply gives me the creeps. Whenever I run up against her, she starts and stares, and then begins crying; or, if she doesn't, her face is enough to upset you for a week."

Lady Dartworth hastened to change the subject; but chancing to glance across at Judy Slade, Lord Raymond found her eyes fixed upon him in silent comprehension, although she said nothing; and he got the impression—as indeed she meant that he should—that she alone of the party understood him, although he had only known her so short a time.

Nevertheless, when the men joined the ladies in the drawing-room, Geoffrey crossed at once to Veronica, the wine he had drunk having somewhat quenched his resentment. His face was flushed and his eyes restless; for a very little wine tended to excite him, and he never knew when it was wise to stop.

Veronica, who had been talking to Lady Northbridge, looked up as he approached, and a slight flush of dislike and displeasure at his heated appearance stained her usually pale face. He stood a moment biting his thumb-nail, and looking down at her with a somewhat rude stare; then he drew a chair to her side, and sat down.

"I say, Vee," he said, using the name he alone applied to her, and which she hated accordingly, "what made you ride off this morning, when you jolly well knew I was in the house?"

Veronica hesitated in her reply, half-tempted to tell him the truth.

"I sent you word that I had a headache, and thought a ride might do it good," she answered, casually.

"That's the truth, I suppose?" he said, with a discourteous suspicion. "You know, I thought you did it to get out of my way; and that just riled me, I can tell you. It was enough to make any fellow wild, wasn't it?"

Veronica made no reply, for in a moment it flashed across her mind how much she hated this man, who in every way showed himself such a contrast to others of his race.

"Of course I was wild," Lord Raymond continued; "and I meant you to see I was. That was the reason why I wouldn't speak to you all through dinner. I guess it riled you a bit, didn't it, Vee?"

"No, I can't say that it did," replied Veronica, quietly, with that intense scorn which is too contemptuous to openly proclaim itself.

"Well, you only *say* so," he answered, with an incredulous sneer; "you wouldn't own it, naturally. No girl would, I suppose; and you're too proud, anyway. I say—suppose we make it up, and you sing that dreamy sort of song I liked so much the other night."

"If you ask Judy, she'll sing you something you'll like much better than my German songs," answered Veronica, not very willing to oblige him.

"Well, I jolly well guess I will. You're too disagreeable to sing, I suppose. Anyway, your cousin looks a decent sort; I'll go and ask her."

Judy Slade had been covertly watching the pair, and quickly saw that they were not on the very best of terms with each other.

"I say, Miss Slade, I've come to ask you to sing—Vee won't; she's too disagreeable," said Lord Raymond, as he came over to her.

"Oh, how unkind!" answered Judy, with a smile, though Geoffrey thought she looked across at Veronica somewhat reproachfully, a belief which sent her up a good deal in his estimation. "What would you like?" she asked, softly, as she walked over to the piano. "Italian Opera—Musical Comedy——?"

"By Jove, yes!" exclaimed Lord Raymond, as he stood leaning over the piano. "Let's have something out of 'The Twilight of Love.' You've seen it, I suppose? Ripping, isn't it?"

Judy Slade's gifts were of the popularly versatile order; and she greatly pleased Lord Raymond by playing to him selections from most of the successful comedies which he cared to ask for.

"I say, I do think you're a sport," he said to her later, when the Dartworths were saying good night. "We'll have some ripping times, I guess, while you're down here."

"I hope so," replied Judy, casually, careful not to infuse too much warmth into her good night to him, seeing that Lady Dartworth's eyes were upon them.

That night, when the maid deputed to wait upon her had brushed out Miss Slade's hair, and helped her into a dainty dressing-wrapper of silk and lace, Judy sat down at an escritoire and began to write a letter. She wrote quickly, for she had been preparing it while she sat before her looking-glass; and when it was finished she did not trouble to read it through. This fact was characteristic of her: she invariably thought out beforehand her plan of action, and when it was accomplished, gave herself no chance either for regret or hesitation.

"DEAR OLD HUBERT," she wrote, "I sincerely hope this will catch you before you go north, for you have got to change your plans altogether—it will be worth your while.

"Didn't you tell me you knew Raymond—Lord Northbridge's son? I suppose you could get an invitation to his place, couldn't you? I have already mentioned Veronica Dartworth to you; and since you were 'cute enough to cram Debrett from cover to cover, when you were young, you will be fully aware of her position.

"It is rumoured that she *may* marry Lord Raymond.

"This, however, I do not intend she shall do—not if I can in any way prevent it. It would be a tremendous pity to throw them away on each other, when you and I stand in such urgent need of increasing our slender incomes.

"These few remarks will, I am sure, give you a clue to the little game I have on hand. When you come, I will explain more fully. I think I know you well enough to be aware that you are not likely to let the grass grow under your feet.

"Au revoir, then.

"JUDY."

This curious letter was carefully folded and put into an envelope addressed to

"HUBERT DENVILLE, Esq.,
"The Barbarian Club,
"Piccadilly, W."

CHAPTER V

On Metherston Common four caravans were drawn up, a pitiable remnant of the tribe which twenty-two years before had camped almost upon that very spot.

Two brown-looking tents also formed part of the encampment, though they were set a little apart from the caravans. The flap of one of the tents was fastened back, and beside it stood a camp-stool and a vessel of water. A leopard-skin, that had seen better days, lay spread out upon the ground in front of the tent, upon which Tazoni lay, his face turned towards the fire.

Above, the moon shone down in clear, cold splendour, which rendered the gipsy forms about the fire mere grotesque shadows. But Tazoni did not heed them, for his mind was full of a girl's face in a misty setting of golden hair, with soft brown eyes that were a very pool of shadows. She was proud, and she had scorned both him and his people; but she was none the less fair for that. She had looked down into his eyes—looked his heart away—and now he could do nothing but dream that he was no longer a poor gipsy, but some prince of great fame and fortune, who humbly ventured to ask her to marry him.

Presently the bitter disenchantment of unreality came to him. It was time he put these dreams away from him, he told himself. What good could possibly come of it all?—since Fate had allotted to him the destiny of a vagabond, and *she* —she was one of God's angels upon earth; and therefore he had no right to think of her, save as the pleasant dream of an hour, born at the same moment as the spring sunshine, the flowers, the birds, the perfumes of God's earth—and Love! But still his thoughts continued to revolve in this circle of futile question and bitter answer.

A girl, on the verge of a beautiful womanhood, emerged from the second tent, and with a swift, graceful tread approached the rug upon which Tazoni lay. She was a handsome specimen of her kind, with a softly tinted olive skin, regular features, oval face, and hands and feet curiously small as befits those of true gipsy blood. As a contrast to most of her kind, however, her forehead was high, and like all gipsies she had beautiful teeth. Her large eyes were shadowed by long, drooping lashes, which gave them a half-dreamy, half-melancholy expression.

For a moment she stood looking down upon Tazoni in silence, her hand on her hip in just the same attitude that Veronica had noticed in the man on the previous morning.

"Dreaming, Tazoni? What are your thoughts? They seem troubled, and I would ease you of their burden?"

Her teeth flashed white beneath the curve of her mouth, as the quaint Romany words fell from her lips. Tazoni raised himself upon his elbow, and took her hand.

"Little sister," he said, softly, "when the moon is full, a man will think upon a woman—a woman, perhaps, of a man; but the man will think the hardest, for he has been given the power to love most."

"No, you are wrong; you are wrong," she whispered, and her eyes sought his face in the half-darkness; but he fell back into his original position upon the leopard-skin, and between the moonlight and the half-light from the camp-fire she could not see its expression.

"And you," she asked after a moment, "you are thinking of a woman, too?"

This was a thought that made her heart beat fast for a moment, and she could not understand why; but when his answer came back to her, she grew calm again, and wondered why she had felt a sense of something like fear at his words.

"Maya, little sister," he said, "in my books I read of many women, and I ponder to myself what they would be like if they were flesh and blood like you and me."

"Then—then the woman you were thinking of so deeply, so sadly, was only a dream-woman after all?" she asked, wonderingly.

"Yes—she is only a dream to me, little sister," he answered, after a pause, during which his lips grew straight suddenly. "She can never be anything but a dream to me—that is why I am sad."

Had he chanced to be looking up into her face, he would have seen a smile of quiet contentment resting upon her lips.

"I am glad she is only a dream-woman," she said, softly.

Tazoni turned his head sharply towards her.

"Why?" he asked, with a curious abruptness, which she was too absorbed to notice. Then he sat up and made room for her on the rug, as he added more gently: "What made you say that, Maya?"

"Indeed, I don't know. I would not like you to care for anyone but me," she answered, in such a bright manner that he could not guess that for one moment she had been jealous of him.

"Of course, I shall not, little sister," said Tazoni, tenderly pressing her hand. "You will always come first, I hope."

"Always?" she persisted.

"Naturally," he replied, trying to evade a question which he could not answer truthfully. "Maya," he added, suddenly, "when do we move from here?"

"That is for you to say," she returned. "Are you weary of the place already?"

"No, you are wrong—it is not for me to decide whether we shall go or stay," he answered, ignoring her question.

"But you are the master," said Maya.

"No, I am only your lieutenant," he replied, with a smile.

"I don't know what that means," said the girl, quietly; "neither do the rest. You are our master, Tazoni."

"Do you remember, Maya," Tazoni said, suddenly, "the night Zera, your mother, died, how they came from many long miles to see her, as she lay in the tent yonder—men and women of many trades—often unsuspected gipsies—from far distances? I was just a thoughtless boy then; but I could not resist a feeling of enthusiasm, when I realized that it was the secret unity and brotherliness of our race that had kept them always apart from the Gentiles, even though, to all appearances, they had been absorbed into them."

He broke off with a sigh; for to-night he realized that to be a gipsy meant to be outcast by all the world—an outcast from the being who typified that world for him.

Anxious to raise his spirits, Maya took up the subject at the point at which he had dropped it.

"And do you remember," she said, "how—on the night my mother died—it was decided that I, being of her blood, should take her place; and how I refused because I said a man should have a man for a master?"

He bent his head for answer; and she, stirred to enthusiasm by the memory of that night, continued:

"Oh, how the men shouted when they knew it was you I was speaking of; and they knew I was right. You were very modest, Tazoni, and resisted a long time; but when the men came and asked you themselves, you gave in. I think you should have given in when I asked you," she added, laughingly.

"I will tell you now, Maya, why I felt I could not give in at the first. I had made a resolution, from which I thought nothing could keep me. You remember I was always dissatisfied, always restless. Colin said once that I was only half a gipsy; and I had grown to believe that he was right. That very night I had determined to leave the camp."

"To leave the camp!" repeated the girl, almost inaudibly; and a sudden flush, which, however, he did not see, swept over her face.

"Maya dear," said Tazoni, sadly, "forgive me if what I say appears to be a wrong against you and my own people; but it always seemed to me that a gipsy was a term of reproach to everybody, though we on our side gloried in it. No man would trust us, or give us anything but contempt. We were nothing but a poor, ignorant people; our hand was against every man, and every man's hand was against us."

"But you are happy now, Tazoni?" asked the girl, eagerly.

"Yes," he replied. "Fate was kind to me; otherwise I should never have come across that old schoolmaster. He was starving for bread, while I hungered for knowledge."

"Aye, he taught you much—too much for a gipsy, I sometimes think—in return for your kindness," she said, almost wistfully. She forgot that she had been quite as eager to sit at the feet of the old schoolmaster whom they had befriended six years before; although Tazoni had far outstripped her in rapidity of learning. "Anyway, you are happier when you are with your books, and so I, too, am content," she went on, her eyes resting softly upon him in the moonlight.

"You are a dear, unselfish little sister, Maya," he answered, kissing her hand tenderly. Then he rose, as he added: "I must go and see after the horses that Colin brought from the village."

"So they trust their young colts to the gipsy to break in," said Maya, with an unconscious bitterness called up by Tazoni's words to her that evening.

"Yes," he replied, with a careless laugh. "They know there are none better than the gipsies for horse-breaking, Maya; though perhaps they would not trust all our people."

"It is you who have worked this change in us, Tazoni," she replied; "you, who, as Colin said, are only half a gipsy. Even during my mother's lifetime your quiet, strong influence was felt among the men; and it needed a man of indomitable will to bring about this transformation."

With his mind full of the subject they had been discussing, Tazoni walked towards the camp-fire. It was true he had well-nigh brought about the impossible, through his great influence over those of this curious wandering people with whom he lived. But nevertheless he knew that he and his people must always be of the Ishmaelites of the earth; and this thought was doomed to bitter confirmation within the next few minutes.

"Well, Colin," he said, addressing one of the men, when he reached the camp-fire, "what luck to-day?"

"There they be," said the man, in answer to his question, pointing to three fiery colts.

The two men went together to inspect the animals, at present wild and unmanageable.

"Three good ones," remarked Tazoni, as he examined them with the eye of a connoisseur.

"Yes, an' there would 'a' been two more—a beautiful pair of bays from that house on the hill—but the young lady stopped them as the groom was a-giving 'em to me."

"What young lady?" asked Tazoni, sharply.

"The daughter of old Lord Dartworth," said the man, sullenly.

Tazoni's face looked graver than usual in the moonlight; but when he spoke his voice was steady.

"They were hers, then?"

"Yes; and the groom had promised us two pounds if they was broken well; but the young miss said she wouldn't trust gipsies; so the man took 'em back to the stables again, and I come away empty-handed."

The man accompanied the words with an expressive gesture of loss and regret; while Tazoni, scarcely heeding him, took several paces to and fro in silence.

"What time was that?" he asked, suddenly.

"Before midday," answered the man.

"A little later she drove me from her father's woods in utter contempt!" thought Tazoni, bitterly.

"Tether the colts safely apart, and I'll break them in to-morrow," he said aloud, not wishing that the man should notice his chagrin.

After supper, of which he partook with Maya, Tazoni took a walk through the little camp to satisfy himself that all was right for the night. Then he rolled himself in a rug and was soon asleep.

But his dreams were troubled, for they were full of Veronica Dartworth. He thought that he met her riding through the woods, and that she stooped from her saddle and kissed him on the mouth. Yet when he whispered that he loved her, and that his heart had been hungering for her, she struck him with her whip. Then he cried out that he would have nothing more to do with her, that her pride had killed his love for her.

He awoke with this thought in his mind, to meet the dawn of a beautiful spring morning.

CHAPTER VI

Having resolved to leave the neighbourhood as soon as possible, and to keep out of Veronica's way in the interval, Tazoni rose, and went to the stream that divided the stretch of common from the woods. Pure air, plain food, and a daily plunge into some cold, fresh river were the secrets of his sturdy healthfulness.

His passage through the camp had been the signal for the general rising; and when he returned he found the fire already alight, and breakfast in course of preparation. He ordered the colts to be brought, and occupied himself with them until the meal was ready, when he gave them once more into Colin's charge.

After breakfast, which was eaten in common, some of the gipsies occupied themselves with the manufacture of articles in bark and wicker-work; but Tazoni himself took a huge axe and started for a plantation, where he had been employed to cut some saplings. He worked hard and well, rejoicing, as he did so, in his own magnificent strength when it was brought into contact with that of Nature.

Presently a girl with a mist of golden hair slightly ruffled by the wind, and soft brown eyes that were full of dreams, came riding through the sweet-scented wood. She wore a well-fitting habit that showed off her slim figure to perfection, and upon her head was perched a three-cornered hat—a headgear more becoming than conventional.

Tazoni had caught a glimpse of her through the trees; but though the colour flushed his face for an instant, he still continued his work, and made no effort to hide himself, or the fact that he was doing the work of an ordinary labourer. He did not think for a moment that she would speak to him—he was too mean a thing in her eyes—and it was with a start that he heard the voice that had rung in his ears all through the long night, calling to him. He turned, and his eyes met hers.

Veronica looked down at him with a cold scrutiny. "I wish to speak to you," she said, somewhat imperiously.

"I am listening, lady," he replied, with a quiet dignity which Veronica could not help admiring.

For a moment she did not reply, and her eyes wandered restlessly over the tops of the tall trees.

"Before I met you yesterday, I saw my groom giving a pair of ponies to one of your men to break in," she said, forcing herself to look down at him again; but Tazoni's eyes were bent upon the ground; and gaining courage, she continued: "I stopped him, for I was afraid they would be stolen; and I had no wish to lose them."

The gipsy said no word, and Veronica, who had expected that he would have answered in the same proud way that he had done on the previous morning, was surprised at his silence.

"I am sorry now that I did so," she went on, with an obvious effort; "for I have since heard that your people bear a good character in every respect. I have therefore changed my mind, and was on my way to your camp to tell you so."

"Thank you, lady," Tazoni said, raising his eyes to her face. "The ponies shall be broken in most carefully. I will train them myself."

"Oh, so you don't spend all your time making music in the woods?" she asked, with a little laugh; and Tazoni, sensitive to every change in her voice, thought there was a slight strain of sarcasm underlying her words.

"No, lady, not always. I work—sometimes."

Veronica caught the tone of bitterness in his voice, and felt rebuked for her question. To lighten the sudden tension that had sprung up between them, she asked:

"How long have you been able to play?"

"All my life it seems to me, lady. Our people are very musical, and the violin is their favourite instrument."

"Do you read much?" she asked, suddenly, seeking the explanation of his educated voice.

"Yes, lady," he replied; "that is—when I can. I have not many books, it is true; but what I have I know by heart. Sometimes in our journeyings I pick up old, cheap books, and then I am very glad."

"Where did you get your education?" she asked, wonderingly.

"An old man my people found starving, and befriended, taught me all I know; and I've never ceased to be grateful."

"What did he teach you?"

"English grammar, some Latin, arithmetic, and a little astronomy, among other things," was the smiling reply. "Above all, he taught me to know and love Shakespeare."

"And you are satisfied with your life?" she asked, and as she spoke her horse moved impatiently.

Tazoni stretched out his hand to seize the bridle; and their hands met. Veronica noticed that his hand, although tanned, was well-formed, and one that indicated an artistic temperament. Drawing her own away hastily, she glanced at his face, and saw that it had suddenly grown white, while his lips were quivering.

In another instant he had regained his accustomed self-control, and his voice showed nothing of the emotion which the touch of her hand had aroused in him, as he said:

"Your horse is timid, lady."

"I'm afraid she is," Veronica acknowledged.

"She has been frightened at some time or another. If you will let me have her, lady, I could break her of it," said Tazoni.

"You shall have her, then," replied the girl, kindly. "How long have you been head over your people?" she asked, after a moment, a faint interest showing itself beneath the hauteur with which she had so far spoken to him.

"For three years, lady; but I have no right to the title. It is a woman who should be at our head by right."

"A woman!" exclaimed Veronica. "How interesting!"

"Yes, lady; she is the daughter of Zera, our queen, and should have taken command in succession to her; but she chose to place me in her stead."

"And how old is she?"

"Younger than I am, lady," he replied.

"I suppose she's very beautiful?" she asked, almost unconsciously.

"Yes, lady; Maya is very beautiful," he answered, without enthusiasm; but Veronica did not notice the tone, only the words; and with a touch of her usual hauteur, she said:

"Very well, then; you shall have Bess when you bring back the ponies."

Tazoni loosened his hold of the bridle; and Veronica was on the point of turning homewards when, chancing to glance up, she saw the figure of a horseman coming towards them. The gipsy, who was watching her intently, saw her start and change colour. So earnestly had they been talking that the new-comer had been able to approach them unheard and unnoticed.

"Morning, Vee," he said, with studied politeness. Then he looked at the gipsy standing beside her; and for a moment the two men regarded each other with a fixed intentness. "One of your men?" Lord Raymond queried, as Tazoni took up his axe and resumed his work, as if no interruption had occurred.

"No," she replied, her voice sounding cold and formal.

"Then what the dev——" Lord Raymond checked himself as Veronica lifted her eyebrows with surprise.

"I have been speaking to him about my ponies; he is going to break them in for me," she said, calmly, in a tone that plainly showed she did not wish to be questioned further. "I am going home."

"I'll come with you," said Lord Raymond, without waiting to see if his company were desired.

They had ridden in silence for two or three minutes when suddenly Veronica pulled up.

"What's the matter?" asked Lord Raymond.

"I've forgotten to tell the man he was to come for my ponies to-morrow morning. I must go back."

"I'll go," Lord Raymond volunteered, with more than his usual courtesy. "Wait for me, won't you?"

"Thanks," she replied, coldly; and plunging his spurs into his horse, her companion galloped back to where the gipsy was still at work.

Hearing the sound of hoofs upon the turf, Tazoni looked round.

"Here, you!" said Lord Raymond, coarsely. "You're to go up to Dartworth Manor for the ponies to-morrow morning."

Tazoni nodded silently.

"D'you hear?" said the other man, with overbearing insolence, bringing his horse nearer.

"I heard," said the gipsy, quietly.

With a muttered oath, Lord Raymond raised his whip. "The next time you speak to a gentleman——" he shouted; but the eyes of the gipsy were quick, and before the other could strike him, he had wrested the crop from his hand.

With a smile of scorn, untinged by embarrassment or fear, Tazoni handed it back. "I think you have dropped your whip," he said, calmly.

Lord Raymond's face grew crimson with fury; but the next moment, as his blazing eyes met the intense regard of the other, it changed to a deathly white. A mysterious, indefinable fear had suddenly clutched his heart, and without a word he snatched the whip from the strong, brown hand, and rode away.

Veronica was waiting for him beneath the shadow of an elm tree; but as she heard the sound of his horse's hoofs coming nearer and nearer, she made no attempt to meet him. Try as she would she could not banish the thought of the gipsy-musician from her mind.

It was all so extraordinary, that Veronica felt she must be dreaming. There was a peculiar fascination about the man; but what it was she could not tell for the moment. Then, through her musing, there passed the thought that Tazoni held his position by a girl's favour—she was probably very much in love with him, and had thought of this means whereby to increase the already strong friendship that existed between them. A feeling of regret—she could not call it anything more, for it was indefinable—took possession of her; but at last she roused herself.

"What am I coming to," she asked herself, "to bother my head about a gipsy vagabond?" But in her heart she knew he was more of a gentleman than the man who presently overtook her. Lord Raymond had to speak twice before she heard him.

"Wherever did you pick up that dog, Vee?" he asked, brutally. "Of all the insolent——"

"I didn't find him insolent," the girl interrupted, coldly.

"You were more fortunate than I was," he retorted, with a scowl. "But you wait till I'm master at Northbridge, and then you see what'll happen! I'll keep a pack of bloodhounds to hunt up every man-jack of them that comes within a mile of the place."

"You're not master yet, you know," Veronica, said, quietly; "and candidly speaking, I hope it will be a long time before you are, if that is the line you intend to adopt."

Lord Raymond stared at her in surprise, but did not reply.

"I think, if you don't mind, I'll cut across the park. Please don't bother to come; it's much too hot to take you out of your way," Veronica continued; and before Lord Raymond was quite aware of what she was saying, he found himself alone.

"Well, I'm blessed!" he remarked in angry astonishment, as he looked after the girl's retreating figure. "I'll be jiggered if she doesn't beat me every time!"

CHAPTER VII

The next morning Tazoni made his way to Dartworth Manor to fetch the ponies. The groom received him in an almost respectful spirit, due perhaps to the manner in which his young mistress had spoken of the gipsies—for a well-trained servant is never slow to follow up a cue from his superiors.

"You'll do your best with 'em, won't you?" he said, as he led out the bays, " 'cos that 'ere pair is a particular fancy of our young lady's."

"I'll be responsible for them myself," Tazoni replied; and the groom nodded with satisfaction, while he regarded the gipsy with increased curiosity. Here was an ordinary gipsy horse-breaker with the manners and speech of a gentleman, and to his mind the facts were irreconcilable.

"Our young lady be mighty fond of 'osses," said the groom, by way of an opening to a conversation which he hoped would be a lengthy one. "And yet," he went on, "she's a-going to marry that Lord Raymond what don't know how to treat a good 'oss any more than a green fig. He's a reg'lar brute with 'em."

There was an imperceptible pause before Tazoni asked:

"Is that true—what you say about Lord Raymond marrying Miss Dartworth?"

"O' course it is," replied the groom, piqued by the bare idea that he did not know the affairs of his own particular "family." "And ain't it very fitting that it should be? Ain't it plain that there's nothing else for 'em to do, seeing as the 'All and our place joins each other, and them two young people is openly made for each other?"

Not wishing to encourage him to pursue the conversation any further, Tazoni prepared to take his departure.

"Oh, but you must come in and have a drink, and summat to eat," protested the groom. "Miss Veronica said as I was to be sure to offer you some lunch."

"Miss Dartworth will not doubt my gratitude for her kindness, I know; even if I do not take advantage of it," replied Tazoni, with a smile; and then he drove the ponies away, while in his brain were whirling the words he had just heard concerning Veronica and Lord Raymond.

"She's going to marry that brute," he thought. "He doesn't love her, nor she him—I saw it in their eyes—and I—I could have made her love me had Fate been kind, even as I came to love her in a moment of time."

Half-way across the common, and within sight of the encampment, an open carriage met him, containing Veronica and Lord Dartworth, accompanied by Miss Slade. The horses were brought to a standstill, and the coachman signalled to Tazoni to draw near. With a tightening of the lips as he caught sight of Veronica, he led the ponies to the carriage. The girl herself gave him a quick glance of recognition, but made no outward sign that she knew him.

"I wanted to speak to you, my man," commenced Lord Dartworth; but he broke off suddenly to remark, as he looked at Tazoni with a long and steady gaze: "I think there is some mistake, though; you are no gipsy, surely!"

"I am, indeed, my lord," was the reply.

"H'm, I should never have believed it," commented Lord Dartworth. "Anyway, I wanted to tell you that I think some of your men have been poaching on my estate."

Tazoni frowned; but he said nothing.

"Two or three nights ago, my keepers caught sight of a man trespassing in the preserves, and, searching the covers, they found a hare or two. Last night the rascal was seen again, and more distinctly. From the description they give of him, I should say he was one of your party. Now, I can't have anything of that sort. I'm a magistrate, you know, and could easily have the whole lot of you moved on. Besides, I think it is very ungrateful, considering that my steward has found work for several of your men."

Tazoni's eyes were stern and angry.

"My lord," he said, drawing himself to his full height, but speaking in a lower tone than usual, "if I find that the poacher is one of our people, I promise to hand him over to you within twenty-four hours; but I very much hope you may be mistaken. I venture to think that not one of our company would be guilty of such vile ingratitude as to steal from the man who has protected and befriended us. If you will give me your permission to track the thief through your estate, I will give you my word to discover and capture him."

Lord Dartworth nodded his head in frank approval. "That is but fair," he said. "I will tell my keepers that you shall have the run of the preserves for a night or two. You see I'm trusting you implicitly, to how great an extent I've no doubt you are fully aware."

"I appreciate your confidence, my lord, and am grateful for it. Believe me, it shall not be abused."

Then he waited in silence, one strong, tanned hand resting unconsciously upon his hip in his favourite pose.

"Very well, then. Good day," said Lord Dartworth, with an affable smile.

Tazoni raised his cap in silence; and the carriage moved on. Never for a moment had his eyes sought Veronica's; but he had felt her gaze fixed upon him several times during the conversation, and his heart beat uncomfortably fast. For one swift moment he had had a hope that she might speak to him, so that he might hear once more the music of her voice; but instantly he knew that she was too proud to acknowledge that she had ever even seen him before.

"What a handsome man!" remarked Judy Slade, when Tazoni was out of earshot. "No one would think he was just a common gipsy."

"Indeed he is not a *common* gipsy," replied Veronica, suddenly up in arms to protect the man who had won her interest and admiration.

"No, I think you're right," said her father. "He is certainly out of the ordinary run. He speaks excellent grammar, and really has the manners of a gentleman. By the way, Veronica, did you notice anything else about him—he doesn't remind you of anyone, does he?" added Lord Dartworth.

"No, I don't think so," answered the girl, thoughtfully. "Why do you ask?"

"Oh, it was nothing—nothing; just a mere fancy, that was all," was the reply, which intimated that Lord Dartworth did not want to impart his idea; and nothing more was said.

Meanwhile a sad, white-faced woman was making her way through the woods to the village. She did not look very strong, and often paused to rest. She was leaning against a tree for a few moments, when the figure of a man crept stealthily out of the undergrowth behind her. The woman was about to proceed upon her way, when something caused her to turn her head, and she found herself face to face with a tall, dark-featured individual who peered at her from behind the tree against which she had been resting.

"Luke!" she exclaimed in a faint whisper, while her lips grew white with fear.

"Aye, old woman, and not my ghost neither; so ye needn't stare yer eyes out."

"You here! What does it mean?"

"Well, and why shouldn't I be here, same as you? It means as I've come to have a look at old faces again, that's all. But ye've no call to trouble about me. Fancy me dead; same as ye wish I was, eh? And as for me, why I'll fancy ye're out of your mind, and stowed away quietly and safely—or ought to be," Luke concluded, with a sudden ugly savageness.

The woman shrank back against the tree for support.

"Don't, Luke! God knows I'm not likely to be here much longer, and——"

"So much the better," interrupted the man, brutally. "Now then, just ye keep a still tongue about me, will ye? If ye don't, I'll pretty soon hear about it, and I guess ye'll know what to expect."

It was evident from her eyes that she did. Suddenly she stretched her hands towards him with an appealing cry. "Oh, Luke! My boy——" she began; but he interrupted her with a threatening gesture.

"Yer brat is dead, isn't he? Ye'll do well to remember it; nobody but a mad woman 'ud forget it, anyway."

There was a significance in the words that made her shudder.

"I sometimes think I am mad," she said, in a hushed voice.

"Aye, and ye're not the only one as thinks so," he retorted, with a brutal laugh; "Lord Raymond, for instance. He'd never have ye here, if he had any choice in the matter."

The woman uttered a low, heart-breaking cry.

"Luke! Luke! Do you want to kill me?"

"Not while ye keeps quiet," he growled. "Ye can't be too careful up at the house. If ye take my advice, ye'd go away for good an' all. It's like carrying a light through a gunpowder factory. A slip o' the tongue, and we'd be blown up; and don't ye forget it."

"I will be careful; I will indeed; only let me stay near him."

35

"That's all right, then. Just ye bear in mind that Lord Raymond is very nice and comfy all on his little own," said Luke, significantly—"plenty o' money, which he don't forget to spend. I happen to know something of his little games in Lunnon that 'ud make the old earl sit up a little, I bet."

"I don't know what I've always been afraid of," said the woman, sadly. "I thought, somehow, that because of our sin—I mean——" she added, quickly, as the man scowled at her, "I mean, I'd better be getting along now."

"Yes, ye'd better," advised her husband, harshly. "Remember what I've told ye; and don't forget as I'm not a hundred miles away, and that I generally knows what's a-going on. There, off with ye! Here's someone coming down the road, and I'm travelling incog., as ye might call it, just at present."

Before Marion could utter a word Luke Smeaton had disappeared into his hiding-place amongst the undergrowth.

A week passed, and with the near approach of summer the days had grown considerably hotter.

Judy Slade had several opportunities of meeting Lord Raymond; and in her clever, subtle way she had confirmed the good impression she had made when she first met him. She played her cards so well, however, that no one had even the faintest inkling of her carefully laid plans. Indeed, Lady Dartworth, for her part, really believed that her cousin was doing her utmost to bring about the marriage between Veronica and Lord Raymond which both their families desired.

"Judy is such a mouse that one scarcely knows she is about you," Lady Dartworth once remarked to Lord Northbridge, who, however, was restrained by innate courtesy from reminding his guest that mice work a great deal of mischief, which their quietness only serves to conceal.

One morning, Veronica and Judy Slade were walking in the old rose-garden belonging to the Manor when, chancing to look up, Veronica saw her mother coming towards them, accompanied by Lord Raymond and another man, with whom she was unacquainted.

"Why, Judy," she said, "who is that with my mother and Lord Raymond?"

"It's Hubert Denville!" exclaimed Judy, her eyes bright with satisfaction. "Who on earth would have expected to meet him here!"

Meantime Veronica had had time to notice that the man designated as Hubert Denville was tall and looked distinguished. As he came nearer, she thought she had never seen a face which wore an air of such utter boredom. His eyes, too, as he looked into hers while they were being introduced, had the same expression. He was smartly dressed, with the hall-mark of good taste about everything he wore; and by contrast, there seemed a lack of refinement about Lord Raymond which was certainly not prepossessing. This fact did not, naturally, escape Judy Slade, who thought that it should be a point on her side in the game she was playing so skilfully.

"I thought you never left town until quite the end of the season! I certainly never expected to meet you down here!" exclaimed Judy, as she shook hands with Hubert Denville.

"Is that a reproach or a welcome?" he asked.

"Scarcely a reproach, since it is surely a virtue to go in for Nature-worship in these strenuous times," laughed Judy.

"A virtue which has its own reward," said Denville. He looked at Veronica, and gave her one of the swift smiles that stirred the habitually bored expression of his face like a ripple upon a pool. It was this smile which had made Hubert Denville so popular with women generally; and Judy Slade hoped it would have its due effect upon her cousin.

As for Veronica herself, she felt that she had been paid some clever compliment, too subtle to be resented or even accepted; and she felt herself flushing hotly beneath Hubert Denville's eyes, in a way that annoyed her considerably; for she fancied he must think her some silly schoolgirl, altogether unused to men's society. To cover her unaccountable confusion, she asked after Lord Northbridge; but she still felt the new-comer's eyes upon her face, and bungled terribly. Presently they retraced their steps; and it happened that Lady Dartworth and Judy Slade were accompanied by Lord Raymond, while Veronica found herself walking with Hubert Denville.

"Are you fond of the country, Mr. Denville?" she asked, more to make conversation than for any other reason.

"Dear lady," replied Denville, in his lifeless voice, "I love all things beautiful."

Once more his eyes were upon Veronica's face, giving a subtle point to his words which again brought the colour to her cheeks. This time she changed the subject abruptly; and then, almost before he could reply, she drew Judy into their conversation. Miss Slade was walking only a very few yards in front of them, and as she fell back by Veronica's side, her glance sought Hubert Denville's, and she smiled faintly. She joined in the conversation with a *verve* which broke the curious tension that had existed between Veronica and her companion.

But in her mind Judy Slade was saying:

"She is frightened of him—like all women when they first meet him—they all flutter into his net in the end, though."

Indeed, Hubert Denville's *affaires* had become notorious. A pretty woman once said that her sex usually fell in love with him out of pique, because of his utter indifference to them; but, when he did make up his mind to fall in love, there was no man about town who was a more perfect lover than he. As a matter of fact, if Hubert Denville set his heart on winning a woman, he generally succeeded. Now, however, the time had come when his own financial position demanded that he should make a profitable marriage; and Judy Slade—who, in some incomprehensible way had become his staunch friend and ally—had hit upon the person who would most easily fall in with Denville's tastes and requirements.

It had been said that Judy Slade was Denville's only woman friend who had not fallen in love with him; and she was clever enough not to get her name mixed up with any scandal; although, perhaps, had her friends witnessed a certain little incident that occurred upon the day of Denville's first visit to Dartworth Manor, they might have found that they had made some mistake regarding her own feelings towards him.

Lord Raymond had refused, not over graciously, it must be confessed, Lady Dartworth's invitation for himself and his friend to stop to lunch; and when the two men had gone, Judy Slade went up to her room and locked the door. She scribbled a hasty note to Hubert Denville, and when she had addressed and carefully sealed down the envelope, she took from her writing-case a rather faded snapshot of a man in flannels punting on the river. For a moment she stood looking down at the photograph, and as she put it away again, she murmured:

"We're much too clever to throw ourselves away on each other—but I—well, I'd like to marry Hubert Denville all the same. Anyway, I'd appreciate him a great deal more than that silly schoolgirl ever will, I know."

Nevertheless Judy Slade carefully schemed to attract Lord Raymond more and more by pandering to his egotistical weaknesses. She would listen for hours while he recounted some of the antics of his over-fast life in town—coarse, stupid stories in their way, but things he gloried in. She knew every turn of his passionate, distorted nature, and played upon it with careful forethought. Often she sickened of the man who was slowly, but surely, entering her toils, as she compared him with Hubert Denville; but she had put her hand to the plough, and would not turn back. Besides, she told herself, that whether she became Lord Raymond's wife or not, Hubert Denville would never marry her; therefore she must snatch from life what she could, for her future welfare.

During the next few days Veronica saw much of Hubert Denville, for he and Lord Raymond were often at Dartworth Manor. Seeing them together, Veronica could not help comparing the two men, greatly to Raymond's disadvantage. She felt flattered, too, by Denville's manner towards her. Gradually he seemed to emerge from his chrysalis of boredom, and would often talk with animation when they had a discussion upon any point of art or literature.

Denville was careful she should see, however, that this departure from his usual manner was called forth by her alone—a supreme form of flattery at which he was an adept—for he knew that to win Veronica, all his powers were needed. She was intellectual, and also highly educated; but, above all, she was proud. All this he remembered; he noticed quickly, too, that she was pleased when he came to see her, while she took a keen interest in all he said and did.

Veronica could not help wondering about Hubert Denville, for he had made a curious impression upon her, as indeed he had meant to do; but a peculiar question dominated her mind. She had an instinct that he had come into her life for some purpose; and inwardly she asked herself whether it would be for good or ill.

Only Time could answer that question; but not yet.

CHAPTER VIII

While matters were thus running with such dangerous smoothness at the Manor and Northbridge Hall, Tazoni seemed to have found life almost unbearable.

All day long he went about hoping for, yet dreading, a sight of Veronica. Sometimes he saw her in the distance, riding with Hubert Denville or—less frequently—with Lord Raymond; and during the bitter hours of jealousy and self-humiliation that followed, he would ask himself how he could imagine for one moment that she would even remember his existence, much less think of him kindly.

How little he slept, only Maya, whose attentive eyes were always watching his every movement, could really tell. From the tent which she occupied with old Martha—who had quarrelled with Luke, and had resumed her connection with the tribe soon after the birth of Lord Raymond—she would see his stalwart figure rise from the rug beside the fire, and pass into the outer darkness, invariably disappearing in the direction of the Dartworth woods.

Anxious eyes watched Tazoni in the camp. The old woman, Martha, would place before him her choicest dishes, and when he turned away from them with an impatient gesture, she would remove them in stolid silence. The men, too, noticed the change in him; but it was not for them to annoy him with questions or idle gossip. He was just and generous with them all, giving every penny he earned to the common fund. All of them regretted the change that had taken place in him; and, at last, Maya, with an inward trembling, broke the silence which her instinctive fear and awe of him cast as a spell upon her. He had come into the camp one evening, his axe upon his shoulder, looking wan and weary. The men had gone to a horse and cattle fair some miles distant; and Martha sat fanning the flame of the supper-fire.

Tazoni flung himself down on the rug, and fell into a moody silence. From a short distance away, Maya watched him in silence; then, softly approaching him, she placed her small, brown hand upon his shoulder. He started at her touch.

"Well, little sister?" he said, with a smile that had but the shadow of its former brightness.

"Tazoni," asked the girl, "why do you work so hard? You are quite tired out. For six days you've worked like a slave, and eaten scarcely anything; for six nights you've not slept more than an hour—unless you sleep in the woods yonder? Tazoni, what is the matter with you? I've never had a secret from you—will you shut your sister out of your life, and make her utterly unhappy?"

He tried to smile, as he took her hand and fondled it with the casual affection of a brother.

"Maya dear, I have turned spy and thief-catcher," he said; "that is why I haunt the Dartworth preserves."

"*You!*" she cried, with flashing eyes. "And at whose bidding?"

A flush dyed his face at her scornful question; but he answered, calmly:

"Some rogue has been poaching; Lord Dartworth said it was one of our men. I denied it; and, to give some body to an empty denial, I have promised to catch the thief. As yet, he's proved the smarter man. I've been on his heels three separate nights; but he's always managed to slip through my fingers. I go round the camp to make sure of every one of our men before I start—otherwise I'd have sworn it was one of our people; for no one but a gipsy could be so swift of foot and keen of ear. But I'll catch that dog of a poacher, whatever happens."

Tazoni was vehement; but quickly fell into silence again.

"And is this all?" asked Maya, after a moment.

For Tazoni the embarrassment of a reply was avoided by the appearance of Martha with his supper; and Maya did not dare to reopen the subject.

That night, as usual, when the camp was still, Tazoni took his rifle, and set out in pursuance of his self-imposed task.

It was a beautiful night; the sky overhead was bright with stars. He went cautiously along, stopping to listen attentively every now and then. His thoughts were divided between the matter upon which he was engaged, and a train of fancies centering about the sweet, proud face of Veronica which stirred his soul to its very depths, though they were yet so intangible that he scarcely dared give them freedom of thought. With an effort, however, he cast them from him, and sternly set himself to the task he had in hand.

The night was a favourable one for poaching. Once or twice Tazoni fancied he heard the crisp crushing of leaves which denoted a footstep; but the result proved only the advent of a keeper, who nodded or stopped to talk to him, and then went his way, gun in hand, and eyes on the alert.

At last, Tazoni heard the peculiar rustling amongst the leaves which had always preceded the appearance of the mysterious poacher; and, with heart beating fast and straining eyes, he crouched behind a bush, and waited.

The noise seemed to be near him; and presently, when he had almost despaired of keeping his patience within bounds, he saw the dusky outline of a tall, lithe man rise cautiously from the ground, dragging what he had little doubt was a trap behind him. Tazoni raised his rifle, and covered him; then, in a voice suppressed with excitement, he said:

"Move a step, and I fire!"

The figure paused for a second; then, instead of facing the gun, as Tazoni had fully expected, swiftly turned its back, and, with the utmost audacity, sprang on one side.

The movement had been so sudden and daring, that Tazoni, who had not given the poacher credit for so much courage, hesitated a second before firing. When he did so, it was with an aim rendered uncertain and ineffectual; and the man quickly plunged into the undergrowth, and disappeared.

Tazoni dropped his gun, and dashed after him; but although he ran as swiftly as the poacher could have done, he was unable to overtake him. He stood still, and listened; but there was not the slightest movement of the leaves nor did the bushes rustle. He felt absolutely certain that his prey was hiding near at hand, and without delay began to make a cautious and exhaustive search; but he was doomed to disappointment. He waited for some few minutes longer, and, going back to the spot where he had dropped his gun, regained it, and returned to the camp.

He had not left the wood more than three minutes, when a tall figure detached itself from the undergrowth, and stole away in the opposite direction.

CHAPTER IX

It was Lord Raymond's amiable custom to breakfast in bed; for he was not a man who looked well in the keen light of the early morning, his eyes being puffy generally, and his skin sallow. Nights of dissipation in town had left their mark; and the habit of secretly drinking more than was good for him while under his father's roof, did not tend to improve his personal appearance.

On the day of Tazoni's encounter with the mysterious poacher, Lord Raymond woke rather later than usual, and was disgusted to find a pile of letters of a very uninviting appearance by his bedside.

"Bills! Curse 'em!" he muttered, as he glanced at one or two. "Why they can't let a fellow alone, I don't know. They might be sure I'd pay them some day."

But although Lord Raymond's creditors were well aware of the fact that, should matters come to the worst, the Earl of Northbridge would undoubtedly settle his son's debts, yet they evidently thought that a little pressure might not be amiss. As for Raymond's own opinion of the situation, he thought it was certainly more than a trifle worse than his creditors imagined.

His father was indulgent up to a certain point; but Raymond knew that there were items in his bills that Lord Northbridge would refuse to pay. His enormous wine bill was not even to be justified by the fact that he had given a great many dinners and supper-parties in his flat in town. Heavy bridge and betting debts had led him into the hands of the Jews, a thing that Lord Northbridge would certainly look upon with abhorrence. Then, too, there was a little party at the Savoy given to the ladies in the cast of "The Twilight of Love," at which each guest had received a handsome jewel hidden in a bouquet. That would not look well, when brought to his father's notice in plain black and white.

In his son's eyes, Lord Northbridge was too much of a Puritan to be really human; yet he had been very indulgent with him, and Raymond never knew what a grief it had been to him when he had been expelled from Sandhurst. If ever he did feel a pang of conscience, he consoled himself by saying: "Well, I suppose I *am* a 'rotter.' But that's no fault of mine. I was made like it, wasn't I?"

On this particular morning, Lord Raymond was in something like a panic, as he saw some of the bills that had been sent to him. He dared not give his father so much as a hint of his difficulties, otherwise the whole business would come out. His own income was owed twice over in a hundred different quarters; his only resource, therefore, was to try and raise more money from the Jews upon the strength of his inheritance.

Yet even that particular way might possibly be barred; for he had had an angry dispute with Levy Jacobs—a rich Jew from whom he had borrowed much. This unfortunate quarrel had influenced the money-lender to send in an urgent application for a settlement of a certain little bill, whose proportions, however, were far from small. Jacobs might influence his brethren to cheat Raymond yet more than he himself had done, or else he might refuse to meet his demand under any conditions. Lord Raymond felt he was *dans le consommé*, as Hubert Denville, who was no French scholar, might have described the situation.

Through the entire day Lord Raymond was sullen and depressed; but that night at dinner his manner underwent a change. He launched out into a flood of pointless jokes and questionable levity, which, although intended to please his father, disgusted and pained him to such an extent, that he rose, and said:

"Geoffrey, you forget yourself, I think. I cannot conceive where you heard or learned such things."

"The world's grown old since you were young," retorted Lord Raymond, with covert insolence.

"Then I'm afraid it has not improved in manners, or gained in humour. Don't stay long; but come and have a game of billiards with us, will you?"

"Thanks," said Geoffrey, filling his glass, his finer sense being much too blind to take the kindly hint. "I'm going to have another glass of port. What do you say, Denville?"

But Denville had risen from the table with Lord Northbridge, and declined Raymond's suggestion; so the latter was left alone to indulge his alcoholic craving. He drew one of the carved chairs towards him, to make a resting-place for his feet.

The dining-room looked out upon the shrubbery; and it was in this direction that Lord Raymond's face was turned. He had emptied the decanter, and was rising to leave the room, when a man's face appeared, pressed against the window. It was only for a moment; but Lord Raymond managed to catch the outline of a swarthy face, and the gleam of a pair of coal-black eyes.

In blank astonishment he dropped back into his chair; and before he could once more rise to his feet the apparition had disappeared.

Recovering his presence of mind, which had been utterly routed for the moment, Lord Raymond strode quickly across to the window and, throwing it open, stepped on to the gravel path outside. Looking swiftly from right to left, and discovering no trace of his visitor's presence, he walked into the shrubbery to continue his search. But it was all to no purpose; there was not a trace of the intruder; and so he returned once more to the dining-room.

"It's worry, that's what it is," he muttered to himself; "sheer worry, and that beastly port. It's only fit for farmers. I'm out of sorts—want something to pull me together."

He went to the sideboard and mixed himself a stiff brandy-and-soda, which he apostrophized as a jolly good "pick-me-up," and promptly repeated the dose, without any other result, however, than that of partial intoxication. When he presently rose to go to the drawing-room, he had sufficient wit left to understand that it was an unwise thing to do.

"I'll take a stroll in the woods to get cool; or else there'll be a row," he remarked aloud, with a vacant face. "A man's a good deal better without a father, I think—he can do as he likes—be his own master. I'm regular screwed—all through that vile Jew—vile Jew."

With the reiteration of these words he stumbled into the open air. The influence of the spirits he had drunk proved greater than he expected; and, hiccoughing and swaying at every step, he passed from the grounds adjoining the house into the woods beyond.

Suddenly, almost out of the ground beneath his feet, rose the dark figure of a man. There was so little light in the woods, although the night itself was clear, that Lord Raymond rubbed his eyes with all the perplexity of a drunken man. But he came to the conclusion that it was no alcoholic apparition; and when his mind had mastered this fact, he put out his hand and grasped the man's arm, half in fear, half in anger.

"What are you doing here?" he exclaimed. "You're a poacher, and want to rob me, I know you do—yes, I'm sure you do. But it's no go—no go, I assure you. There's a dozen keepers somewhere about."

"But ye won't call 'em, my lord," said the poacher, with cool ferocity, not unmingled with sarcasm.

The man's sudden appearance had done a little towards sobering Lord Raymond; his words and manner did more.

"Why not?" asked Raymond, instinctively grasping the man's arm more tightly.

"Because if ye open yer mouth wider than it is now, I'll shut it for the last time."

Lord Raymond fell back a step, his eyes glaring into the darkness with vicious longing. He could not see anything more than the mere adumbration of the poacher's face; but the tone of his voice told him plainly that, whoever its owner might be, he was not a man to be trifled with.

"Who are you?" asked Lord Raymond, with sullen anger.

"One as means what he says, and says no more than what he means, my lord," was the reply.

"You know me, apparently," said Lord Raymond.

"Better than ye thinks for," retorted the man, with curious significance.

"Then you know, perhaps, that I'm not a mere nobody, whom you can molest and rob with impunity, my fine fellow," said Raymond, with a pompous display of courage he was far from feeling, seeing the possibilities of the situation. "So now I warn you to give it up as a bad job, and do a bolt. I'll let you off this time ——"

"That's all very nice and kind," said the man, interrupting him; "but I'm a-thinking it's all the other way about. It's a question whether I'll let *you* off, my young shaver."

"—and here's a sovereign for your impudence," continued Lord Raymond, holding out the coin, and pretending not to notice the interruption.

"Thanks; that'll do as a small instalment," replied the other, with a grin; and, as he took the money, he seized the hand that proffered it, and drew off a gold signet ring.

At the man's touch, Lord Raymond felt a thrill of fear and something else, which he took for a feeling of repulsion, pass over him like a shudder.

"Now, go," he said, with an assumption of calmness, which, however, did not hide the true state of his feelings.

"I'm in no hurry," answered the poacher, with an irony that Lord Raymond did not altogether appreciate. "I've been wanting ye for some time, and been dodging ye about for a week."

"You came to the dining-room window to-night, didn't you?" asked Raymond, not without natural curiosity.

"Ye're right there; and I should 'a' come in, only I saw ye weren't in a fit state for a gentleman to speak to. Ye drink too much for a young fellow. Take the advice of a man old enough to be yer father"—he grinned secretly at the word—"and drop it."

"Keep your advice and your insolence until they are asked for," said Lord Raymond, angrily. "If you have anything to say to me, be quick about it; or else I shall call the keepers. I'm a match for you, I think. You want money, I suppose?"

"That's it," said the man, utterly disregarding the threat. "I want a hundred pounds."

Lord Raymond laughed unpleasantly.

"To be quite candid," he said, "so do I."

"I know that," replied the man, coolly.

Raymond started, and peered with still greater curiosity at the face confronting him.

"You do, eh?" he said, rudely. "Well, perhaps you know all my affairs?"

"Pretty nearly," retorted the other. "But what I know is neither here nor there. I want a hundred quid, and I mean to have 'em. That gold watch and chain of yours is worth a bit. I'll take 'em instead of the cash; though the ready money 'ud be more convenient."

Lord Raymond was subconsciously wondering how on earth the poacher could see the things in the dark; until he remembered that the man had been watching him through the window, and must have seen them then.

"And suppose I won't give them to you?" he said, drawing a little further away.

"Then I'll knock ye on the head with this stick, and help myself," said the man, quite unruffled; "or, better still, take the liberty of writing to yer papa, and give him an account of that little nobbing job ye did so neatly at Newmarket."

In spite of his assumed *sang-froid*, Lord Raymond could not help uttering an exclamation of alarm.

"Who the devil are you?" he asked, hoarsely; "and how in the name of goodness did you get to hear of that—that affair?"

"That's telling," said the man, with a grin. "Ye see, I do know of it; that's enough, ain't it? But I can't stand gossiping here all night; give me the ticker and I'll be off."

"If I give them to you, will you leave the country?" asked Lord Raymond, into whose voice there had come an anxious note.

"Not me; I'm too fond of England and you, my boy. I'm going to watch over ye, and give ye lots of advice."

"Advice!" sneered Lord Raymond, in derision.

"Yes, advice. Don't trouble the wine-bottle so much; keep clear of the Jews, and make up to Miss Veronica Dartworth."

"Veronica Dartworth!" exclaimed Lord Raymond. "What do you know——"

"That ain't your business. Take my advice, and marry her as soon as ye can; it's safer."

"What *are* you talking about?" asked Raymond, not knowing whether to be amused or angry at the man's impertinence.

"Ye've got ears—listen!" said the poacher, shortly. "Dartworth Manor's a nice little nest-egg to fall back upon, if anything should happen to ye. This is a rare uncertain world—up to-day and down to-morrow—and ye might lose North-bridge one of these fine days."

"You're out of your mind! Lose Northbridge! Impossible."

"So ye may 'a' thought o' these 'ere bits o' jewellery," retorted the man, who had taken the opportunity of securing Lord Raymond's watch and chain whilst his mind was occupied with other matters; "but they're gone, ye see. Take my advice—marry the Dartworth girl and ye're safe."

Lord Raymond laughed outright.

"I'm afraid you're slightly touched in the upper storey, my good fellow. You've picked up some cock-and-bull race-meeting story, and think you've got a hold on me; but you've made a mistake. I'm not to be bullied or frightened out of money or other things. I'm Lord Northbridge's son and heir, I'd like to inform you; there isn't much chance of the property slipping through my hands. So, if it's all the same to you, I'll please myself whom I marry; and if I see your face again——"

"You haven't seen it at all yet," said the man, with a broad grin.

"That doesn't make the slightest difference," replied Lord Raymond, begin-ning to think that he had won the day. "I could pick you out blindfolded amongst a thousand; and, if you don't take care you'll get nabbed as it is, for all your im-pudence, long before the week's out."

The poacher stooped down, and a sudden, senseless panic seized Lord Ray-mond. He opened his mouth to shout for help; but he was both frightened and fascinated by the man's movement, and no words came. The next instant, how-ever, the poacher struck a match.

"Have a look at my face, my boy," he said, with a sardonic grin; "it'll help ye to remember me."

Lord Raymond looked and stepped back. The features, from the thin-cut lips and dark eyes and hair, seemed to reawaken the curious sensation he had experi-enced when he first heard the man's voice, and felt the touch of his hand.

"Who—who are you?" he demanded, hoarsely.

"I am——" the man began, but suddenly checked himself, and looked with unmitigated scorn at Lord Raymond's craven face. "I am a man who doesn't know what fear is," he said, with a threatening movement.

Completely unhinged, Lord Raymond lost his presence of mind, and uttered a faint cry. With an oath, the poacher knocked him down and plunged into the bushes, dragging after him the trap which Tazoni had noticed earlier in the evening.

Suddenly, the silence of the woods was broken by the shrill sound of half a dozen whistles, and through the trees lights began to dance up and down like so many will-o'-the-wisps. Two minutes later, three keepers had reached the spot where Lord Raymond was lying. For a moment he was unable to speak, and returned the amazed stare of the men with a glare of alarm. At last, he gained breath.

"It's all right, Rogers. I'm Lord Raymond. Came into the woods for a stroll, and caught sight of a poacher. I nearly had him; but somehow he managed to knock me down, and bolted off."

"Which way, my lord?" asked the head keeper, excitedly.

Lord Raymond pointed in the opposite direction to that taken by the poacher; and the men started off like hounds unleashed.

"I think you'd better stay here with me, Rogers," said Lord Raymond, faintly, as the head keeper was preparing to follow his subordinates. "The fellow has given me a nasty knock; I think you'd better help me home."

"I hope you're not hurt, my lord," said the keeper, with a look of concern. "Good heavens! you've lost your watch and chain!" he added, as his eyes fell upon Raymond's waistcoat, which had come unfastened when the articles had been removed by the poacher.

Lord Raymond uttered an exclamation of annoyance. "I thought I felt the fellow tug at my chest," he said; "I suppose that was when he took them."

"Did you see him, my lord?" asked the keeper.

"N-o," said Lord Raymond, with a slight hesitation. "We struggled for a long time; but I couldn't see his face. He was tall, and sounded like a beastly gipsy."

"I wouldn't mind taking my oath as it was that vagabond, Luke Smeaton, my lord," said the keeper, emphatically. "He's been hanging about this part for the last day or two; and he's as tough a customer as you'll find, for poaching."

"Why, that's Marion Smeaton's husband, isn't it?" said Lord Raymond, who knew Luke only by name.

"That's him, my lord; he's a regular bad lot. But, if you like, we can have him arrested on suspicion?"

"Oh, no, don't do that," replied Lord Raymond, with a touch of authority. "From what you say, I'm sure my man can't be this fellow—it was a much bigger chap, I'm certain. No, don't make any fuss about it; but keep a sharp look out, and—er—Rogers, take my advice and put a bullet or two into 'em. That'll teach them a lesson."

"We can't do that, my lord," replied the keeper, with a laugh. "That 'ud be murder, I'm thinking."

"Oh no, it wouldn't," said Lord Raymond, with conviction; "my father's a magistrate, and he'd call it justifiable homicide in self-defence."

CHAPTER X

Lord Raymond spent the remainder of the night in a state of uncomfortable perturbation. However he might try to dismiss the matter from his mind with contemptuous disregard, he could not help confessing to himself that there was something mysterious—not to say extremely unpleasant—in the familiarity which the poacher displayed with his affairs.

Had his valet been gossiping? he wondered; or could it be possible for some connection to exist between the gipsy and the Jew, from whom he had been compelled of late to borrow freely?

For more than an hour Lord Raymond paced his room in listless uncertainty. His encounter with the poacher was so fresh in his mind that at present he could not bring himself to think the matter over in detail; but after a time his brain grew clearer, and he came to the conclusion that it would be absolutely necessary to silence the gipsy—how and in what way he was yet to discover.

As soon as it was light he rang peremptorily for his valet; and, for a time at least, the subject was dismissed from his mind. But when he descended after breakfast, the story of his adventure was the sole topic of conversation; for Lord Northbridge had already learned from the keeper of the incident of the previous evening.

"It's a most extraordinary thing," said Denville, as he and Lord Raymond paced up and down the terrace; "but I suppose you'll have no difficulty in tracing the fellow? There's a tribe of gipsies camping on the common, isn't there?—that's where you'll find him, you mark my words!"

"Oh, for heaven's sake chuck it!" exclaimed Lord Raymond petulantly. "I'm about fed up with the whole business."

"All right, old fellow," said Hubert Denville, soothingly. "But why I really mentioned the subject was to see if you'd care to come down to the common with me, and have a look at them—you might spot your man, perhaps. In any case, you'll get your money's worth in the shape of a jolly nice little gipsy girl."

Lord Raymond was interested; and as he had been wondering what excuse he could make for visiting the camp, he seized upon Denville's suggestion with avidity.

"Come on, then," he said, throwing his half-finished cigarette into the flower-bed nearest the terrace; "we'll go now."

"I'm awfully sorry, old chap, but I can't come this morning. I'd forgotten that I'm booked to go motoring with Miss Slade—it had gone clean out of my head till a minute ago. But don't wait for me, if you're keen on going. By the way, you'd better be careful of the gipsy girl's watch-dog—he's a tall, handsome chap; rather hot-headed, I should imagine."

Lord Raymond's face darkened. "D'you mean a big, heavy sort of brute, with ideas a few sizes too large for his station?" he asked.

"Yes, that's the chap—rather 'uppy,' as you say."

"Well, I guess he won't forget the lesson I gave him the other day—insolent puppy!"

Hubert Denville laughed, exclaimed "Good!" in a tone of apparent amusement, and mentally called his companion a liar in the space of two seconds.

"Well, you'd better be careful all the same," he advised; "gipsies aren't the sort of people to forget an injury—even when it is merited. There's a kind of she-dragon, too, about the place—looks like an Egyptian mummy. But go and try your luck, my boy, in spite of the watch-dog and the witch. I'd like to know what you think of the girl."

"All right," said Lord Raymond; "but where did you say you were off to?" he asked, with faint suspicion.

"I've promised to go motoring with Miss Slade. I'm rather keen on seeing that little Elizabethan cottage they talk so much about. You've seen it scores of times, I suppose? I can't very well funk it now I've promised."

"Is Vee going?" asked Lord Raymond, in a voice that he tried to make careless, but in which the note of suspicion had deepened.

"I really don't know," replied Denville, with admirably feigned indifference. "It was Miss Slade's idea, you see. I can't say I'm exactly keen about Veronica Dartworth—clever girls make me nervous. I don't want to come on the *tapis*—if that's what you mean to infer?"

"Oh, I don't doubt that," returned the other man, with something like a sneer. "Well, if you're not coming, I'll be off."

Lord Raymond walked quickly through the shrubbery, turned sharply to the right, and in so doing came face to face with the individual he most wished to see. Marion Smeaton smothered an exclamation, and, with a white face, drew back closer to the bushes to allow him to pass. Conscious of that indescribable and unpleasant feeling which her presence always produced in him, Raymond swerved a little aside, and then stopped.

"Good morning," he said, abruptly. "You've got a husband, named Luke, haven't you? Where is he?"

"I—I don't know, my lord," was the hesitating reply.

"D'you mean he isn't in Northbridge?" asked Lord Raymond.

"No—yes—that is, I don't know, my lord."

"What d'you mean? Can't you speak the truth when you're asked a simple question?" he asked, harshly.

The woman began to tremble.

"I—I am telling you the truth, my lord," she faltered. "I saw him some days ago in the woods; but I never know where he is, or when he's likely to come to Northbridge."

"Then why couldn't you say so?" said Lord Raymond, angrily; "instead of shaking and shivering like a lunatic!"

As he strode away, the woman looked after him with misty eyes; and, as she turned to continue her way, tears rolled down her sunburnt face.

The morning sunshine lit up the gipsy encampment with dazzling brilliance; and to any other eyes but Lord Raymond's the scene would have seemed unusual and picturesque. Its appearance, however, only served to deepen the frown on his narrow forehead.

"A rotten lot of thieves, I bet!" he muttered, as he swaggered between two of the caravans. He looked about for someone to whom he could address his enquiries; but the place seemed almost deserted, the women having accompanied their men-folk to the surrounding farms; for hay-making had commenced, and labour was in great demand.

He was on the point of entering the tent nearest to him, when a small, brown hand pushed back the flap from within, and Maya confronted him. For a moment Lord Raymond stared at her in amazement and unconcealed admiration. From what Denville had told him, he had expected to find a rough, if pretty girl; but the calm, dark beauty of the gipsy somewhat overpowered him, and it was quite a moment before his surprise vanished and his usual insolence returned to him.

"I thought you'd gone and left your rubbish behind you," he said, his eyes still fixed on her face with unpleasant intentness.

The gipsy regarded him steadily in silence.

"Where are all the others?" he demanded, rudely.

"In the fields," she replied, with quiet reserve.

"Gone to find an excuse for some of their thieving work!" he said, with a sneer.

The girl's dark eyes flashed, but with a great effort she controlled herself.

"No; they have gone hay-making."

Lord Raymond laughed unpleasantly.

"And left you—the best of the whole bally lot—at home, eh?"

"If you will please tell me what you want," the girl said, with quiet dignity, "I will see if I can get someone to attend to you."

"Oh, I guess you'll be able to help me quite as much as I need. Perhaps you can inform me as to which of your honest subjects happened to be poaching in my woods last night?"

Maya started; and the movement was not lost on Lord Raymond.

"Ah, I see you know all about it," he said, with a cunning twinkle in his eyes. "Perhaps you've got my watch and chain tucked up nice and snugly somewhere?"

The gipsy's small hand clenched by her side.

"Oh, take your time about denying it," continued the man, leaning against a gaudily painted caravan, and lighting a cigarette. "I know you gipsies too well to expect the truth for nothing. Look here, my girl, here's a bargain. Tell me the name of the man who robbed me last night, and I'll give you a quid."

The gipsy looked at him with contemptuous eyes.

"Well, look here, let's make it a fiver," he went on, thinking that he had not offered enough.

The girl laughed; and Lord Raymond came two or three steps nearer to her.

"You refuse?" he said, in astonishment.

50

"Yes, I refuse to sell you the truth; but I'll give it to you for nothing."

"That's what I call generous," said Lord Raymond, a smile for the moment lighting up his dark face. "Well, what was his name?" he asked, eagerly.

"I don't know," was the calm reply.

For a moment Raymond was staggered; it was impossible to doubt the truth that shone in the clear, dark eyes.

"Do you mean to tell me that none of your men were in the woods last night?" he said, threateningly.

"I didn't say so; there was one."

"Oh, there was, was there?" he said, with a sneer. "You're candid, I must say. Perhaps you wouldn't mind telling me his name?"

"Tazoni, my brother," said the girl, readily; "he was watching for a poacher, by Lord Dartworth's permission."

"Oh, really!" said Lord Raymond, in whose mind a sudden idea had fixed itself.

"Curly-haired chap, isn't he?—grey eyes, don't yer know—a big, clumsy ox?" he asked.

The girl was about to contradict him; but before she could do so, he continued:

"Well, that's all I want to know; I guess I'll be going—not before I've said good-bye, though," he added, as he saw a spasm of relief pass over her face. "Here's the five pounds I promised you, and now what d'you say for it, eh?"

With savage violence he drew the girl towards him. Maya set her lips tightly, and struggled with all her force to avoid the threatened embrace; but his strength was greater than hers, and he had almost succeeded in touching her white lips with his own, when, in answer to a cry of hers, the shrivelled form of old Martha hobbled from behind the tent. So sudden was her appearance, and so hideous the sight of her almost fleshless face and fierce eyes, that Lord Raymond relinquished his grasp of the girl, and fell back.

"What in the name of goodness be all this scuffling about?" she said, harshly.

"I—I'm having my fortune—er—told," replied Raymond, with some embarrassment.

Martha grinned.

"Well, the next time as ye come ye'd better keep yer distance, young man. A gipsy girl isn't for the likes of ye. Did I hear ye say as ye wanted to know the future?—well, I'll tell it ye for nothing. Ye'd better make the most of the present, and not think about the future—it won't be a long one for 'ee, if I can read your face aright. Make yer hay now; the sun won't always shine."

"I'm dashed if I know what you're talking about," said Lord Raymond politely; and he made more haste than was absolutely necessary to get clear of the camp.

No sooner had he gone than Martha turned upon the still trembling girl, and asked her how she dared degrade herself by gossiping with a stranger. With fierce indignation, Maya told her the truth; and the old woman changed her tactics.

"And what did he ask ye?" she enquired.

Maya told her; and her anxiety on Tazoni's account was not lessened by the look of apprehension which clouded the old woman's cunning eyes.

"Did ye tell him Tazoni was in the wood?" she asked, with something like contempt.

"What else could I do?" asked the girl, in surprise. "He can't do Tazoni any harm."

"Right can't stand against might," muttered the old woman. "If Tazoni hears that ye've been insulted, he'll be after thrashing the fellow; and who'll suffer for it but the gipsy?"

"No, no," said Maya, her cheek blanching before the prospect of harm to Tazoni. "Tazoni must know nothing of this. You must give me your solemn word that you won't tell him."

"Will ye be more careful and keep in yer tent, then?" asked Martha.

"I will, indeed," said the girl, relapsing into her old dignity.

Satisfied with this, but refusing to answer any questions as to the danger that might accrue to Tazoni from Maya's ill-advised admission of his being in the woods, the old woman hobbled away.

Meanwhile Lord Raymond retraced his steps towards the Hall with an unpleasant expression in his eyes.

"At any rate," he muttered, as he entered the shrubbery, "I've got that insolent puppy under my thumb. I'd better not be too hasty, though; better wait till I can pay him off in full. Snatched my whip from me, did he! I'll teach him what's what; and the girl, too. By Gad! though, she's worth a little trouble—much too pretty for such a crow's nest."

He had almost reached the house, when his thoughts were suddenly interrupted by something that fell at his feet, thrown apparently from behind the hedge. He started back with an oath, expecting a second stone—for such he had imagined the missile to be. But none came; and, after peering through the hedge and listening for a moment or two, he stooped down and looked about the gravel path.

Then he saw that the supposed stone had only served as the means of carrying a missive of some kind; for a small piece of paper had uncurled itself from a pebble, and lay under the hedge. He picked it up, and, with a suspicious glance right and left, read the following words, written in a crabbed and illiterate hand:

> *Tell the Jew ye'll pay him his money in a week from to-day, if he'll keep his mouth shut. Meet me in the wood, at the same place, this day week, at the same time as before.*

There was no signature; but it needed none to tell Lord Raymond that his correspondent was the poacher whom he had encountered upon the previous night.

CHAPTER XI

As Hubert Denville had said, the little motoring trip was Judy Slade's suggestion, but Veronica had also seconded it; for, against her will, she had become interested in Lord Raymond's friend; as indeed did most women who came into contact with him. That she was in love with him was not probable, but Hubert Denville calculated that, although she was different from most women, he had only to play his cards with a little more *finesse* than usual to win the prize he so greatly desired.

He returned from the visit to the Elizabethan cottage in a contented frame of mind, and the bearer of an invitation for himself and Lord Raymond to dine at Dartworth the same evening.

Of course the main topic at the Manor that night was the assault and robbery of Lord Raymond, who, curiously enough, did not seem to wish to discuss the matter.

Hitherto, Judy Slade had found that her plans as regards Lord Raymond had worked almost too easily. He had shown a marked preference for her; and she had had to devise many little stories of conversations she had had with Raymond about "dear Veronica," in order to keep Lady Dartworth's eyes blinded to the real object of her manœuvres.

That night, however, both Judy Slade and Hubert Denville were to receive a surprise. Great as was Raymond's temptation to drink, and drown the memory of his difficulties, he refused several times to have his glass refilled—a fact which did not pass unnoticed by the two allies. Again, when the men returned to the drawing-room, instead of going up to Judy Slade as usual, and asking her to sing some of his favourite musical comedy songs, he went at once and seated himself beside Veronica.

But his enforced abstinence from wine, even though it had kept him clear-headed, had not improved his temper; and Veronica soon grew tired of his sullen ways. She proposed a walk upon the terrace, so that they might see the moon rise above the hills, and gave Denville the opportunity of being her companion, leaving Lord Raymond to follow at will with Judy Slade. This, however, he was in too bad a temper to do; and, having passed through the long windows, he suggested that they should walk in an altogether different part of the grounds, hoping to spite Veronica—much to Miss Slade's secret delight.

Veronica and Hubert Denville stood leaning against the stone balustrade of the terrace, and watched the moon sail up above the distant hills, purple-tinged by the summer dusk. He knew how to play upon a woman's mood so delicately and intimately, that it was no wonder he had found women easily accessible. Now he seemed to enter into Veronica's silence and become part of it, making her cognisant the while of his thought and existence.

Upon the balustrade his arm touched hers—inadvertently at first, it may have been; but it lingered in that position with fixed intent, and Veronica was too absorbed by the beauty of her environment to notice it. Her pure, æsthetic joy in the beautiful was greatly increased by the relief she felt in having congenial companionship. While her soul was rendered softly pliable by this mixture of glad sensation, Hubert Denville's voice came to her through the twilight—soft, and exquisitely low, with a throbbing under-current that thrilled her through and through—playing upon her emotions like a harpist's hand upon the strings of his instrument.

> "O Moon of my Delight that knows no wane,
> The Moon of Heaven is rising once again.
> How oft hereafter rising shall she look
> Through this same garden after me in vain?"

Once more there was a slight silence between them; then Veronica asked, with an attempt to escape from the world of emotional thought and sensation that his words had called up to her:

"This garden in particular?"

For a moment he made no answer, and she felt rebuked; for she saw he understood that she had been too much of a coward to leave her customary groove of conventional expression.

"Life is a garden in which Fate has placed us," he said. "We may choose our flower from its many treasures—I'm sure we have some choice given us—and by that choice we stand or fall. Love is the flower that most of us strive for; but we generally make the mistake of never plucking it at the right moment. Men love too soon; that is our tragedy. You women love too late; that is yours—to convert a paradox of Oscar Wilde. We men often cast down our soul's treasure before women who don't matter the least bit in the world. We learn our lesson; then some of us help to swell the list of suicides; the rest become hard and cynical."

His voice stirred Veronica to a feeling of real interest.

"I leave you to decide which is the more commendable," he continued. "But to some of us there comes, sometimes, the happy fortune to light upon a chance oasis in Life; to find a woman whom one grows to appreciate with that tense, inner self that shows us what might have been ours, had Fate been kind."

After the slightest fraction of a pause he went on, almost irrelevantly:

"Have you ever envied a certain environment—objects, scenes, walls, flowers—that have the sweet privilege of being even near to one of whom you are never weary of thinking, day or night?"

Veronica's mood had been so skilfully played upon, that she had unconsciously been drawn out of herself—she could not say what she thought or felt. Hubert Denville hastily threw away his cigarette; and she watched its glowing descent into the garden, though not aware that she did so.

Then she felt his hand upon her arm, and her heart began to beat with rapidity.

"Veronica!"

The name came through the scented night like a throb of pain and love. His arms were closing about her, and she was only dimly conscious of it. Perhaps it was the moonlight, the music of his voice, and the perfume of the sleeping flowers in the dusk.

"Veronica!"

Suddenly the scene seemed to change. She thought the sun was shining, and she was riding through a wood; a tanned, delicately shaped hand touched her own. She looked down into a quivering face and grey eyes raised to hers, full of pain, and something more—what was it?

"You have no right to look upon us with scorn and hatred—Veronica!"

It was strange; it was even ludicrous; and yet she felt on the verge of tears. Why should the memory of Tazoni have come between her and this man who was making love to her? Another moment, and she might have permitted him to kiss her, sealing a compact between them that could only end in marriage.

Still the memory of Tazoni obtruded itself, persistent, compelling; yet he was only a gipsy, while Fate had placed her in such a station that convention, wealth, birth, and position—the whole world, in fact—separated him from her.

Hubert Denville felt her shiver a little. He raised her face in his hands, so that the moonlight fell upon it, and he saw there were tears in her eyes, even while her lips smiled. He thought she was his at last, and bent his head to kiss her; but she stopped him with a nervous little laugh.

"I—I think we have made a mistake—Mr. Denville."

He had often won a seemingly lost game by treating women as though they did not know their own minds.

"You are excited and nervous," he said, soothingly. "We will speak of this on some other occasion. It is time we went in; the night is cold for you."

Then through the garden rang Lord Raymond's voice, calling her name.

"Vee!—Vee!—Veronica!"

A sensation of repugnance passed over her, throwing up into striking contrast the pleased, restful feeling she invariably felt when in Hubert Denville's company, and then she wondered if after all she had made a mistake, as she had said.

Judy Slade and her cavalier came upon them round a bend in the terrace.

"Veronica," she said, in her sweet way, "Lord Raymond has promised to take us in his drag to Hindworth for a picnic the day after to-morrow."

Lord Raymond had evidently forgotten his ill-temper, for he seemed in the best of spirits, and held Judy Slade's arm in a somewhat over-familiar manner. She, however, seeing Veronica's eyes upon her, said laughingly:

"Lord Raymond said he had sprained his foot and pretended he couldn't walk."

"I didn't," replied her not very astute companion. "I held your arm because I wanted to—if that's what you mean."

Judy Slade and Hubert Denville exchanged glances of amusement; but Veronica was disgusted by Raymond's coarseness, and turned towards the house.

Denville, who accompanied her, maintained a careful silence until he took his leave. Then he said softly, as he bent over her hand:

"Good night—*Veronica.*"

Beneath his eyes she flushed, and for a moment she felt like a trapped bird. Then she looked away from him; and he passed on to say good night to Judy Slade.

That night, when her maid had brushed out Veronica's long, fair hair, she was bidden to leave her mistress alone. Veronica looked into her glass, scanning her every feature as though to seek an index to her innermost thoughts.

Presently she rose from her low seat before the mirror, and switching off the light, crossed the room to the window. All the casements were latticed at the Manor, and Veronica threw hers wide open. The moon was high in the heavens; and she stood and watched it for some moments. From her lips fell a soft, low murmur like a prayer.

"Oh, I want to know what Love is—really, truly, whatever it may bring. If it brings joy I shall be glad—and if it be sorrow, I shall be satisfied still."

While Veronica stood looking out into the night, praying Fate for a dangerous boon, Tazoni was in the woods, thinking of her, loving her, with all the strength of his true manhood.

In his room at Northbridge Hall, Hubert Denville was smiling over his thoughts as he smoked his final cigarette, and, as he threw the glowing end away, he murmured to himself:

"All women are fools—thank goodness! *She's* like all the rest."

CHAPTER XII

The following morning Tazoni—who had been kept blissfully unaware of Lord Raymond's visit to the camp—proceeded to Dartworth Manor with Veronica's ponies.

It had not been without a struggle between prudence and desire that he was taking this course. He knew that it was possible he might meet Veronica, whom, he told himself, he should do well to avoid; but inclination, under the guise of duty, conquered. He silenced the voice of wisdom by reminding himself that he had promised to break in the ponies himself, and had given Veronica to understand that he would bring them back personally.

It must be confessed, however, that Tazoni was very disappointed when he did not see Veronica after all. A groom took the ponies from him, and gave him Miss Dartworth's horse, as it had been arranged. Then, with an abrupt good day, Tazoni strode once more down the drive, chagrined and disconsolate.

But Veronica had witnessed his approach and departure from the library window; for she had pleaded a headache as an excuse for not accompanying Miss Slade in her morning ride, knowing the possibility of meeting Hubert Denville, whom she wished to avoid, for that day at least.

At the sight of Tazoni, Veronica had experienced a strange thrill of pleasure, which, however, she chose to put down to the fact that he had unconsciously saved her the previous night from being drawn into an act which she was sure she would have regretted afterwards.

In the cold light of early morning, Veronica had frankly confessed to herself that she was not in love with Hubert Denville. He interested her; but she nevertheless wondered if his attraction were not due to the contrast between him and Lord Raymond, who every day seemed to grow more odious. She owned that Denville was clever, and she certainly liked him; but Veronica understood her real feelings too little to know whether that sense would ripen later on into a deep and veritable love for the man who inspired it.

One thing, however, struck her as exceedingly curious. When comparing Hubert Denville with Lord Raymond, the contrast was dazzling; yet when she subconsciously placed Hubert Denville beside Tazoni, there somehow seemed a lack of sincerity about him which detracted much from his splendid gifts. A gipsy and a gentleman! The contrast was ludicrous; and yet a questioning of inner self told her that the gipsy gained by it. Veronica had realized it last night, when she fancied she had heard Tazoni speak her name an instant after Hubert Denville had done so actually.

When Veronica saw Tazoni again pass down the drive, she realized that he had not been paid, and crossed to the fireplace, but paused as she was about to ring the bell. It needed no extraordinary penetration to see that Tazoni was very proud—indeed it had been that trait in his character that had first claimed her attention. It was not at all unlikely that a servant would give him the money with some insolent remark, after the manner of the servant class; and her soul shrank from the idea of hurting his feelings. Her nature was impulsive in many things; and, hastily donning the hat she held in her hand, she made her way quickly down the terrace steps, thinking to intercept Tazoni by taking a short cut that would bring her to the bridle-path leading through the woods.

Tazoni's disappointment had been so keen, however, that he had not taken the usual road, but, leaping upon the horse's bare back, had followed a by-path in order to keep away as long as possible from the tenderly enquiring eyes of Maya and old Martha.

Presently he came out upon a little plot of rising ground that dipped down into a glen, through which ran the stream that watered the Dartworth grounds. The turf was an enamelled patch of glorious colour—gold, white, and dainty blue —by reason of the flowers of early summer.

Having reached this earthly paradise, Tazoni dismounted, gave Bess her freedom to nibble the sweet, succulent grass about her, and flung himself down upon the moss, to calm his thoughts by dipping into the leaves of the book that he carried in his pocket. But his mind was too turbulent; and presently he flung the book away, causing the horse to refrain from her nibbling to eye him with surprised curiosity.

After a few moments, passed apparently in deep thought to judge from his contracted brows, Tazoni once more drew the book towards him; and, taking a pencil from his pocket, began writing rapidly upon the fly-leaf. Then, discarding the book, he rose to his feet and began to pace restlessly up and down the limit of shade cast by the trees.

Meanwhile Veronica, finding that she had missed him, felt greatly annoyed, for she thought that in her attempt to spare his pride, she had subjected him to an even greater inconvenience. She feared he might be wanting the money, for she had heard that gipsies were generally poor, and sometimes even without enough to eat. Suppose he should be wanting that very money to buy food for himself and others?

The thought was not pleasant, and it led her on to one, curiously enough, even less so; for an imaginary picture rose before her of Maya—the girl who had abnegated her position as chief of the tribe in favour of Tazoni, the handsome gipsy.

Had it not been for the thought of meeting Maya, Veronica would have gone to the camp to take the money to Tazoni; but, instead, she deviated from the path leading to the common and took one that led deeper into the woods. Presently she came to the stream, and followed it along its course until it brought her to the very glen where Tazoni himself had stayed in his homeward journey.

Bess was the first to hear her light footstep, and gave a whinny of delight; whereupon Tazoni, turning quickly to see who the new-comer might be, found himself face to face with Veronica. With a curious reverence in his bearing that made her heart beat quickly, he uncovered his head, while his eyes shone with the happiness he felt in being once more in her presence.

"Good morning," said Veronica, as she patted the horse's neck. "So you've taken Bess in hand at last. You and your people have been kept very busy one way and another, I've heard; I hope Bess will not take up too much of your time," she added, kindly.

"No, lady," he replied, with a new humility that sat strangely upon him; "I shall be glad to have her, and redeem my promise."

He still stood uncovered before her; and Veronica smiled up at him as she said:

"Please put your cap on."

As he complied she noticed, for the first time, that there was a pallor in his face which had not been there when she saw him last.

"You've been at work at night, too," she went on. "It's not right to tire yourself too far."

"One can scarcely call it work, lady," he replied. "I have rested in the woods while I sought for the thief Lord Dartworth spoke of."

"I remember," she said. "Have you found out whether it is one of your men or not?"

"I am sure it isn't," Tazoni answered, his face darkening for a moment. "For the last two nights I've been on the thief's very heels; but he has far more cunning than I could ever have given him credit for."

"Did you hear that the night before last, Lord Raymond was attacked and robbed of his watch and chain while walking in the Northbridge woods?"

"Did he see the thief?" he asked, with an eager look.

"I cannot say," answered Veronica; and there was a momentary silence between them, while Tazoni's eyes scanned the ground thoughtfully. Then, with the crimson colour flaming over her face, the girl said:

"I am glad I have met you, because I wished to pay you for the ponies. I have brought the money with me. Here it is."

She took some money from a gold chain-purse she carried, and held it out to him. With a slight start, and the tightening about the corners of the lips by which she had discovered his pride, he opened his hand to receive it, and she placed in it five pounds.

"It is too much, lady," he said, selecting two sovereigns, and holding out the remaining three as if they had bitten him.

"No, it is not too much," Veronica replied, hesitatingly. "I——"

"Forgive me," he said, decisively. "There is no shame in accepting fair wages for fair work; it is no more than the highest and lowest of us do daily; but he who takes a needless charity soils his honour and his soul. Take them back, lady; and forgive me for daring to speak to you like this."

Her lips quivered a little as she took back the money, and the wistful look in the man's eyes grew tense. He knew that had he accepted her charity, he must have fallen in her eyes; yet it hurt her that he should have reproved her by the very act that called forth her admiration of him.

Suddenly his eyes rested upon her hand, and she guessed what he was about to say before the words came. Might he tell her her fortune? he asked; and, with a little laugh, she stretched out her hand. Her heart began to beat curiously fast as his strong fingers took it in his grasp, while he scanned the palm with interest.

There was a curious white look of repression upon his face that Veronica could not understand, and she could not help noticing that his hand holding hers trembled a little. Forced to speak from pure nervousness of the silence that had come upon them, she said:

"Would you mind beginning, please? I am curious, although somewhat sceptical."

Beneath his gaze Veronica's eyes dropped shyly to her hand, as he commenced:

"Lady, I would have life's path before you all smooth and shining; roses should shed their leaves about your feet, and you should know nothing save pure happiness. But I see in your hand a cloud overhanging your life—a secret pain, a deep unhappiness—shall I go on?"

"I would like to know all you can tell me," she said, her pride falling round her like a cloak, as she wondered what this gipsy could read in her heart and life.

"I see you walking in the garden of your youth—happy and serene is your life, with never a cloud in the sky. But into that life comes a man, with lust of gold and the love of self in his heart. His voice is like the tempter—sweet and seductive, calling your soul out of your body to the everlasting destruction of your happiness."

In a flash Veronica became aware that he was warning her against Hubert Denville; and that very thought awoke an obstinacy in her, which made her draw her hand away in a quick access of pride. What right had Tazoni—a mere gipsy —to hint at the honour of a man like Hubert Denville? Her pride of class was piqued; and, for a moment, she felt that she actually disliked Tazoni, forgetting that she had herself given him permission to say to her the words that had aroused her anger.

"I—I don't think I want to hear any more, thank you," she said, with an assumption of proud reserve that made Tazoni look at her in surprise.

"I am sorry if I have offended," he said, coldly.

She could only be just, and replied:

"There was no offence, since I asked you to tell me"; adding: "You will take care of Bess, I know."

"You may trust me, lady," was the quiet answer. "You shall have her back again within a week."

Tazoni whistled to Bess, who was reluctant to part from her mistress; raised his cap to Veronica, and went his way towards the camp; leaving the girl, ashamed of her pride, angry with him, and discontented generally.

As she, too, prepared to return home, her eyes fell upon the book Tazoni had been reading, which he had forgotten. As she picked it up, the fly-leaf fell back, and she saw some verses inscribed in pencil beneath her own name—*Veronica*.

Urged on by something more insistent than mere curiosity, she read them to the end, and when she closed the book her eyes were full of tears. All the man's restless, hungry longing had been put into that short poem—all his striving for high ideals, all his desire for the beautiful. Over all, like the soul rippling beneath a wonderful passage of music, breathed his despairing love for her.

Veronica looked in the direction in which Tazoni had gone, and her lips murmured, softly:

"If you hadn't been a gipsy, I could have loved you with all my heart, I think."

CHAPTER XIII

Lord Raymond possessed neither the courage, coolness, nor strength which are absolutely necessary to the making of a good whip. But the road leading to the ruined chapel which had been fixed upon for the picnic, was almost straight, except for one awkward curve, and he had managed to keep his temper and guide the drag safely to its destination.

It was a glorious day; and Lady Dartworth had consented to accompany the party. Lord Raymond condescended to be good-tempered, having, for the time, cast the memory of his troubles to the winds. He was filled with elation, too, at his success in bringing the drag along without mishap. On their arrival he helped to lay out the luncheon, occasionally swearing at the servants, and he ended up by rearranging everything that the rest had done.

With good appetites, they sat down to an admirable repast, while the horses were rested and refreshed.

"What a lovely drive!" said Judy Slade, as Raymond helped her to champagne. "You must have good nerve to drive a team like that."

Raymond smiled, pleased at the flattery.

"Think so?" he said. "Well, it isn't every fellow who could do it—'specially with this team. That off mare is as touchy as a bear with a sore head. But I think I managed to bring her along right enough. It's more than Denville could do, though; he's no good for anything."

"Perhaps you're right," drawled Hubert Denville, very bored.

His attitude towards Veronica that morning—the first time he had met her since he had made love to her two nights before—had been a reversion to his old indifferent manner, a fact that might have piqued her exceedingly, as it was meant to do, had not her thoughts been occupied with someone else.

After lunch, he asked Lady Dartworth to accompany him over the ruined chapel, if she were not tired; and Veronica and Judy Slade stayed with Lord Raymond, who showed a marked disinclination to leave the champagne.

When Lady Dartworth and her companion returned to the clump of trees under which they had lunched, they found Lord Raymond greatly excited, and his champagne glass still in his hand. The luncheon basket had already been packed up; and a servant had twice suggested that the remainder of the champagne should also be included, only to be sworn at soundly for his interference.

Hubert Denville ventured to glance with significance at Veronica, who, however, looked straight before her, too disgusted for words by their host's behaviour.

"Come, my dear fellow," said Denville, touching Raymond on the shoulder, "don't you think we had better be starting? The ladies are waiting."

"What's that?" asked Lord Raymond. "Oh, no; I say, let's have some more champagne, eh, Judy?"

Miss Slade, who felt, rather than saw, that Lady Dartworth's eyes were fixed upon her, declined; and Lord Raymond filled up his glass. Hubert Denville then signed to a groom to take the hamper away; and, looking after it with an ill-tempered scowl, Raymond rose to his feet. Several champagne bottles lay near the spot where he had sat, and he sent his glass to join them; then, with a coarse laugh, he strode towards the drag, utterly ignoring the ladies, whom Denville assisted to their places.

"Raymond," said Denville, in a low voice, loud enough, however, to reach Veronica's ears, "I say, don't you think you had better let me drive? The horses seem rather restive and——" the shrug that completed the sentence was expressive.

Lord Raymond stared at him angrily.

"Do you think I can't manage my own team? What are you driving at?" he said, and sprang on to the box, with an accurate celerity highly commendable after the amount of champagne he had taken.

Judy Slade and Lady Dartworth glanced at Hubert Denville with ill-concealed fear; and the slight frown that ruffled his habitually smooth forehead did not help to reassure them. Veronica, however, who was by nature fearless, sat looking down upon the splendid, fidgety bays, and seemed unconscious of impending danger.

At a signal from Denville, the groom let go the leaders' heads, and the horses sprang forward. With a cut of the whip, Lord Raymond tightened up his reins, and for the moment the occupants of the drag felt reassured. But after a few minutes' careful driving, the wine he had drunk began to stir his blood to fever heat, and the long whip coiled too often round the sides of the excited horses.

"The off mare's very touchy, my lord," the groom ventured to remark; but his master glared at him and struck the restless animal viciously. With a start and a plunge, it dashed forward: the drag rocked to and fro, and Lord Raymond rolled in his seat.

"Hold them in," said Denville in his ear, and, for a few moments, Raymond managed to do so.

"If we can pass the corner he may bring us in with whole skins," said Denville to Judy in an undertone; and then he relapsed into silence, watching the road and Lord Raymond's whip.

Every moment the excited animals were gaining fresh strength and command over their incapable driver. The drag began to lurch to and fro like a ship in a storm; the dust rose in a blinding, choking cloud; and the clatter of the horses' hoofs, as they beat the road, sounded fearfully distinct and threatening.

The corner came in sight, and Miss Slade's face grew paler than ever.

"For goodness' sake be careful of the corner," she said, anxiously, to Lord Raymond. But either he did not hear, or chose to disregard her warning, for with a hoarse laugh he cut the leaders across the ears, and let them have the rein.

With a combined dash, like a stone from a catapult, they swerved and rushed forward.

Denville rose in his seat, and threw his arm around Veronica. The groom shouted warningly, and Judy Slade and Lady Dartworth entirely lost their heads. Only one person seemed fearless. Pushing back Hubert Denville's arm, Veronica grasped the rail, and rose to look before her. The bays were close upon the corner, careering at full speed. The foam was flying across their straining backs.

"It is certain death," she said, calmly.

The words had scarcely passed her lips when a figure rushed from the woods; stood for the space of a second, then, with a smile which only Veronica saw, sprang at the near leader's head and drove her from the fatal point. There was a confusion of hoofs, a tossing of heads, a fearful kicking and snorting; then the drag was brought to a standstill; and Veronica knew that they were saved.

Hubert Denville leapt to the ground, and, with the groom, secured the horses' heads. Amidst the confusion Lady Dartworth's voice was heard to ask: "Who was it that stopped them?"

No one could say. Only Veronica had seen and recognized the rescuer; but she remained silent. An innate sense of delicacy had shown her that Tazoni's disappearance meant that he wished to remain unrecognized; and could she refuse to comply with his desire for secrecy?

The almost miraculous escape, from what must undoubtedly have been a frightful accident, had somewhat sobered Lord Raymond. He was considerably shaken, and did not hesitate to make everyone acquainted with the fact.

Beneath his lowered eyelids Hubert Denville watched Veronica, and was astounded at her self-possession. In a clear, steady voice she gave orders that the drag should be taken to the Hall, and that a car from the Manor should pick them up as soon as possible. There was a peculiar light in her eyes, but neither Judy Slade nor Hubert Denville noticed it.

Veronica did not attempt to explain, even to herself, the feeling that had taken possession of her; she only knew that in her heart there had sprung up an intense admiration for the man who had risked his life to save her.

Half an hour later a car arrived from the Manor, and the three women entered it with no small sense of relief. Hubert Denville declined to accompany them, saying that it would be wiser to deliver his friend into safe keeping.

That night, while Veronica and Judy were dressing for dinner, Lady Dartworth told her husband of the mishap; but refused to attach any blame to Lord Raymond, whom she wished, as the son of her dearest friend, to see the husband of her daughter.

"I am sure it was more excitement than the wine he had drunk, my dear," she said. "You know he so easily loses his head."

"I am afraid that he drinks more than he ought to do," replied her husband, gravely; "it is not the first time he has been intoxicated, to my own knowledge."

"Oh, no; surely not!" said Lady Dartworth, looking grieved.

"Well, I may be mistaken," he rejoined; "but if I find I am right, all hope of a union between him and Veronica is at an end. We could not expect her to love her husband, if she had no respect for him."

Meanwhile, in her own room, Veronica stood with the copy of Shakespeare in her hand, reading some verses pencilled upon the fly-leaf, while a vision of Tazoni's determined face as he stopped the drag, rose between her and the lines she sought to read. Finally she closed the book, and hid it in a secret drawer.

"I owe him my life," she said to herself; and in her heart Veronica knew that she was on the verge of something that would light up the darkness of doubt in which she had been groping for so many days.

CHAPTER XIV

On the following morning, Lord Raymond possessed but an indistinct idea of the events of the previous day. That there had been a picnic, and that some mischance or other had occurred, were dimly conceived notions in his mind; but in what way things had ended, he was unaware, and too lazy to enquire. He had a splitting headache, and a presentiment of coming ill which was partially fulfilled by the appearance of a further relay of bills accompanied by unfriendly letters. With an unsteady hand he wrote to Levy Jacobs, the Jew, promising, as he had been directed to do, the complete payment of his claim in a month from that date. The least pressing of his bills he tore up, tossed the others into his bureau, and then, with uncertain steps and a gloomy countenance, descended to the morning-room.

It was empty, for Hubert Denville had been called up to town, where he was to return definitely in a day or two; Lord Northbridge, too, had breakfasted, and was busy with his correspondence.

Lord Raymond was particularly thankful for his father's absence. Owing to a lucky accident, Lord Northbridge had been out when he had been brought home the day before, and, by keeping away from him as much as possible, he hoped to escape all unpleasant scrutiny. He mixed himself a stiff brandy-and-soda, which he imagined to be a good tonic for persons in his condition; and after swallowing this down in one gulp, he sauntered out into the grounds, his hands in his pockets, and his eyes fixed upon the stones which his restless feet kicked from the gravel path.

But Lord Raymond did not find himself congenial company; and the large number of bills waiting to be settled had an unpleasant knack of recurring to his mind. He would have liked to ride over to the Manor and be petted by his ever-devoted admirer, Miss Slade; but he had enough sense to know that his reception at the hands of Lady Dartworth and Veronica might be anything but cordial.

"I think I'll go and see that little gipsy," he said to himself. "I guess the rest of the tribe will be out of the way; so that if the old woman doesn't spot me, I shall be quite all right—plucky little thing, that gipsy!—Vee's not a patch on her."

He stifled a yawn, and set out languidly for the gipsy encampment. He could scarcely have chosen a more unfavourable moment for his visit.

On the previous evening, when the time for Tazoni's return drew near, Maya had spread the soft mat before his tent, arranged some of his favourite books at its edge, and in various other ways prepared a woman's welcome for the man she esteemed above all others. Six o'clock chimed from the Northbridge stables, but he did not come. He was usually so punctual that Maya began to experience that sense of fear which visits those who love and wait.

Seven o'clock passed; the sun set; and still he did not return. By this time the men had returned to the camp, and were waiting, with stolid patience, for their supper, which Martha was preparing for them. They were all in good spirits, for work had been to hand in plenty; but every now and then they would glance towards the woods, where they hoped first to see Tazoni. Suddenly, with a step singularly unlike his usual strength-denoting stride, he emerged from the gloom of the trees, and passed into the glare of the fire; and instantly the men knew that something had befallen him. His face, though calm as usual, was stained with blood; there were cuts upon his temple, while his right arm was thrust into the breast of his coat.

Instantly the men sprang to their feet. Had anyone dared to do him harm? Not one of them uttered a word; but the gleaming eyes and clenched hands were more eloquent than a thousand vows of vengeance.

Tazoni understood them; and, with a smile that was faint and weak, held up his left hand.

"It's all right," he said. "Go on with your suppers. I have had an accident."

They obeyed, reluctantly; but one, more curious than the rest, asked:

"What accident?"

"Runaway horses and a clumsy driver," said Tazoni, in his short way; and passed on to his own tent, hoping to avoid Maya, who, however, heard his footstep and sprang to meet him.

"Tazoni, what has happened?" she asked, anxiously, as she caught sight of his pale, blood-stained face.

It was useless for him to assure her that it was of no moment; for, seemingly heedless of his indifference, she arranged the rug inside his tent, helped him to remove his coat, and, when one of the men had fetched some water, herself bathed his lacerated face. But when she came to his arm the matter looked more serious. He groaned when he tried to move it, causing her to grow as pallid as himself.

"I'm afraid I've got a bad sprain," Tazoni said ruefully.

Without a word, she rose from her knees and fetched Martha, who examined the limb and confirmed Tazoni's fears.

"I'll go and find Zillah," said the old woman at once; "she'll soon see to it."

Zillah was a small, dark gipsy, with large, soft eyes. Her skill in medicine was remarkable; and it was asserted by the men that she knew more of bone-setting and sprains than all the doctors in England. With gentle, yet skilful touch, she bandaged up Tazoni's arm, and put it in a sling; then, after vainly endeavouring to drink some soup which Martha had specially prepared, he turned in for the night.

When all was quiet, and the stars shone down upon the embers of the deserted camp-fire, the curtain of Maya's tent was pushed gently aside, and she stepped out. Without a sound she crept to Tazoni's tent and listened anxiously. It was as she had suspected. He was neither asleep nor resting, but turning from side to side in uneasy pain. Now and then, he would mutter an unintelligible remark, and Maya heard something about horses and drags, sharp corners and broken necks.

Suddenly, after a pause, during which she hoped with a feverish longing that he might have fallen asleep, she heard him speak a woman's name. There could be no mistake, for it came again.

"Veronica! Veronica!"

With a dazed sense of some great sorrow, she closed her eyes. That, then, was the reason of his absent, silent moods. He was in love, and with a proud, cold-hearted woman who would bring only sorrow and suffering into his life. A passion of jealousy, and a bitter sense of the mockery of it all, came over her, and with a suppressed moan she crouched at the door of the tent, and watched through the night till the summer dawn had broken. All night long the delirium lasted; and it was not until the sun was high in heaven that Tazoni had fallen into a sleep of sheer exhaustion. The men had been sent to their work in the surrounding countryside, for Maya wished the camp to be in perfect silence, lest the slightest sound should awaken Tazoni.

It was, therefore, with no small amount of astonishment and anger, that she saw Lord Raymond making his way jauntily between the caravans. She sprang hastily to her feet, and, before the new-comer could utter a word, she increased his surprise—for he had expected her to run away rather than come to meet him —by saying in a whisper, intensified by anger:

"How dare you come here again! For God's sake, don't speak or make a noise, for there is someone ill in the camp, and he is sleeping for a time. Please go!"

Her face was white and drawn; and beneath her dark eyes were the shadows of sleeplessness.

Lord Raymond grinned, and put out his hand to push her aside; but the next moment he stepped back with a low exclamation of alarm, for he was a bully and a coward, and the sight of a heavy whip that Maya had caught up in her extremity had the effect upon him which she so greatly desired.

"There'll come a time perhaps when you may think it worth your while to be civil, my girl," Lord Raymond said, threateningly, an evil look in his eyes; and with that he turned on his heel and left the camp.

The next day Dartworth Manor was flooded with guests, whose advent had kept the large staff of servants busily engaged for some weeks beforehand.

Veronica had wished to go over to the gipsy encampment and seek an opportunity of speaking with Tazoni, in order to tell him that she had recognized him, and that she should always consider herself under an obligation to him for the immeasurable service he had rendered her. But the unexpectedly early arrival of some guests prevented her from carrying out her plan; for her duties as assistant hostess kept her busily occupied.

Some days passed, and she neither saw nor heard anything of Tazoni. There were motoring excursions, picnics, dances, bridge parties, and a host of other entertainments for the amusement of the visitors at Dartworth; and Veronica felt that she had scarcely time to breathe.

Hubert Denville had been kept in town much longer than he had expected, but was coming down for a big ball, for which many other guests had been invited, in addition to those already included in the house party.

It had been some little while before Lord Raymond could summon up courage to visit the Manor, after his not very praiseworthy exhibition upon the day of the picnic; but when he did put in an appearance, both Lady Dartworth and Judy Slade received him with a warm welcome; although Veronica's attitude was certainly far from encouraging. This fact drove him more than ever into the society of Judy Slade, who made him feel that she not only understood him perfectly, but fully appreciated where Veronica seemed only to despise.

After dinner one evening, just two days before the date fixed for the ball, Saidie Maddison, a little American millionairess, suddenly suggested that they should "try their legs" instead of spending the night at bridge as usual. Judy Slade was pushed into the seat at the piano, and commanded to play a waltz, while the rest sorted themselves into couples. Veronica had Sir Harry Beriford for a partner, and, almost before she was aware of the fact, she was being whirled round the room in an altogether breathless fashion.

Meanwhile, through the Manor grounds stole the figure of Maya, the pretty gipsy girl, her heart beating fast as she thought of the errand upon which she was bent.

Tazoni's delirious ravings had filled her with a jealous curiosity to see for herself the woman who had won his affections. Night and day she wished that they had never come to Northbridge—for herself, and for him she loved, since to both of them it had brought a great unhappiness. Now, her one desire was to see Veronica, and if possible to speak to her. She was childish enough to dream that if she begged Veronica to release Tazoni from his yoke of bondage to her, he might become once more the happy mortal he had been before he saw the woman who had enslaved him.

Maya skilfully managed to extract a description of "the young miss at the Manor" from Colin; and feeling sure she would be able to select Veronica by instinct from among a thousand others, she secretly made her way to Dartworth.

When she reached the terrace, however, the many lights from the windows made her afraid, and the sound of music and high-bred voices struck her with an unpleasant thrill. She would go back, she told herself. Why should she give herself fruitless pain by looking on the face that Tazoni loved?

For an instant she half turned, but only for an instant; the next she ran up the flight of stone steps, and glided into the dark shadow of the laurels. From her position, she could clearly see the moving forms of the people within, as their feet danced in rhythm to the beat of the music. The highly polished floor reflected the many clusters of lights, which were again reflected, in sparks of glorious colour, in the jewels worn by the women in their hair and upon their necks.

To Maya the scene was so wonderful—since she had never seen anything of the kind before—that she could only gaze and gaze in mute admiration.

Presently one of the couples came to a stop quite close to the open window near which Maya was crouching. The woman had a wealth of golden hair dressed round her head in classic bands; the face was sweet, though a trifle weary; and as she turned her head towards the window for a moment, Maya was near enough to see that her eyes were dark. From Colin's description and her own instinct, Maya knew that this was the woman who had wrought so much havoc in Tazoni's life; and she caught her breath for very pain, as she realized Veronica's loveliness, and the utter hopelessness of her own mission.

Veronica spoke to her companion, and he went away as though to fetch something which she had asked him to get for her. Then she herself turned towards the open window, and stood looking out into the silent night. Suddenly she stepped outside, and in that moment Maya could have touched her with her outstretched hand. Veronica walked along the terrace a little way; then turned, somewhat startled by a footstep behind her, to find herself confronted by an unknown gipsy girl. Instantly her mind flew to Tazoni, and she asked hastily:

"Were you watching for me? What do you want?"

"Yes, I was seeking you, lady," began Maya, quietly; then suddenly she burst out passionately: "Oh, lady, be kind and let him go. We were happy before you came into our lives; and might be so again, if you would turn away your eyes from him, and leave him in peace. He has been ill; he is not better yet. It was to save your life—I heard it while he tossed and turned in the night; his brain was on fire. All night long he cried out 'Veronica'—and I knew he meant you, lady, though he had said never a word to me——"

Veronica laid her hand upon the girl's arm, and interrupted her wild raving by asking quietly:

"Will you tell me of whom you are speaking?"

"Of Tazoni," replied the girl, her passion calmed a little by Veronica's even tones. "Oh, he loves you, lady; as high as Heaven above, as deep as hell—that's what love means to him."

The fervid earnestness underlying the quaint words caused a strange choking sensation in Veronica's throat; and for a moment she did not speak. Then she said:

"Did you say he was ill?"

"Yes, lady," was the answer. "He hurt himself in the accident."

"What accident?" asked Veronica, quickly.

"I do not know, lady; but when he was ill I heard him cry out, '*The drag*' and '*Oh God, Veronica!*'—it may be that you know, lady, more than I."

"Oh!" said Veronica, and the word sounded like a sob. "Is—is he ill now?" she added, after a pause.

"He is getting better, lady."

"Tell him"—Veronica hesitated—"tell him that to-morrow I will come. Say to him——"

What more she would have added remained unsaid; for Lord Raymond's voice came floating out to her in his usual harsh tones.

"Vee! Vee! Are you there? Can't you spare a moment to say good night to a fellow! I'm going home."

As she recognized the voice, Maya slipped away in a flash; and Veronica saw her no more that night.

In the privacy of her own room, Veronica trembled from head to foot as she realized, at last, the truth that had been dawning slowly on her, ever since the night when the memory of Tazoni had come between her and Hubert Denville's love-making.

Sobbing, she flung herself down upon her knees before her open window, her face turned in the direction of the gipsy encampment. That she loved Tazoni, she could not deny; but that, for that very reason, they two must part for ever, she was forced to confess as well; and the bitterness of her despair sank upon her heart like a pall of blackness.

When Maya returned to the camp, she found that Tazoni was awake, and had been asking for her.

"Well, little sister," he said, with a welcoming smile; and the girl was glad that he seemed to be his own self again; "where have you been?"

She made no answer to his question, and, scanning her closely, he noticed that she looked pale; though it might have been owing to the half-light thrown by the lamp.

"Maya, you have made yourself ill in waiting upon me; but I am fit to play the man again now."

"Indeed, I am quite well," she answered, quickly; "but you must lie down and rest—for another week, at least."

"That is impossible," he said, decisively. "There is work to be done, and——"

Seeing that he hesitated, the girl averted her gaze, and said, softly:

"Are we going to leave the common then?"

He started slightly, and threw back the hair from his forehead with an impatient gesture.

"Leave the common?" he repeated. "Have we been here too long then, Maya?"

"No, no," she replied, quickly. "Why should I think so? It's true we have stayed here longer than anywhere else; but as long as you are content——"

"That is not it," he said, in a quiet voice. "If the men are tired of the place—and it is their nature to rove——"

"And yours, too. You are a gipsy, Tazoni."

"Ours, I meant to say," he corrected himself, with a slight flush. "It is our nature to love change; and if they wish to move on, we will go—to-morrow if they like."

"No, not to-morrow, that's impossible," she said. "I don't know whether the men do want to move on. Why should they? There is plenty of work, and food, and money."

"Very well," he replied, his brow clearing a little. "If they are contented, we will stay a little longer—that is, if you are willing, Maya?"

"It is not for me to say," she said, softly. "But you have been talking too long; you must rest. It is well you should sleep, Tazoni; for to-morrow—to-morrow the young lady of the Manor will come to speak with you."

She saw his face turn deathly white; then suddenly a flush crept over it like a crimson stain. Flinging aside the rugs that covered him, he crossed to the open door of the tent. He stood there in long, deep silence—his hand resting upon one of the tautened ropes—a black silhouette against the moonlight. Maya sat and watched him while the tears ran down her cheeks, washing away all jealousy and bitterness from her heart, and leaving in their place only a sweet, tender love and pity for the pain, for which there could be no remedy, in Tazoni's life.

CHAPTER XV

The same night—being that which the anonymous poacher had fixed for the second interview—Lord Raymond stole down from his own room, and slipped unseen through the great hall into the grounds. Though the night was anything but cold, he had put on a large overcoat, and wore a scarf so arranged round his neck that it effectually concealed the lower part of his features; while a cloth cap, pulled carefully over his eyes, completed his disguise. Thus armed against recognition, he made his way cautiously through the huge elm-woods, and, after some little difficulty, found the fallen tree which had been fixed upon by the poacher as a rendezvous.

The faint chimes of the stable clock proclaimed the hour of twelve; and, seated on the trunk, his hands in his pockets and his eyes impatiently alert, Lord Raymond waited, with something approaching fear, the coming of the mysterious being who seemed so fully cognisant of his most secret affairs.

Half an hour passed; and with an imprecation he rose, with the intention of returning to the Hall. As he did so, a mass of leaves quite close to him was agitated; and from them uprose a tall, thin form, causing Raymond to start violently.

"Did I frighten ye?" queried the man, in his thick, guttural voice, and with a familiarity that was not lost on Lord Raymond.

"Where did you come from?" he asked; "through the ground?"

"Not quite *through*; but I've been here at yer feet, trying yer patience, for the last half-hour. It's a good job ye kept yer word," said the poacher, with a slight menace in his tone.

"I'm here; and that's enough," replied the other, with a futile attempt to be haughty. "And now, what do you wish to tell me, my good fellow?"

"What do ye want to know?" said the poacher.

"A great deal; but, first of all, you'd better tell me what you've got to say. I can't stay here all night."

The poacher sat down on the bank; but although the posture was a careless one, his eyes were wary, for they detected a movement of Lord Raymond's hand in his pocket. Before he could bring the hand out again, the poacher had sprung upon him, and, with a grin, had wrenched it away. Taken unawares, Lord Raymond had not the presence of mind to release his hold of the revolver that he had, concealed.

"Thought so," said the poacher, not at all surprised. "Quite right of ye to take precautions; but they're thrown away on me, I can tell ye. It would be the very worst little job ye ever did, to put a bullet through me. There's a little secret o' yours, shut up, as ye might say, in a barrel; and, if I'm moved out o' the way, I've left instructions for someone else to deal with the matter—kind o' last will and testament, d'yer see?"

"What d'you mean about a secret?" asked Lord Raymond, harshly.

The poacher smiled knowingly.

"It wouldn't be a secret any longer if I told you; so you bet I don't. It ain't for that I've brought you away from all your fine friends. I mean business to-night, I warn you. Before I begin, I'd just like to ask you a simple question, though. Why didn't ye keep clear of the drink, when I told ye ye was to? I guess as ye had a good many fillips of something, to make ye play the fool with that drag the other day."

Lord Raymond scowled.

"Don't attempt to do things ye don't understand," continued the man, coolly. "Ye can no more drive a four-in-hand than ye can fly. Don't attempt to; or ye'll come to grief, as sure as yer name's what it isn't—I mean——"

"You don't know what you do mean, and that's about it," said Lord Raymond, angered by what he was unable to understand.

The poacher laughed quietly.

"Well, suppose we gets to business," he said, soothingly. "You wants money badly, so do I; so we're in the same tub together. I suppose Mr. Levy Jacobs has been a-tightening the screw lately, ain't 'e?—then there's a lot of other little bills to be paid. Two thousand 'ud just cover it, eh?"

Lord Raymond was silent; but, with an uneasy feeling of wonderment, he felt that the man had hit the mark.

"Two thousand pounds ain't a large sum; but it's more than yer father will give ye, isn't it? Well, suppose we say two thousand five hundred—the five hundred for me, eh?"

Raymond laughed scornfully.

"You're amusing, if nothing else, I must say. But for goodness' sake be quick. I'm tired; and this isn't the best of places to spend the night in."

"Oh, all right," said the poacher, cheerfully. "What we've got to consider now is how to get the money."

"Exactly," sneered Lord Raymond. "I was wondering how long you'd be before you came to that point. Perhaps, as you think you know all my affairs, you can tell me how to do the trick?"

"Ain't as hard as ye think. Ye've apparently forgot the saying, 'Where a man won't give, take!' Yer father won't give ye the tin; well then, ye'll have to take it."

"You mean steal it," put in Lord Raymond.

"That's vulgar," sneered the other. "Call it 'borrow.' After all, that's only what it comes to. It'll be yours some day—if ye don't lose yer head; so it's only borrowing what's yer own."

Lord Raymond's lips twitched with nervous indecision.

"Ye know the old man's strong-room," continued his companion, in an undertone; "well, in that room's the safe, isn't it? There ought to be plenty of money in that—ye know the old earl thinks as his strong-room's securer than any bank. I know for a fact as he keeps a lot of his wife's jewels there still; in fact, it 'ud be quite as easy to get the lot as part."

Lord Raymond raised his cap, and wiped off the great beads of perspiration which had gathered upon his forehead.

"Well, I'm blessed!" he said. "You seem to know the house—the very position of—of—the valuables; what do you want with me?" he asked, hoarsely.

"Half a mo'," said the poacher, calmly; "we're a-coming to that. There's going to be a ball up at the Manor pretty soon, isn't there?"

"The day after to-morrow."

"Good!" replied the man. "There'll be no moon to speak of, and every chance of a dark night—well, that's when we'll land the swag, my boy."

"*We!*" said Raymond, beginning to tremble, although he did his best to revert to his former jauntiness. "If you want it, you may steal it yourself."

"With the greatest of pleasure," assented the poacher; "but *you've* got to have a hand in it. Well, now for the modus hoperandy, as they calls it. Ye're going to that ball, of course?"

Raymond nodded.

"All the Northbridge servants are going up to help, I've heard; so it's ten to one they'll come home dog-tired—every man-jack of 'em! That's the night for us then; the strong-room opens out of Lord Northbridge's dressing-room, doesn't it? and he's an uncommon light sleeper. I suppose he never takes anything in the shape of a drink before he goes to bed?"

"No, he doesn't," said Lord Raymond surlily.

"Well, ye'll have to manage so that he does, then," replied the poacher. "It'll be quite easy to do the trick."

The man put his hand into his breast pocket and drew out a small, flat packet.

"Just drop this 'ere powder into his glass, and it'll mix with the grog in a jiffy —no sediment or discolouring, or anything like that—makes ye sleep like a top."

Lord Raymond took the packet, but made no comment.

"Well?" asked the poacher, finding that he did not speak.

"I'm hanged if I'll do it!" said Raymond, with more spirit than the other man would have given him credit for.

"Why not?" asked the poacher. "Ye're going to gain more than I shall."

"No, it isn't that," returned the other. "I wouldn't mind if it had been any other man but my father. Hang it all! a man's got a certain amount of respect for his family—I mean he can't stoop to such dirty jobs as burglary—besides, I might get nabbed."

"Oh, that's it, is it? Afraid ye'll get copped; and so ye talk about respect for yer father, and yer family, and all that rot, on purpose to hide yer funk."

Lord Raymond stirred uneasily. He could not understand the attitude of the mysterious poacher; but he firmly made up his mind that he would have no hand in the proposed burglary of his father's strong-room. It was not only the fact that the risk he ran would be great, but, even to such a nature as his, the idea of robbing his own father was revolting. He was in a quandary; for he wanted money badly, and did not know how he should raise it if he did not take the poacher's advice. At last he decided to adopt an intermediate course.

"It's not a question of funk," he said, endeavouring to speak quietly and un-concernedly. "I won't do it; so there's an end of it—unless—unless—well, why don't you do it yourself?"

"Because I don't want to. Look here," said the poacher, for the first time get-ting impatient, "supposing I tells ye that the man we wants to—er—borrow from, isn't yer father at all; what 'ud ye say to that?"

"Why, that you've lost a button somewhere," said Lord Raymond, with his usual coarseness.

"Well, he isn't—because I'm your father!"

"*You!* Get off! You're pulling my leg," said Lord Raymond, getting jocular, and quite under the impression that the poacher had suddenly taken leave of his senses.

"Ye don't believe me," remarked the man, not at all ruffled by the other's at-titude. He had expected it, and was therefore prepared. "Well, suppose I told ye that twenty odd years ago my wife nursed two kids—one her own, and the other Lady Northbridge's——"

"I know all about that."

"Well, suppose Lady Northbridge's brat died, and Marion Smeaton's—that's you, my boy—was put in its place, unbeknown to anyone but three people; what would ye say to that?"

"That you can't prove there's a word of truth in it," said Lord Raymond, putting on a bold front, but with a horrible fear clutching at his heart.

"Can't I! What about if Lady Northbridge's brat didn't die after all, and we can put our hand on it whenever we like?"

"You can't prove that Marion Smeaton's child didn't die, though. Why, it was buried—my father told me so."

"Merely a coffin stuffed with rags and a stone or two," said Luke Smeaton, with a grin. "Lady Northbridge's child had a fit, and my wife thought it was dead; so I didn't undeceive her. We put her child in place of Lady Northbridge's —that's why Marion's always behaved so funny-like when she's met ye. Ye've only got to dig up the coffin; and then there's three people to prove as ye're my son, while the trump card—in the shape of the real Lord Raymond—is always to hand."

"Tell me who it is," said Raymond. "Seeing's believing."

"Well, if ye must know—only don't blame me for upsetting yer apple-cart— it's Tazoni, the gipsy."

The other man gasped. "Do you mean to say," he said, as yet hardly compre-hending what it all meant, "do you mean to say, that that insolent puppy is Lord Northbridge's son; and that I'm nothing but the son of a low-down dirty gipsy!"

"I do," said Luke Smeaton; "and what's more, I'm prepared to take my oath on it—when it suits me, of course—and so's old Martha, if need be; and my wife'll have no difficulty in proving it, into the bargain."

"Good Lord!" said the other man.

"Funny, ain't it!" remarked the poacher.

Lord Raymond stood for some minutes in deep thought. Although what he had heard had "knocked him flat," as he would have put it, yet somehow he did not experience the astonishment that any other man would have done in the circumstances.

He felt as if he had always known that he was alienated by some unseen force from the people with whom he lived. Now that everything had been made plain to him, the cunning which had been his natural birthright, and which had been kept somewhat in abeyance by his environment and position, came to his aid. He had no intention of relinquishing his rank, even if he had no right to it.

The idea that Luke Smeaton was lying, naturally occurred to him; but then everything went to prove his assertion; and if the real heir did make his claim known—it was possible, however, that Tazoni was totally unaware of his good fortune—there would certainly be some test by which he could be proved to be Lord Northbridge's son. The only thing to do, then, was to sit tight and get all the fun he could while it was possible; and, if anything did come out, he could always deny that he had ever known the truth. Possessed of this knowledge he decided to act accordingly.

"Look here, your story may or may not be true," he said, suddenly; "but the fact still remains that I want money. So I've changed my mind; I'll come in with you after all."

"That's right," replied Luke. "Ye can please yourself about believing what I told ye—ye'll be an ass if ye don't, though; for ye can depend upon it, I can prove what I say in more ways than one."

"Well, what's to be done?" asked Raymond, impatiently.

"Take care of the packet I gave ye, to begin with. The next thing is, that to get into that room we shall want the keys, which must be taken from the old man's pocket."

"What, when he's asleep!"

"Of course," replied Smeaton. "It's better than when he's awake, isn't it? That powder will send him off like a top. Ye'll have to get the keys; and exactly as the clock strikes three, open the double doors of the strong-room, and then let me in by the side entrance to the house. I'll be there as true as life. What'll be easier than to walk upstairs, open the safe, and make off with the swag? I'll do that part while you go back to bed, and sleep like a baby."

"It's absurd!" said Lord Raymond. "Why, the slightest noise, and there'd be a fine hullabaloo. You might get away; but I should be recognized at once."

"Not if ye wears the togs I'll rig ye up in."

"But how am I to get them?"

"They'll be under this tree to-morrow night—just as if they'd grown there like a mushroom," replied Luke.

"Oh, yes, that's all very fine; but directly it's seen that the doors were opened by keys, suspicion will fall on someone in the house."

"We'll manage all that easy enough," said Luke, cryptically. "For days there have been tramps hanging about the roads. Gipsies——"

Lord Raymond started, for an idea had occurred to him by which he could get Tazoni well out of his way.

"There are gipsies in the neighbourhood, and they generally get the credit for anything that goes wrong. Can't we throw the scent on them?" he asked, eagerly.

Luke Smeaton smiled.

"I thought ye'd want to pay him back before long," he said. "Well?"

"One of them must be got out of the way—one whose absence will be missed."

"Tazoni, you mean," said the poacher, grimly.

"He'd do," returned the other, with an assumed indifference.

"Of course he would. D'ye think I'm a luny, and can't spot yer little game! But you must get him out of the way, or it wouldn't be worth much."

"You're duller than I took you for," said Lord Raymond, with an ugly sneer. "They tell me the girl's sweet on this Tazoni; and that he looks upon himself as her guardian and protector."

"Well?"

"Don't you see?" asked Raymond, irritably.

"Can't say as I do," retorted Luke, coolly.

"Goodness knows it's simple enough. This girl must be got out of the way by some trick. A message must reach him, supposed to come from her, saying that she's been carried off, and begging him to follow her—of course, in the opposite direction to the one that she has really taken. He'll be off like a shot; and, if the thing's properly managed, he'll be missed just about the time the—the affair takes place."

Raymond looked at the man opposite for approval; but Luke Smeaton did not answer.

"You must manage the man, and I'll arrange about the girl," Raymond went on, hurriedly. "I suppose you know something of the Romany dialect? Well, both messages must be given in that, and delivered by a gipsy—preferably yourself— then it won't arouse any suspicion."

"Ye'll manage the girl?" repeated Luke, who was beginning to find out that his offspring was not such a fool as he had imagined. "Where will ye take her?"

"Oh, somewhere—anywhere—that doesn't matter to you," replied Raymond, carelessly. "I'll take care of her, trust me."

"I dare say ye will," said Luke; "but it can't be done. Ye know precious little about gipsies, my friend; or ye'd know that they don't sell one another in that fashion. Why, it's more than my life's worth!"

"What d'you mean?" demanded Lord Raymond, angrily. "There's no danger in your part of the business. All you have to do is to take a message in their own language."

"Don't sound much, I own, but d'ye know what 'ud happen if I did it? Why, they'd hunt me down like a rat; and they wouldn't stop at nothing until they'd reckoned they'd paid me out for running off with the girl. Besides, it 'ud be at least two years if we got caught, without the risk of the other affair. We'd much better leave the girl out of it."

"No," said Lord Raymond, decidedly; "if I play your game on Wednesday night, you've got to play mine in return. I'll have the girl, or you don't get the money, and you can go hang with your lies about my not being what I'm supposed to be."

Luke Smeaton considered a moment.

"All right, then, I agree. Where shall the girl go, and when?"

"You must get her to the cross-roads at nine o'clock. A motor shall be there waiting," said Lord Raymond.

"Not the Northbridge one?" interrupted Smeaton.

"Of course not, you fool! I'll have one sent from a garage in London."

"What about the messages?" asked Luke.

"We'll have to get Tazoni away on some business to the farther end of the woods; meanwhile, you can take a message from him, asking the girl to meet him at the cross-roads. Once there she'll be quite all right to manage."

"How?" asked Luke. "You can't be there."

"If I can't, I know a man who will—he owes me money, so he can't afford to play me up. I'm too useful to him," replied Raymond, with a sneer.

"Ye mean Hubert Denville?" said Smeaton.

"Well, you are a one-r!" exclaimed Raymond, with surprise. "You seem to know every blessed thing!"

"Go on; time's getting on," said Luke, imperturbably.

"Get her to the cross-roads, and he'll take care of her."

"And Tazoni?" asked Luke.

"I'll leave him to your tender care; you're a gipsy and ought to know how to manage that."

"And what's to become of him?" asked the poacher, sardonically. "You're disposing of 'em pretty quickly, it seems to me."

"He doesn't matter. Get the girl away, and suspicion will fall on him; circumstances will do the rest."

"All right then; it's a risky game we're playing; but I dare say we'll manage it. We'd better be going, I think."

Lord Raymond reached the side-door, through which he passed when he chose by means of a private key, and glided noiselessly to his own rooms. Quietly removing the overcoat and cap, he smoothed his dark hair to its usual appearance, and sitting down to his writing-table, dragged out some note-paper, and commenced to write hurriedly.

"DEAR DENVILLE," the letter began, "I needn't remind you of your many promises to do me a good turn if ever the chance came. This *is* the chance.

"You are coming down by an early train on Wednesday afternoon, I think. Well, *don't.*

"What I want you to do is to get a good car from a garage, and bring it down here to the cross-roads at nine o'clock on Wednesday evening. That gipsy girl has got to be taken to 'The Cottage,' and you're the man to do it for me. If you will, we'll make it five hundred quid, and a cancelling of the sundry little debts you owe me.

"You won't miss the fun at Dartworth; because, if you get a decent motor, you can do the job and be back by twelve, in good time for supper. Is it a bargain? Wire me 'accept' on receipt of this, and the thing's done.

"Yours,
"RAYMOND."

At dinner the following evening, a telegram was handed to Lord Raymond and as he glanced at the two words it contained, a smile of satisfaction lit up his vicious eyes.

CHAPTER XVI

The next morning Veronica, accompanied by Saidie Maddison and Sir Harry Beriford, rode over to Northbridge Hall with a message from Lady Dartworth referring to the many preparations in connection with the supper. If it had been possible, Veronica would have sent the message by a servant, for she wished to fulfil her promise to visit Tazoni; but her mother specially wished that she should go herself; and Sir Harry and Saidie Maddison had volunteered to accompany her.

Wondering how she could possibly contrive to visit the encampment privately, since it seemed she must invariably be accompanied by one or other of their guests, and yet not wishing that Tazoni should wait for her coming and be disappointed, she decided upon sending him a message. Here, however, arose another difficulty. Who could she send?—for the servants were all so busy, and she did not wish it to become known that she herself held any intercourse with the gipsy encampment on the common.

They took the bridle-path through the woods to Northbridge; and here it was that they came upon Luke Smeaton, at the sight of whom Veronica immediately drew rein, allowing her companions to ride ahead of her. She did not know the man for Marion Smeaton's husband; but from his swarthy appearance she took him to be a gipsy.

"Are you one of the men from the encampment on the common?" she asked, kindly, and from her tone Luke took up his cue and answered:

"Yes, lady."

"How is your master, Tazoni? Is he better?"

"Much better, lady," replied Luke, who knew it for a fact, as he knew most other things.

"Will you tell him from me that I will visit the camp the day after to-morrow? He will understand. Good morning."

"Good morning, lady," answered Luke, and stood looking after her as she rode away.

"*He'll understand.* So that's the little game, is it?" he muttered to himself. "Well, p'raps I'll take your message, young lady, and p'raps I won't; but anyway, I see my way a bit clearer over to-morrow night."

Veronica was glad to think that she was not likely to meet Lord Raymond that morning during her visit to Northbridge; for he had arranged to take some of the guests forming the Dartworth house-party on a motoring expedition to some bits of show scenery in the neighbourhood.

Since Luke Smeaton's advice to secure Veronica Dartworth as his well-dowered wife, Lord Raymond had paid less attention than formerly to Judy Slade, a change of affairs which neither the latter nor Veronica quite appreciated, though for very different reasons.

Miss Slade chafed at Denville's absence, though she had been informed that it was inevitable. She did her best, meantime, to keep Veronica's interest alive in him; although she could not close her eyes to the fact that the girl generally sought to change the subject as soon as Hubert Denville's name was mentioned. Naturally enough, Judy Slade had heard full details of the scene upon the terrace; and although she had implicit faith in Denville's knowledge of women and their varying moods, she did not quite understand why, if Veronica had liked him—as it was certainly quite plain she did—she should have repulsed him in that manner, unless she cared for someone else better.

Denville argued, however, that the very fact of allowing him to take her in his arms had formed a bond between himself and Veronica; but that, like a nervous horse, she had shied at the supreme moment when she thought of an irrevocable yoke.

"If you are right in what you think, I should advise you not to leave her too long without the light of your presence. You can never tell what secret influence may be at work; especially where the heart of a woman is concerned," Judy wrote.

Miss Slade, however, hoped that all would go well the instant her ally returned; and for her own sake, as also for his, she expected much from the Dartworth ball. She gave a considerable amount of careful attention to the selection of her toilette, with a view to the complete conquest of Lord Raymond's wavering attentions. How much of her slender income went towards paying for the Paris frock she wore, Judy never cared to think when all was over; although, at the time, she looked upon it as money well invested. Her gown was of a delicate gold, sheathed in chiffon of a softer shade, and at her throat she wore a necklet of imitation diamonds, which deceived all who noticed them.

Altogether, Miss Slade looked remarkably well, and a smile of quiet satisfaction lit up her face when Lord Raymond exclaimed, upon seeing her:

"My word, you do look ripping!"

Veronica was very nearly late for dinner that night; for she had managed to send word to Tazoni to meet her in a part of the rose-garden that nobody visited. So, at an hour when most of the other guests were resting in order to be fresh for the fatigue attendant upon all such festivities, she, for whose sake the ball was being given, might have been seen making her way unostentatiously towards the ruined arbour, situated just where the rose-garden became part of the woods.

It was greatly at variance with her own principles for Veronica to arrange a meeting, which could not necessarily be otherwise than clandestine. But she felt she must let no time pass without telling Tazoni that she alone had recognized him, when his courage and forethought had saved herself and others from probable death. For another reason she wished to see him—to ask him to go away out of her life for ever.

Veronica knew it was a great and difficult thing to ask of a man, but she felt that Tazoni would understand, and of his upright manliness and honour would respect her desire.

She had also to ask his pardon for her manner to him upon the last occasion on which she had met him in the woods; for during Hubert Denville's absence it had become clear to Veronica that he had only appealed to her very superficially; although she could not quite see why Tazoni should have felt he had cause to warn her against him—for that Denville was the man in question she had very little doubt.

Tazoni was the first to keep the tryst, and in a wistful sadness he awaited Veronica's coming. He could not understand why she had sent for him—since to him it seemed impossible that she should love him in return—but something told him that she was not wise in asking him to meet her in this fashion. Ever careful for his lady's welfare, he did not wish her name to be associated in any way with his; and he had been greatly worried ever since the loss of his book, lest anyone should find it, and gain possession of his secret by reading the verses he had inscribed to Veronica in the dreamy half-consciousness of the act of creation.

When at length he saw Veronica coming towards him, he leant against one of the stone pillars of the arbour for support—she looked so beautiful in her white dress with the glow of sunset on it, and he had not seen her for so long; besides which he had not quite recovered his former strength, although the accident had taken place some days ago.

As for Veronica, her face was suffused with colour, and her heart beat unusually fast; but outwardly she was her calm, sweet self; and, suppressing all signs of his excitement by a marvellous effort, Tazoni came forward to meet her.

"Lady," he said, in his low, musical tones, "I am here."

With a tender impulsiveness, she held out her hand.

"I am so glad you are better," she breathed, vainly endeavouring to keep her voice from trembling. She entered the arbour and sat down, motioning him to sit beside her; but Tazoni felt that to comply would be like daring to ascend a throne with a goddess; and so remained standing.

"There is so much I want to say to you," said Veronica, looking up at him; "so much, that I don't quite know where and how to begin. First I want to tell you that I recognized you on the day you stopped the drag; and ever since I have been waiting to thank you."

"It was nothing, lady," he interposed, quickly; "any other man would have done the same."

For a moment she did not speak, though her eyes said much, if he could have read them; but Tazoni voluntarily blinded himself for her sake; and Veronica's love for him grew, even as she respected him the more. What other man, given such an opportunity as this clandestine meeting afforded Tazoni, would have borne himself in such an irreproachable manner?—certainly not a man of the world like Hubert Denville.

Suddenly she held out both her hands to him in charming wistfulness.

"I wanted to ask your pardon for being so rude to you on the day you told me my fortune."

The little laugh that finished her words was very pitiful, for it was nearly akin to tears.

Tazoni stood for a moment speechless. He could not trust his voice, lest its tones should proclaim his heart's secret; and he dared not touch the hands she voluntarily stretched out to him, for fear the temptation to take her in his arms should prove too strong for him. The bonds that held his passionate love to silence nearly broke beneath the strain which the delight of her sweet presence, and the sound of her voice, imposed upon them.

Veronica's hands dropped to her side, for she suddenly realized the temptation she was putting in his way. Round the arbour were trails of roses that had grown luxuriantly wild. Her thoughts occupied with the problems life presented to her, Veronica unconsciously drew down a cluster until it caressed her cheek. Idly she plucked one of the blossoms, and fastened it in the bosom of her gown, letting the branch slip back to its original position above her head.

"If I can, will you let me help you in some way?" she asked, her tone changing to one of candid friendliness.

"You cannot help me, lady," he said, gently. "I am a gipsy, and I shall always remain a gipsy. I want for nothing."

"My father has a great deal of influence," she replied, eagerly; "is there no way——?"

"No, lady," Tazoni answered, with respectful firmness. "You have no idea how you are tempting me to break my oath to the tribe."

"You won't let me help you," said Veronica, sadly. "How shall I assure you of my gratitude?"

"I have the assurance treasured in my heart already," he replied, his eyes fixed tenderly, passionately upon her face. "But if you would be kind, I'd ask you just one thing——"

"And that?" said Veronica, eagerly.

"The rose you wear in your dress, lady," he answered.

For a moment Veronica's cheeks flushed with colour; then, with quick, nervous fingers, she complied with his request.

"Only this?" she murmured, her face wistful.

"I dare not ask for more," he said, hoarsely.

With trembling fingers she held out the rose towards him, and their eyes met. Then with a low, broken cry he bent and passionately kissed the flower, and her hand with it, not once, but many times. When he raised his head, ashamed of his momentary weakness, Veronica's eyes were wet with tears.

"It is good-bye, isn't it?" she asked.

"Yes, it is good-bye," he said; and turning hastily on his heel he went away.

CHAPTER XVII

"Oh, miss, you never looked so beautiful before!" exclaimed Veronica's maid, with sincere admiration, as her mistress stood before her glass, looking absently at the reflection of herself, and the wonderful Paquin creation she wore—a robe of white satin, with a panel of embroidered water-lilies.

Veronica smiled indifferently, and turned from the glass.

"Thank you, Bedford; you can go now," she said, quietly.

Left alone, Veronica drew from her secret drawer her carefully prized book, and read the verses that she already knew by heart; then, with her eyes bright with the gleam of unshed tears, she locked it away.

All the house-guests were assembled in the great hall, when Veronica at last descended the staircase; and a murmur of admiration ran through the spectators, as they watched her slow, gracious movements and her beautiful, sweet face.

"Saint Veronica with a vengeance!" murmured Sir Harry Beriford; "especially in that dress! My word, what a magnificent creature she is!"

"Yes, she looks stunning to-night," assented Lord Raymond, who, however, seemed curiously wan and haggard.

"You are looking very well to-night, dear," remarked Lady Dartworth, voicing the general praise of Veronica; but only her father saw the sadness that was in her eyes, in spite of the fact that she was talking and laughing with the rest.

"What is the matter with the girl, I'd like to know?" he thought to himself; and then he noticed, too, the pallor of Lord Raymond's face, and began to wonder whether it had any connection with Veronica's ill-concealed abstraction. "She isn't in love with him, I'm sure; what's the matter with them then?"

But Lord Dartworth had no time to find an answer to his question; for his many and arduous duties as host kept him busily occupied.

Veronica was talking to the Prime Minister when Lord Northbridge passed them, with a friendly nod to the latter and a smile for the girl, of whom he was extremely fond.

"*Apropos* of Northbridge, he and I were school-fellows, you know," said the Prime Minister. "We are both old and grey now; although he is younger than I am. You'd never think it, to look at him, would you? He seems to have aged a great deal more than I have, during these last two years; in spite of all the incessant worry and anxiety I have had to endure."

Looking over to where Lord Raymond stood leaning sullenly against the opposite wall, Veronica thought she knew the cause of Lord Northbridge's premature decay; but, naturally enough, she remained silent on the matter.

By everyone the ball was voted a great success; and the only one who did not appear to participate in the general pleasure, was Lord Raymond. He wandered about, as if he could find no rest or amusement anywhere. Sometimes he joined in conversations by fits and starts with the various groups of men scattered here and there. Once he joined a circle of some of the older men, and stood listening for a while. He had caught the words: "The most daring burglary I ever heard of!" and seemed chained to the spot, standing behind his father and listening with bent head and compressed lips.

One of the men—a baronet from a neighbouring county—was giving a full and sensational account of a burglary at a friend's house, not far from his own. It seemed that the thieves had succeeded in carrying off a great quantity of plate, in addition to some valuable jewels; and when Sir William Blathewaite had finished his story, a murmur of indignation and astonishment escaped from his hearers. Lord Northbridge lifted his grey head with a quiet smile.

"I venture to think, Blathewaite, that if the rascals ever pay a visit to my place, they will meet with a rather warmer reception than they had at Elsfield—I always keep a loaded revolver by my bedside, and should not hesitate to use it in defence of my life or even of my property."

Lord Raymond covertly drew his hand across his low forehead, which was covered with beads of perspiration.

"But I'm not afraid of anything of that sort," continued Lord Northbridge. "I keep my valuables securely locked away; and my strong-room is far more secure than any bank, I assure you."

Lord Raymond walked quickly away to hide himself in one of the smaller drawing-rooms that had been fitted up as a sitting-out place, but was, however, at present untenanted.

"Good gracious!" he thought to himself, as he sank down on one of the lounges. "It nearly turned me sick to hear him talk like that!"

At this most inopportune moment, Judy Slade tracked her intended victim to his hiding-place.

"Oh," she gasped, "I'm suffocating! It seems we both had the same idea of running away. I thought this place was empty, at least."

"It shall be, if you like," Raymond answered, with a sarcastic smile, rising and pretending to go.

"How horrid of you!" she said, sweetly. "I've no doubt you mean to be nice, though. Get me an ice, will you? I'm very nearly dead."

He did not take the trouble to actually comply with her request, but yelled the order out to a servant who was passing in the distance. Somehow, it seemed that that night the desire asserted itself in Lord Raymond to be what he really was— the son of Luke Smeaton, the gipsy, and not of Lord Northbridge, the aristocrat. It may have been that to insist upon this plebeian parentage to himself, gave him the courage of which he stood in such great need for the dastardly work that he was meditating.

To Judy Slade, he seemed even more despicable than ever; but she had determined that his position and title should be hers by marriage, and when she set her hand to the plough she never turned back—in blank contradiction of the impression conveyed by her sweet, mouse-like appearance.

Lord Raymond sat and watched her eat her ice, not aware that she was as critically watching him.

"Well, mouse?" he said, after a moment, with a rough attempt at lightness; "had a good time?"

"So, so," answered Judy, smiling at him under her lashes, in a way she had carefully practised before her glass. "The men are always a bit tame down here—chosen with such discretion, don't you know. You never get a really 'bad hat' under Cousin Mary's roof, and I *do* like 'bad hats,' you know."

"What about me?" asked Raymond, with a smile that was a near approach to a leer.

"That's the attraction about you," laughed Judy, nestling against the cushions with a careful regard to her *coiffure*. "I say, have you got a cigarette? I always think you want one after an ice. Do you know, you've been my only salvation down here? Cousin Mary objects to a woman smoking; and it's only when I'm with you that I dare brave the risk of incurring her displeasure. Two 'bad hats' together, you see, can accomplish a great deal," she added, pointedly.

"H'm, yes," commented Lord Raymond, as he offered her his cigarette case. But his thoughts suddenly reverted to the task that was to be accomplished that very night by two 'bad hats,' as Miss Slade called them; and his smile went all awry.

Judy saw that something was wrong with him, and began to chatter her hardest, in order to divert his thoughts from what appeared to be a painful subject.

"Give me a light, will you?" she demanded, presently, having dabbed her cigarette upon the back of her hand for at least two minutes, until Raymond demanded surlily whether she wanted to spoil it altogether.

She bent forward, and brought her eyes on a level with his. The lighted match cast a charming glow upwards that made her face look very attractive; so, at least, thought Lord Raymond, who immediately voiced his opinion in his usual blunt way.

"I say, Judy, you don't half look ripping to-night."

"Think so? I'm glad you do. I wanted your good opinion more than anybody else's," replied Judy, ingenuously.

"Sweet of you," answered Raymond, with a grin. "Why mine?"

"Well, we've been such pals, haven't we?" she said, not in the least taken back by his disconcerting manner. "You've been the only one who's made staying with Cousin Mary at all endurable."

Raymond eyed her critically for a moment; then—apparently satisfied by her candour that she was not "gassing" him for the sake of what she could get out of him, as so many girls, chiefly of the "chorus" type, seemed to do—he acquiesced in quite a friendly spirit.

"Yes; we have been a bit chummy. Fact is, I like you, don't you know. I shall miss you a bit when you go to-morrow. Can't you stay longer?"

"No, I'm afraid not—for several reasons," replied Judy—one being that Lady Dartworth had begun to look somewhat coldly upon her, for seeking to spend so much time in the company of Lord Raymond. Although not greatly attracted by the young man himself, Lady Dartworth was anxious that the rumoured marriage between him and Veronica should take place, in order to cement still more closely the lifelong friendship between their respective families.

"Can't you come up to town?" added Judy, sweetly.

"'Fraid not—for several reasons," mimicked Lord Raymond, though not unkindly.

"Anyway, if you change your mind, I hope you'll look me up," said Judy, having laughed a little in careful acknowledgment of Raymond's mimetic powers.

"Right you are! I'll get some seats for the theatre, and take you out," he answered, generously, moved by her appreciation of himself, which came as a balm to his soul, that night of all nights. "You're a jolly little soul; and we'll have some good times together."

"Splendid!" laughed Judy, seeing what wonderful opportunities such plans would afford her for landing her fish. He was too *distrait* to-night to be sentimental as he had sometimes been with her before. She strongly suspected his trouble to be caused by the thought of his many creditors, of whom Denville had duly warned her.

"You make him pay off all his debts before he marries you, Judy; then he will only have yours to settle in the blissful hereafter," he had advised her.

Hubert Denville's absence made her somewhat troubled to find a reason for his delay in making the most of his few remaining opportunities with Veronica. He had written her to the effect that he would not be down until late that night; and she had begun to think that he must be mad to play at hazard with his chances, or else that he had some other game afoot—neither of which solutions brought her any personal satisfaction, since it would throw Veronica very much in Lord Raymond's way after she had gone.

Judy knew that the girl despised and disliked the husband whom rumour and her parents' wishes had selected for her; but she imagined that pressure might ultimately be brought to bear upon her in some way, to influence Veronica to marry him.

Fearing this, Judy Slade determined to bring Lord Raymond to a certain point that night, in spite of its obvious inopportunity. She knew he liked her much better than Veronica; and he had on one occasion tried to be sentimental with her in a clumsy, pointless fashion. Unfortunately, before she could bring her destined lover to the mark, Sir Harry Beriford came to claim her as his partner; and Judy had to confess to herself that she had lost her chance, for that night, at any rate.

At the encampment the gipsies—except Tazoni and Maya—were asleep early upon the night of the Dartworth ball; for they had been working very hard during the day.

Tazoni was seated by the dying embers of the camp-fire, fighting out a battle within his soul between duty and inclination. Sometimes he lifted his head, and looked wistfully towards the woods, behind which he knew that Dartworth Manor was the scene of light and music and laughter; at other times he glanced towards Maya's tent, in which he could hear her still awake and restless; then he would stir the red, smouldering embers, sighing with the bitterness of his inward struggle.

A great change had come over Maya during the last two days, and Tazoni had noticed it. Duty was whispering in his ear, that he should give the word, and take her to a change of air and scene. He knew that the parting with Veronica also pointed out to him, that he should leave the neighbourhood as soon as possible—for her sake and his own. Yet the passionate love within him pleaded that he must see her just once more, if only from a distance—one last farewell to all he held most dear in life; then the black loneliness of eternal separation. The day upon which he turned his back upon Veronica Dartworth would be the hardest of his life—he knew it well.

With his mind full of these thoughts, and fighting for supremacy over his passionate inclinations, he was suddenly startled by the advent of a man, who came hurriedly through the camp and addressed him.

"What's the matter?" asked Tazoni, with some alarm.

"I've come with a message from the Manor, as all the servants was busy," said the stranger.

"For me?" asked Tazoni, with astonishment. "From whom?"

"Miss Dartworth," said the man. "She sent word that someone was to come up here and say that she wanted to see ye most particular. She'll be in the rose-garden, and if she's not there, ye're to wait till she comes."

"Who gave you the message?" Tazoni asked, a little incredulously.

"Her own maid," replied the man, ingenuously. "Ye see, I'm a-walking out with her; and I was up at the house running messages and givin' a helpin' hand, all the servants being very occupied like. But if ye don't want to come, say so; and I'll be getting back—Miss Veronica will be wanting to know."

Tazoni hesitated no longer.

"Very well, I'll come," he said. "I suppose you don't know anything further, do you?"

"Well, no; I can't say I do," replied the man, frankly. "She'd hardly be likely to tell me, would she?"

"No," agreed Tazoni, tingling with the sweet thought of seeing Veronica again—perhaps being of use to her. Yes, that was it, he told himself; she needed him. He would go at once. As he passed Maya's tent, the girl heard his step and came out.

"Where are you going, Tazoni?" she asked in surprise. She placed her hand upon his arm, as if with the faint hope of restraining him.

"I am wanted, little sister."

"Who is wanting you?" she demanded.

"I have just had a message from the Manor," he replied, with some constraint.

Her hand dropped from his arm, and a strange light came into her dark eyes.

"Tazoni," she said, earnestly, "will you do something for me? Will you stay here with me? I—I am afraid to-night."

Tazoni looked at her with surprise.

"What's the matter?" he asked, kindly. "What are you afraid of, Maya?"

"I—I don't know; I only know that something will happen if you leave the camp to-night—perhaps I'm mad to say it; but I can't get rid of the idea. Do stay with me, Tazoni," she entreated.

"Very well, Maya," he said, coldly. "You know it is in your power to command me. I will not go."

He turned to the man who was standing near. "Go back to Miss Dartworth, and tell her that it is impossible for me to come," he said, quietly.

The man shrugged his shoulders.

"I'll tell her," he replied; "but seems to me as ye're mighty foolish to take notice of a girl's fancies. I guess—if ye don't mind me a-telling ye—that Miss Veronica will take it as a kind o' slight like. It ain't the way to treat a lady, I'm a-thinking."

Tazoni looked perplexed; but before he could say anything further in the matter, Maya broke in:

"You had better go, Tazoni; I cannot keep you when a lady is wanting you."

"No, Maya," he replied. "It is my duty to stay with you, if you need me."

"I think I am all right now," she said, bravely; "I know you won't be longer than you can help. It is better that you should go."

"Very well," he said, slowly. He kissed her affectionately, and motioned to the stranger that he was ready. A second later they had left the camp; and the girl stood looking after them with a curious sense of depression and foreboding.

For some time Tazoni strode on in silence, the man by his side smoking a short clay pipe, and remaining as taciturn as his companion. When they reached the end of the woods, the stranger said suddenly:

"I think I'll be after getting back to the house again, if ye don't mind. I guess they'll be wanting me for something or other."

"All right," answered Tazoni. "Good night."

The man struck off in the direction of the Manor; but he had not gone more than a dozen yards, before he stopped and looked back with an evil grin on his face.

"Very neatly managed, Luke, my boy," he said to himself. "Lord! and it was all owing to the bait I used. Fancy that fool of a gipsy going in for Miss Veronica! Got his eye to business! Golly! If only old Dartworth knew their little game, the fat wouldn't half be in the fire. If this ain't the rummest muddle I've ever poked my nose into, I'm a Dutchman! Well, I guess I'd better be seeing about the other part of the affair. I'll just have a peep at him to see he's quite safe."

He crept back cautiously from tree to tree, until he saw that Tazoni had entered the rose-garden and, incidentally, the arbour. Satisfied that that part of his work had been safely accomplished, the man made his way on to the high road, and some few minutes' walking brought him to the cross-roads. He looked round cautiously, and, satisfied that no one was about, whistled softly. An answer, like an echo, followed immediately; and a figure in a huge motor-coat stepped from behind a hedge.

"Are you Lord R——'s man?"

"Yes, sir," replied Luke.

"All right, then," said Denville. "Where's the girl?"

"Not here yet, sir; but I hope to get her directly. Is the car ready?"

"Of course, it's been here half an hour or more. You're late, you know. I felt like chucking the whole show once or twice."

"We shan't be long now, sir," said Luke, encouragingly. "I thought I'd just slip across and see if ye was here. The other party's been worked as easy as A B C."

"So you've disposed of him, then?" asked Denville.

Luke smiled, grimly.

"You and I wouldn't be a match for him, if he knew what was up, sir. I think I'll be off now. Keep the car dark; and come the instant I give the call."

"All right," assented Denville, wearily; and the tall figure of the gipsy disappeared.

After Tazoni had left her, Maya returned to the tent. She could not rest; and not wishing to disturb old Martha, who was usually a light sleeper, she returned to the open air again, and began to pace to and fro. Suddenly there loomed up before her the figure of a man, whom Maya had no difficulty in recognizing as the one who had come earlier in the evening to fetch Tazoni, for Luke Smeaton was totally unknown to the camp, except to old Martha, his mother.

"Has anything happened?" she asked, quickly.

"Not as I know of," returned Luke, placidly. "I've only brought a message back for you. Your brother—or whoever he is—says as you're to come with me directly; he wants to speak to you, urgent-like."

Maya drew her shawl over her head; but suddenly the man saw that she hesitated.

"He said summat else in a foreign language. He said you'd understand"; and Luke mispronounced a few words of Romany, which signified, "Come at once, alone, and have no fear."

As he spoke, all Maya's doubt vanished; and a few moments later they left the encampment.

"This isn't the way to the Manor," she said, stopping short as he struck off in an opposite direction.

"No, I know it isn't," was the reply. "He's waiting at the cross-roads."

Maya drew her shawl more closely round her, and sped on at a pace which threatened to outrun the man beside her. Once or twice he grinned, but did not speak. They reached the cross-roads, where Luke stopped.

"He's somewhere here," he said, and whistled.

The next instant, Hubert Denville had stepped from his hiding-place.

"Well, my dear," he said, mockingly, "I'm glad to see you've come."

Then Maya knew that she and Tazoni had been trapped; and as the knowledge came to her, she turned to make her escape; but Luke Smeaton was too quick for her. In an instant her arms were pinioned, and a gag was thrust into her mouth. Then someone whistled, and the girl heard the sound of rubber-tyred wheels upon the hard road. With great haste, and no small amount of force, she was pushed into a car, which her starting eyes had distinguished in the gloom. Then one of the men got in beside her, and the door was shut. There was a sudden jerk, and a moment later they were rushing like the wind along the dusty road.

As the lights of the car at last disappeared, Luke Smeaton breathed a sigh of relief. Then he began to make his way leisurely to the gipsy encampment; for there was still a part of the plot to be completed. On reaching the tent where he guessed Martha slept, he whistled loudly once or twice; then finding that this did not have the effect he desired, he called "Hullo!" and thumped the canvas until he heard a voice from within say:

"Mercy on us! Ye'll have the thing down in a minute. What's the matter?"

"I want the girl who was here when I left," said Luke, in a carefully assumed voice; "it doesn't matter if she's asleep, though. Ye needn't wake her."

At this moment Martha crawled out of the tent half asleep.

"Wake her! Where is she?"

But by that time Luke had disappeared.

"Maya! Maya! Where are ye, child?" called Martha, fully awake now. She searched high and low; and, finding neither Tazoni nor Maya, roused the men.

In an instant everyone was on the alert and anxious for action. They formed themselves into two little parties, the first setting off for the woods, the other to search the roads. They returned very soon, but with no tidings whatever; and when they told the story of their futile search to old Martha, she exclaimed:

"That young limb of Satan has stolen her away from us!"

"Where's Tazoni?" asked one of the men. "He'll be able to help us, if we can find him. Who fetched him?"

All search for the mysterious person who had roused Martha proved as futile as the others; and the men, deprived of their leader, were uncertain what was the next best thing to do.

Meanwhile Tazoni waited patiently for the appearance of Veronica. But the hours passed, and she did not come. Carriages and motor-cars began to pass down the drive on their way homewards; and, not so very long after, Tazoni could see the lights from the windows as they were extinguished one by one. Still he waited; until darkness and silence told him that his watch had been in vain. With a disappointment not the less keen because he struggled to suppress it, he hurried back. As he neared the camp he heard the suppressed shouts of the men, and strode on more quickly.

They were gathered round the camp-fire, which they had revived; they were all fully dressed, and grasped in their hands stout sticks or some other more effective weapon. So engaged were they in discussion, that he was in their midst before they were aware of it. With a cry of welcome they gathered round him.

"What is the matter?" he asked, anxiously.

There was a dead silence; for they dreaded to tell him the truth. He looked round with his piercing eyes upon their downcast faces, and somehow, he could not tell why, he grew afraid.

"Something has happened to one of us. Who is it?" he asked, sharply. Then turning to where the women were huddled together behind him, he asked instantly: "Where's Maya?"

"She's gone," said one of the men, with an oath.

"Gone! What do you mean?" asked Tazoni.

Suddenly he saw it all, as if a flash of lightning had revealed it to him in the darkness. For a moment his face was livid.

"Here's Steve," cried one of the men, as the last of the search-party arrived upon the scene.

"I've got news," said the new-comer, as all eyes were turned enquiringly upon him. "I met a man who said he'd seen a gipsy girl get into a motor with a gentleman—and she went willingly."

"It's a lie!" exclaimed Tazoni. "I'd swear to it. You must have spoken to the same man who played this vile trick upon me to get me out of the way. Did he say which road they took?"

"He said they went Londonwards—if we can believe him," was the sceptical answer.

"Perhaps he thought as she'd be lost to us in London—seeing as we're gipsies," commented Colin.

Old Martha did not give any opinion upon the matter; but only sat and rocked herself, in her sorrow at the loss of Maya.

"You may be right, Colin," said Tazoni. "My men," he added, "I am answerable for this. If I had not been mad they could not have deceived us. But I swear not to rest until I have brought her back to you."

He paced up and down in restless excitement.

"Get me a horse, Colin," he said, suddenly. "The sooner I'm after them, the better."

In a few moments a horse was brought to him, and Tazoni sprang into the saddle. The men watched him, in silence, as he settled himself in his seat; and a minute later he was lost in the darkness.

CHAPTER XVIII

When Hubert Denville put in a smiling appearance at Lady Dartworth's ball just before supper, no one could have imagined, even for a moment, that he had had a run by motor from London to Northbridge, and then through two counties and back, in addition to the capture of a struggling girl.

Veronica greeted him coldly; and he was for once mistaken in putting down her attitude to the pique she felt at his neglect of her, since the scene upon the terrace, even though, when it came to the point, she had refused his advances.

But Hubert Denville was too confident of his power over women, to imagine for one moment that he would not prevail in the end.

"I hope you have saved me one dance at least, Miss Dartworth," he said, his eyes, which knew so well how to flatter, while his lips were silent, fixed admiringly upon her face.

"I'm sorry, but I'm afraid you have arrived too late, Mr. Denville," replied Veronica, and she turned away with the partner who had come to claim her.

Denville looked after her with a bored smile.

"Yes, I'm afraid she is right—you *have* come too late," said Judy Slade's disgusted voice at his elbow. "*I* go to-morrow—*you* can't stay down here much longer—so who's to prevent that young cub, Raymond, from getting her after all?"

"You," replied Denville, with brief explicitness.

"How do you mean? I can only get him to come to my flat occasionally—and that won't be for some time, it seems, owing to his creditors—and in the meantime what can I possibly do to prevent him marrying the girl?"

"Come into that conservatory and I'll tell you. Please look as though you were flattered by my attentions," said Denville, ironically.

"Oh, I am, indeed," laughed Judy, and accepted his arm.

"Now, just listen to what I have to say, without interrupting, and I'll be as explicit as possible," said Denville, when they had reached a secluded corner of the conservatory. Then, in low tones, he unfolded his plot; and Judy's eyes grew bright with excitement.

"You see," concluded Denville, "if he were a shade less mean and despicable, we should fail; but he is cowardly and dishonourable enough for anything. And as regards his point of view of the consequences—well, the biter should never complain when he is bitten. He always takes the risk of that."

"We will only resort to your plan if everything else fails," stipulated Judy, overcoming whatever scruples she possessed.

"Certainly," agreed Denville; then took her down to supper.

Denville drove to the Hall in the Northbridge car, with his host and Lord Raymond. Lord Northbridge looked tired out; but in his eyes shone a tender light when they rested upon Raymond, who had been most attentive to him the whole of the evening, although usually he seemed to avoid the old man on every possible occasion. No one could tell how great a cause of sorrow Geoffrey had been to Lord Northbridge. From his boyhood upwards, day by day he had shattered all the aspirations of his father's love.

The drive homewards was accomplished almost in silence; for Lord Northbridge was tired, while the thoughts of the other two were busily occupied, each in their own way. When the car reached the Hall, Raymond leapt out and ran up the steps, without waiting to assist his father, and made his way to the dining-room, where the others followed him.

"You'll have a drink, won't you, Denville?" asked Raymond, hospitably.

Denville wondered at the "young cub's" access of geniality, and put it down to the fact that the abduction of the gipsy girl had been carried out so well. For he had duly reported the course of events to Raymond before supper, who promised that Denville should receive a cheque for the amount agreed upon the very next morning. Not a word, however, had Denville mentioned to Judy Slade—he never confided in a woman if he could help it; although he trusted her more than most.

"Thanks, old man," replied Denville, to Raymond's invitation, seeing he was busy mixing drinks.

"You'd better have one, too, sir," said Raymond, with unusual solicitude, to his father, who was standing on the hearthrug. "You look tired; it's been a long day for you."

Grateful for Raymond's unusual consideration, Lord Northbridge replied willingly:

"Thank you, Geoffrey; you are very thoughtful."

"Just say 'how,' will you, Denville?" said Raymond, fumbling nervously about with the glasses upon the silver tray, which the butler had placed upon the table; for Lord Northbridge's eyes were fixed absently upon him, and he did not know how to distract his attention.

He mixed drinks for the two men, then one for himself. His glass rattled against his teeth in his nervousness; for he had had no opportunity of dropping Luke Smeaton's powder into the old man's drink, and he was afraid he had lost his opportunity.

Denville finished his brandy-and-soda, and, receiving a sign of enlightenment from Raymond, asked his host's permission to retire, thinking that the young man wished to obtain some money from his father, in order to settle the question of the cheque on the morrow. Raymond had no fear that Denville would be likely to hear anything during the night; for his rooms were in the north wing, while the earl slept in the south.

When Denville had gone, Lord Northbridge could not help noticing his son's restlessness and the haggard look upon his face. Drawn towards him by the unusual attentiveness he had displayed throughout the evening, the earl said, kindly:

"Geoffrey, is there anything the matter? You don't look quite up to the mark. My boy, if there is any trouble or anxiety weighing on your mind, why not confide in me or your mother? We have never shown ourselves unworthy of your confidence, or unwilling to help you as best we can."

Raymond's face turned very white. If the old man had but preserved silence, or had been harsh with him, he could have borne it better; but the kind, generous words lashed him like a whip, and for the first time in his life he shrank from his own nature.

Almost the next moment, however, he realized that what he had set himself to do must be done that night, or never; and money he must have at any price, he told himself.

"I'm quite all right, sir," he said; "and I haven't any confidences to make, thanks. Have another drink?" He asked, eagerly.

"No, thanks, my boy," replied Lord Northbridge, stretching out his hand to finish the rest of his brandy-and-soda.

But Raymond was too quick for him, and took the glass before he could reach it.

"Let me give you some more soda. You won't get a headache in the morning, then."

Lord Northbridge smiled indulgently.

"As you will, for once. I'll let you prescribe for me."

Raymond's face, as he carried the glass to a syphon on the sideboard, was ghastly. With trembling fingers he emptied into it the contents of the packet hidden in his hand, taking care to keep his back turned to Lord Northbridge.

"This thing won't work," he said, nervously, in order to cover the length of time before he turned on the syphon.

"Try the one on the table, then," suggested Lord Northbridge.

"Oh, it's all right now, sir. Sure you won't have some more brandy?"

"Quite sure, thank you," replied Lord Northbridge, as he took his glass, and drank the soda-water.

Suddenly he set the glass down on the table, and said somewhat unsteadily:

"I think I will go now, Geoffrey; I'm very tired, my boy."

He pressed Raymond's hand, and could not help noticing that it felt hot and feverish; but thinking his son would be all right in the morning, he left him, with the warning not to sit up any longer.

Lord Raymond waited until the old man's slow, retreating footsteps had died away. Then he turned once more to the table and poured himself out a quantity of neat brandy, and drained the glass at a draught.

In a few minutes the fumes of the spirit had reached his brain, giving him the needful audacity. Stealing quietly to the door, he opened it and listened attentively. In the servants' hall all was quiet and dark. To assure himself of this, he stole down on tiptoe, peered round the lower corridors, and through a window which commanded a view of the stables and the coachman's cottage. There were no lights or sound in that direction, and, with a nod of satisfaction, he returned to the dining-room, gulped down a little more brandy, and tried to pull himself together. Again he stole to the door and listened; but no sound, save the ticking of the grandfather clock, broke the stillness.

Satisfied at last, he stole up to his room. His conscience made a coward of him; and he looked behind him more than once, as though he were afraid of being attacked in the dark by an unseen foe.

From a carefully locked cupboard, he drew out a dark lantern, which he lit, and, taking care to keep the light well screened, he passed down the corridor until he reached the door of his father's room. Here he paused and listened. No sound could be heard; and no light filtered through the chinks of the door. Holding his breath, he laid his hand upon the door-handle and turned it softly.

It made no noise, for he had taken the precaution to oil it the preceding night; and slowly, with cautious footsteps, he entered the room. It was his father's dressing-room. The strong-room opened out of it to the left; and the door of Lord Northbridge's bedroom was exactly opposite to that by which Raymond had entered.

He opened his lantern and glanced hastily round the dressing-room. The thought had crossed his mind, that the drug might not have acted so quickly, but that Lord Northbridge might have had time to undress, and perhaps had forgotten to remove his keys from his pocket. If so, he would be spared the necessity of searching the old man's unconscious body, or from entering the room where he slept.

But, with the exception of his father's dressing-gown, there were no articles of clothing in the room; so he decided to try the door of the bedroom itself. It was locked, as he had expected; but he was prepared. Taking from his pocket a duplicate, and well-oiled key, he inserted it in the lock, and turned it without noise or effort.

But the room was empty!

His heart throbbed excitedly; but with a supreme effort he forced himself to listen for a moment. At last, hearing nothing, he crept on his hands and knees into the room, holding the lantern in his left hand in case he wanted it. He made the circuit of the room, and was about to return, when suddenly his hand touched something soft and almost cold, which he realized was human flesh. In a moment he started up, his whole body trembling, and a horrible feeling, as of someone pouring water down his back, took possession of him.

Something lay extended on the floor!

With a shaking hand he flashed on the light from the lantern; and then he saw the tall figure of Lord Northbridge stretched, rigid as a corpse, beside the bed. His coat was off and thrown across a chair close by; his watch was in one hand, and a key in the other. He had apparently fallen in the act of winding up the watch, unwarned and unprepared.

Lord Raymond knelt beside him and touched his hand. It was cold as ice.

Why did he lie there like that? Was he dead? he asked himself. Had the gipsy, to serve some purpose of his own, deceived him, and given him a deadly poison instead of a powerful sedative? It was not by any means improbable! If so, Lord Northbridge lay there dead; and he whom he had called son, was his murderer! At this thought Raymond's teeth began to chatter violently.

Nerved by despair, he knelt down once more. With an audible sigh of relief, he sprang to his feet again, for his father was still breathing.

"I'm a silly fool," he thought. "What did I expect? Certainly not to find him awake and on the watch! The powder was too strong; it must have overtaken him before he could undress."

His next thought was for the keys. He thrust his hands into the pockets of the coat across the chair and searched, but he had scarcely expected to find them there. Then he knelt down carefully, and felt the waistcoat, of which Lord North-bridge had not had time to divest himself, and something like triumph came into Lord Raymond's eyes as he transferred the keys to his own pocket. He wondered if it would be advisable to lift the unconscious sleeper on the bed; but a moment's reflection showed him that this would be both risky and difficult; whereas if he left him where he was, it would tend to increase the confusion next morning, when his valet came to call him.

He took up the lantern, closed the door after him, and returned quickly but noiselessly to his own room. Setting the lantern on the table, he drew out a small bundle from the cupboard; and, divesting himself of his own clothes, he put on the disguise which Smeaton had provided for him.

It was only by the aid of a clever West-end tailor that Lord Raymond had ever had any pretensions to smartness; but now, in the garb of a White-chapel hooligan, his dark, sinister features seemed in their proper setting.

"Splendid!" he thought to himself, glancing at the reflection in the glass. "I suppose those chaps who said something about fine feathers making fine birds must have known what they were talking about. Why, my own father wouldn't recognize me—whoever he is."

He looked at the carriage-clock that stood on a small table near his bed. It was time to open the door to his accomplice.

He left the room quietly, and now almost fearlessly; his slippers made no sound upon the polished corridor; and he knew the house so well that he could descend without a light, save that which was given by the gleam of his lantern.

He reached the earl's dressing-room more cautiously, however; but he had not the nerve to take a final glance at the still figure lying in the next room. Selecting the necessary keys from the bunch, he opened the double doors of the strong-room. Then he stole downstairs once more to a small corridor at the back of the house. This part, being little frequented, and farthest removed from the bedrooms, had been chosen by Luke as the point of entry.

As Lord Raymond reached the door, a spasm of fear passed over him, and he wished that he had taken another draught of brandy to keep his spirits up. He started suddenly as he heard a slight scratching outside, which told him that Luke Smeaton was there. For a moment a wild idea possessed Lord Raymond's whirling brain. Suppose he returned quickly, gave the alarm, and handed his too-knowing accomplice into custody? But he glanced at his disguise, and abandoned the idea with a curse. Besides, if he did do so, his father would require an explanation of everything; and naturally Smeaton would give him away, if only out of spite.

He drew back the bolts gently, and opened the door a little. In an instant the tall, dark figure of Luke Smeaton entered.

"Ye're quite all right," he whispered, as he scrutinized Raymond's disguise; "but whatever made ye so late? We'll have to buck up, I can tell ye."

"It couldn't be done sooner," returned the other, sullenly. "I almost thought of chucking up the whole show."

"Oh, come off it," said Luke, with a grin. "Ye want such a lot of coaxing before ye'll do a thing. Here, take a pull at this, and for Heaven's sake don't look like a rice-pudding; ye make me sick to look at ye."

He pushed a flask containing brandy into Lord Raymond's hand, and when it was returned to him, he knew intuitively that it was empty. Without another word, they ascended the staircase, and as they entered the dressing-room, Lord Raymond noticed that Smeaton had a small, deadly looking crowbar in his hand.

"All right!" whispered Luke. "Now for it!"

With a trembling hand, Lord Raymond pushed open the strong-room door, and Luke made his way to the safe that stood in the corner.

"Hold the light," he whispered; "and give me the keys. Take care they don't chink."

"The keys?" stammered the other man. "I—I haven't got them—at least I did have them, but I can't find them now."

"Idiot!" hissed Luke, beginning to get angry. "Turn your pockets out."

"I've got them," said Lord Raymond, with less caution than he had hitherto maintained, for the whole affair was beginning to get on his nerves.

Luke snatched them from him.

"Don't make such a row, you fool!" he hissed. "You'll wake the whole house up."

In a few minutes the safe was opened, and Luke thrust his hands into the pile of deeds and threw them on to the floor. The action disclosed an iron casket, which on being opened by one of the keys in Luke's possession, was found to contain some valuable, if old-fashioned, jewellery. This he pocketed as quickly as possible.

"Here's the drawer with the money in it, I reckon," he whispered, when he had done so. He thrust several keys into the lock, but they did not grip. "These ain't the keys, you fool!"

"They must be," said Lord Raymond, scarcely able to hold the lantern, in his anxiety. "I—I took them from his pocket."

"The key I want isn't there, then," replied Luke, savagely, wiping the perspiration from his forehead with the back of his coat-sleeve. "Give us the crowbar; it'll have to be forced."

Lord Raymond handed him the crowbar reluctantly. "But what about the noise?" he asked, tremulously.

"Noise! I'll have this 'ere drawer open if it makes a row like thunder. I'm going to get a little return for all my trouble, you bet." And inserting the thin end of the crowbar into the small crevice of the drawer, he struck it with his clenched fist.

A clear, distinct snap rang through the room.

"For Heaven's sake, be quick!" implored Lord Raymond, looking fearfully round. "Let's leave it; you've got the jewels."

"Not me," returned Luke, angrily. "I'm going to have the money in that drawer. Get away; I can't work when ye're on top of me, can I?"

Lord Raymond drew back; and Luke inserted the crowbar, using all his force. The bar slipped, and rang against the safe with a crash, and Luke, losing his balance, fell over on his side.

"We shall be heard!" exclaimed Raymond, with alarm.

"Be quiet!" hissed Luke, springing to his feet, and listening intently. "Yes, someone's coming!" he said, hoarsely; and, as he spoke, the door opened, and Lord Northbridge stood on the threshold.

CHAPTER XIX

"Darken the lantern, you idiot!" exclaimed Luke; but the warning was too late. With a cry of alarm, Lord Northbridge rushed forward and seized his son by the arm. Luke, who had been concealed in the shadow, sprang up behind him as he did so, and, throwing his arms round him, dragged him off Lord Raymond, who seemed to have lost what little nerve he possessed.

With a cry of helplessness, Raymond dropped the lantern, and stood with trembling knees staring at the two struggling figures. Lord Northbridge was madly endeavouring to remove Luke's hand, which grasped his mouth and prevented him from giving the alarm.

"It's no use!" hissed Luke. "There's two of us here, and a half a dozen within call."

"You ruffian!" gasped the old man, struggling furiously. "You shan't escape if there are a hundred of you. I shan't forget your faces."

He turned as he spoke, and looked at Lord Raymond. It was useless for Luke to cry "The light!" as an intimation that Raymond was standing full in the glare of the lantern; he seemed unable to move, and stood motionless with every feature revealed.

Lord Northbridge uttered an exclamation of horror, and, with an exertion of strength almost marvellous, disengaged himself from Luke and made a rush at Raymond.

"Geoffrey!" he gasped. "Am I mad, or dreaming?"

Lord Raymond seemed suddenly to be possessed with the ferocity of a wild beast; and snatching the crowbar from the ground, he dealt the old man a blow on the forehead which felled him to the ground. Then he stood, panting and breathless, glaring down at him, clenching the crowbar as if prepared to strike again if he should rise.

"Ye've quieted him for a time," said Luke's voice in his ear. "Give me the crowbar, and stand ready at the door."

As he spoke, he forced open the drawer of the safe, emptied its contents into the capacious pocket of his coat, and picking up his cap from the floor, pulled it well over his eyes.

"Get back to your own room as sharp as ye can," he said, hastily. "There's not a second to be lost. I'm afraid ye've let yourself in for a nice job."

Lord Raymond started, and, with a sudden movement, turned to look at the motionless figure on the floor.

"I'm going," he said, hoarsely; "how about the money?"

"I've got that all right," returned Luke; "but for goodness' sake go."

Lord Raymond picked up the lantern like one in a dream; he did not notice on the floor his cap that Lord Northbridge had knocked off in the heat of the encounter. Somehow he gained his father's dressing-room, and was making for the corridor when a shadow, as stealthy as his own, crept out of a doorway to meet him. With a stifled exclamation, he drew back into the room; but the figure followed him. He saw by the light, which the earl had turned on before he came upon them, that it was a woman, and the next moment that it was Marion Smeaton. As she saw who it was, she gave a low cry.

"Be quiet!" he commanded, as he grasped her arm. "If you dare to breathe a word to anyone that you've seen me here, I'll kill you—d'you hear?" His hold tightened on her arm; and she would have screamed in agony, had he not suddenly let go; and, before she was aware of it, he had left her.

In spite of the commotion that had been caused, no one else appeared on the scene; and, for a few more hours, the Hall was enveloped in silence. It was not until the morning that the alarm was given by Lord Northbridge's valet.

He had knocked at the earl's door at nine o'clock; and, receiving no answer, had returned to the servants' hall, remarking that he thought it would be wiser to let his master rest a little longer, after the fatigue of the previous night. At ten o'clock, he went upstairs again and knocked loudly, and again receiving no answer, he at last opened the door. The bed had not been touched, apparently, since the previous day. He knew that his master had returned from the Manor, for he had heard him and Lord Raymond talking together.

It was not until he reached the dressing-room that the valet felt any real alarm; for here his eyes immediately saw the open door of the strong-room, and, looking beyond, his gaze became riveted on something that lay in the centre of the floor. With a gasp of horror he went quickly into the room, to discover that it was his master lying there, white and still, with a stream of blood trickling from a wound in the forehead.

Five minutes later, the dressing-room was filled with a crowd of people, in the centre of which was Marion Smeaton.

"What is it, Peters?" she asked, in a hushed whisper of fear. Then, as she caught sight of the still form, she sank on her knees beside it with a cry of horror. "Someone must get a doctor," she said, quite quietly, after a moment.

With courageous firmness, she beat back the emotion that threatened to overwhelm her and render her useless, and helped to lay the limp form of the master whom she loved upon his bed.

The utmost confusion soon reigned through the Hall; orders were given and countermanded; messengers were dispatched for doctors and the police. Soon all his friends and neighbours knew that Lord Northbridge had been attacked by burglars, who had made off with a great many of the family jewels and a sum of money. As soon as the news reached Dartworth Manor, Veronica ordered a horse to be saddled, and was soon on her way to the Hall.

"Where is Mrs. Smeaton?" she asked, when the frightened servants had told her all that there was to be told. "I will go up to her."

Veronica made her way quickly up the wide staircase.

"I'm so grieved, Marion," she said, as she greeted her. "You must let me stay and help you."

At this moment the doctor, who had been making a hasty examination of his patient, came into the room.

"I know you will be anxious to hear, Miss Dartworth," he said, solicitously. He had attended Dartworth Manor and the Hall for the last ten years, and Veronica liked him exceedingly. "His lordship is still alive, thank God! but his condition is extremely critical. I've wired up to town for Sir John Blake; it's possible he may be here some time this afternoon or evening. Till he comes the house must be kept as quiet as possible. It is Lord Northbridge's only chance of recovery. I wonder if you would mind taking up the rôle of nurse until we can get one down from London?" he asked, turning to Veronica. "It would be too much tax on Mrs. Smeaton, I'm afraid; and her services will be needed in other parts of the house. You're the only one I can think of, whose presence will not tend to disturb his lordship; and I know I can rely on you."

"I shall be only too pleased, Doctor," replied Veronica, earnestly, as she accompanied him to the patient's bedside.

"By the way, Miss Dartworth," he said, after he had applied some powerful restoratives, "has Lord Raymond been informed of his father's unfortunate condition? It is rather curious that no one seems to have seen him."

Veronica started. As the doctor had said, it was certainly extraordinary that Lord Raymond, whom it most concerned, should be unacquainted with his father's state.

"Shall I go and enquire?" she asked, quietly.

"Yes, I think it would be as well."

Veronica went once more to Marion. "I've come to find Lord Raymond," she said, as the elder woman looked up, anxiously.

"I—I really don't know where he is," she stammered. "He must be out; or surely he would have known what has happened before this! I'll enquire."

"Oh, Roberts," she said as Lord Raymond's valet entered the room, "where is your master?"

"He's still asleep, Mrs. Smeaton. I didn't know if I might wake him."

"Call him at once, please," said Veronica; "and tell him to come here as soon as he possibly can. And—Roberts—I don't think you'd better mention anything of—of what has occurred; it might upset him."

The valet knocked softly at his master's door, and, receiving no answer, put his hand upon the handle. The door was locked; but before he could knock again, the key was turned, and Lord Raymond, with every appearance of having just awakened, opened the door.

"Come in," he said, brusquely. "Why didn't you call me before? Is my bath ready?"

"My lord . . ." commenced the man, and stopped abruptly.

"What the devil's the matter?" exclaimed Lord Raymond, with well-assumed surprise.

"Something has happened, my lord," said the man; "and Miss Dartworth has sent me to ask you to go to her as soon as possible."

Lord Raymond stared at him, but made no reply. The man assisted him to dress, and, as he did so, noticed how wan his master looked. Perhaps it was due to the exertions of the previous evening? he reflected; or, more likely, to uncertainty as to what had really happened. However, he had little time for speculation; for when his master was half-dressed, he was sent to tell Miss Dartworth that Lord Raymond would be down directly.

When he was alone, Raymond turned to the glass and, for some minutes, stood looking into it. He certainly did not appear as well as he could have wished; but then, what man would, he reflected, after he had mur——? He stopped abruptly at the word, and shivered miserably. Hastily he opened his door, and made his way to the morning-room, for he could not bear to be alone with his thoughts a moment longer.

When he entered the room he felt that he must immediately make his escape, for the first person his eyes chanced to rest upon was Marion Smeaton. She was seated by the window, but to his great relief, she did not look at him.

"Veronica! What has happened?" he asked; and he felt a little courage return to him as he began to act his part. "Is anyone ill? Anything wrong at the Manor? Where's my father?"

"He—he is very ill, Geoffrey," replied Veronica; and then, as gently as she could, she told him that a burglary had been committed; that Lord Northbridge had been attacked and left for dead; and that he was now lying between life and death.

Raymond listened; and as Veronica spoke, the memory of it all came back to him with horrible poignancy.

"Don't tell me any more," he said hoarsely. "I can't bear it"; and Veronica, for the first time in her life, took him voluntarily by the hand.

"You mustn't fret, Geoffrey," she said, kindly; "you must bear up for your father's sake. Will you come to Lord Northbridge's room with me?—the doctor sent me to fetch you."

Lord Raymond drew his hand away from her hastily.

"Not—not——" he said, shrinking back.

"I certainly think you ought to," said Veronica.

Lord Raymond glanced at the figure by the window; but she made no movement.

"Very well," he said, slowly. "I'll come."

"I'm glad you are here," said the doctor, as Raymond entered his father's bedroom accompanied by Veronica. "My patient is a little better now; and I am anxious that he should see some face he knows."

"You'd—you'd better let him see Veronica," Raymond stammered, and, try as he would, he could not repress a shudder. "I—I should only excite him."

"Ssh!" interrupted the doctor, warningly. "I'm afraid you'll wake him if you make such a noise. In my opinion the sight of you might reassure him, and avert consequences I greatly dread."

As he spoke, there was a slight movement from the bed, and Lord Northbridge opened his eyes, slowly. He looked round with an unconscious gaze for a minute or two, and finally it rested upon the two men standing near the bedside. Instantly a change came over the shrunken features; the eyes lit up with passionate indignation, the blood returned to his face, and, in a clear, emphatic voice, he cried, as he pointed a thin finger at his son:

"That is the thief!"

Then his eyes closed again, and unconsciousness returned to him.

The doctor turned with a sigh of genuine and deep disappointment to Lord Raymond.

"What I feared has happened," he said. "The shock has cost him his reason."

Later that same day, Sir John Blake came down to Northbridge Hall from London, bringing with him two nurses. His examination of the patient lasted some time; but he could only confirm what Doctor Browne had said earlier in the day—that Lord Northbridge had lost his reason, whether temporarily or permanently, time alone would prove. As a consequence of the great specialist's visit, everyone was dismissed from the sick-room but the nurse on duty and Veronica; and if there came a change for the worse, Doctor Browne had implicit instructions as to what he should do.

Heavy loads of straw were strewn along the carriage-drive; and every bell in the house was muffled.

A detective from London had arrived; but, at first, Lord Raymond had been too overcome with grief to see him. Finally Raymond decided that he could not possibly put off the interview and proceeded to the library, where Detective Fraser had been awaiting him for over an hour.

As Lord Raymond entered, the detective glanced at him indifferently; then he rose, and with a slight bow, said:

"Lord Raymond, I presume?"

"Yes," replied Raymond; "will you sit down?" He looked keenly at the detective, and the thought came into his mind that Scotland Yard could not have sent a worse representative to investigate the matter. But he had yet to learn the detective's capabilities.

"You're from Scotland Yard?" he asked, after a pause. "I'm sorry it has not been convenient to see you before, Mr. Fraser. Perhaps you will tell me in what way I can be of service to you?"

The detective smoothed his hair from his forehead in a contemplative manner.

"Well, let me see—perhaps it would be as well if you told me all you know of the affair; one cannot be too well supplied with material to work on."

"Certainly," replied Lord Raymond, affably; and in a clear, concise manner—strangely unlike his usual jerky sentences—he went over the story of the valet's discovery, and the loss of the jewels and money from the safe. The detective jotted down these particulars slowly and thoughtfully.

"I'm afraid that isn't much to go on," he said. "May I see the strong-room?"

Lord Raymond was about to summon a servant to conduct the detective upstairs, when Mr. Fraser, with something almost approaching alacrity, said:

"I should feel obliged if you could spare the time to take me to the room yourself. It is not wise to bring servants into the early stages of an enquiry."

"All right," replied Lord Raymond, who did not feel so kindly disposed towards the detective, whom he began to regard as a somewhat exacting individual. However, he led the way up to the dressing-room. Without any noise whatever, they crossed it and stood at the door of the strong-room; but the detective would not enter.

"Who is in the habit of sweeping out this room?" he asked, in a whisper.

"A woman called Marion Smeaton—she can be trusted implicitly," replied Lord Raymond, not wishing her to be questioned. As he made this reply, he suddenly realized that Luke had got the information he possessed about the strong-room from his wife.

"It hasn't been swept for three or four days, I see," went on the detective.

Raymond turned deadly pale; for though his sight was not keen enough to detect the faint layer of dust noted by the sleepy-looking eyes of the detective, he felt instinctively that some marks of his own and of Luke's footsteps must be visible to this sleuth-hound of justice.

"I shall be glad if you will give orders that the room is on no account to be entered, my lord; and I should like to see the side-door by which the burglars are supposed to have come."

"You think there were more than one?" asked Raymond, with great anxiety.

"There were two," answered the detective.

Lord Raymond took him to the side-door; and the detective, having ascertained that the entrance was hardly ever used, asked to be left to himself to make investigations. Raymond promised to give orders to the valet on guard that no one was to enter the strong-room, and then reascended the stairs. But, suddenly, he came back again.

"Peters," he said, to the valet, in question, "go up to my dressing-room, and bring me the letter you'll find upon my writing-table. If it isn't there, you'll find it in the bedroom. I'll mount guard here while you're gone. But, first of all, send Marion Smeaton to me, will you?"

When Peters returned from his futile search, he saw Mrs. Smeaton sweeping out the strong-room, and washing away the blood-marks upon the floor.

"Lor! Mrs. Smeaton," he exclaimed in a frightened whisper, "the 'tec' said as that room wasn't to be touched on no account."

Marion's face was full of fear, as she asked:

"Are you sure, Mr. Peters?"

"Certain," was the answer; "who told you to sweep it?"

Marion made no answer; but her eyes sought those of Lord Raymond, who had just entered with the detective.

"If you please, my lord," said Peters, in his carefully lowered voice, "Mrs. Smeaton has gone and swept the floor of the strong-room."

The detective uttered an exclamation of annoyance, and fixed his apparently unobservant gaze upon the shrinking woman.

"Who told you to sweep it?" he asked.

"Lord——" she began, her eyes fixed upon Raymond's face. What she saw there seemed to caution her to be silent; and she made no attempt to answer further.

"My good woman," interposed Lord Raymond, in a subdued tone of assumed annoyance, "you have done a very stupid thing. Didn't I distinctly tell you *not* to sweep that room?"

"Yes, my lord," stammered Marion; and then, seeing the foolishness of her assent, she added: "At least—I—I thought you said it *was* to be swept."

The detective, chancing to glance under his drowsy lids at Raymond's face, caught an unmistakable look of relief upon the young man's face, and noted it as a point to be remembered.

"I hope that woman's stupidity won't in any way delay your investigations," said Raymond, when he and the detective were once more closeted together in the library.

"I hope not," was the careful reply.

"Did you obtain any clue from the side-door, Mr. Fraser?" asked Lord Raymond.

"A most important one, my lord—that, whereas two people were engaged in the robbery, only one came, and only one went away again."

Lord Raymond's face was the colour of parchment as he tried to say, in a casual manner:

"You think it was someone in the house, then?"

"Undoubtedly," was the answer.

Just then the valet entered, carrying the cap which had escaped Lord Raymond's notice when he made his hurried flight from the strong-room. One of the servants had picked it up when Lord Northbridge was found. The detective examined it carefully. Then he asked:

"Any poaching lately, my lord?"

"Not anything to speak of," replied Raymond.

"You've had some good neighbours for that sort of thing, too," remarked Mr. Fraser. "I saw the evidences of a gipsy encampment on the common."

"Evidences!" said Lord Raymond, with a palpable start. "Do you mean to say they're gone?"

"Yes," said the detective, who had taken due note of the start, as Lord Raymond had intended him to do.

"They were there the night before the burglary," he said, musingly. "May I see that cap?"

Mr. Fraser handed it to him. He looked at it for a moment in silence, and then he said: "I believe I can help you a little"; after which he proceeded to relate the story of the robbery of his watch and chain by a mysterious poacher, a week or two before.

"That is most important, my lord," said the detective when he had finished. "I wonder if you could possibly remember what the man was like? It would be of the greatest assistance."

Lord Raymond gave the detective a minute description of Tazoni.

"Thank you, my lord," said Mr. Fraser. "May I trouble you to let me have a dog-cart or something? I'd better track those gipsies as soon as possible."

"Certainly," replied Lord Raymond, who was only too glad that the detective was going. "Do your very best to bring the scoundrels to justice, and I won't forget you."

Looking at the detective closely as he said this, Lord Raymond thought himself more than a match for this sleepy person—a thought engendered by the way in which Mr. Fraser had taken the hint about the gipsies, and also by his almost indifferent attitude anent the sweeping out of the strong-room. Had he known the detective's thoughts at that moment, he might have been somewhat alarmed perhaps.

"I wonder why that white-faced young man insisted on having that room cleaned out when I told him not to?" Mr. Fraser asked himself, as he descended the staircase.

Had the detective waited until the evening, and been within sight of the shrubbery, he might have received some enlightenment; for he would have seen the young man in question steal through the darkness towards the lake, and would have noticed with some surprise—if a detective is capable of that emotion —that his lordship dropped into its depths a small, heavily-weighted parcel containing a rough jacket, and a pair of thick corduroy trousers—singular articles to be found in the possession of the heir of Northbridge Hall.

CHAPTER XX

Two hours later, the detective told the driver of the dog-cart lent him by Lord Raymond to stop, and for the sixth time got down and scanned the road upon which they were travelling; for they had come to a point where four ways met. He soon came upon three little handfuls of grass a few feet along one of the roads, and, climbing up once more into his seat, told the man to take the turning to the left.

Presently they came upon a patch of common where four caravans had been drawn up; and descending once more from the dog-cart, Fraser told the man to await him at some little distance, while he went and interviewed the gipsies.

"Is the guv'nor here?" he asked, of one of the men.

"No, he's away," was the surly answer.

"Since when?" asked the detective.

"What's that to do with you?"

"Who's asking for Tazoni?" croaked old Martha, now appearing upon the scene.

"I am, mother," was the detective's bland reply.

"Well, if ye've come from Lord Raymond," she said, "tell him that we'll get our girl back if we have to tear him limb from limb."

"I don't understand," said the detective.

"What have ye come about, then?" demanded Martha.

"To be frank, mother, there's been a robbery up at Northbridge Hall last night; and your man's cap was found in the strong-room."

"Oh, it was, was it?" sneered Martha. "Well, our man had nothing whatever to do with it; 'cos he were away Londonwards, a-looking for our Maya that that fiend up at the Hall stole from us."

"All of which remains to be proved," said the detective, coolly.

"Oh, so ye're a-going to prove that our man's the thief, and let that Raymond go, are ye? Well, I'm just a-telling ye that I'll beat ye at your own game; and now if ye don't go, I'll set the dogs on to ye."

Mr. Fraser went, with the secret hope that the old woman might, in her own way, assist him in the difficult task in front of him.

"Most singular young man!" was his private comment, as he thought of the old woman's association of the name of such a personage as Lord Raymond with a common gipsy girl. "Most singular!"

The next morning he called at the Hall, and asked to see Lord Raymond. His colourless eyes seemed more unobservant than ever; and Raymond began to think him a still greater fool; but beneath his shaggy eyebrows the detective was watching the pale, haggard face of the young man with cunning scrutiny.

"I have been unable to trace the man, Tazoni, I'm sorry to say, my lord," were his first words. "I find that he was away from the camp upon the night of the robbery. I telephoned through to headquarters for a warrant, and also so that they may set the usual machinery in motion to get the man. We're communicating with all the pawn-brokers, so that the jewels can't very well be got rid of; and I really don't think we shall be long in trapping the fellow, seeing there's a woman in the case."

"A woman!" exclaimed Lord Raymond, betraying for the moment his irritability, but he recovered instantly. "What woman?"

Mr. Fraser, who had presumably failed to notice Lord Raymond's sharpness, replied leisurely:

"The gipsy, Maya."

"There I think you're wrong," said Lord Raymond, with conviction. "I don't think she had any hand in it. Why, of what assistance could she be to a ferocious housebreaker? Besides, she wasn't at all that sort of person."

"You knew her, then, my lord?" said the detective, quietly.

Lord Raymond found, with a start, that he was giving the game away.

"Oh yes, I've seen her," he replied, with an attempt at frankness. "They encamped on Metherston Common, you know. I don't know anything beyond that, of course."

"Of course," said the detective, blandly. "But, curiously enough, she disappeared on the night of the robbery; and her people can give no satisfactory account of her disappearance. I conclude that they started for London—the man to keep in hiding, while the girl got rid of the spoil. Women are always better at that, you know, my lord, than men. In almost every case I know of, there's been a woman in it—to act as go-between for the cracksmen and the smelters. Depend upon it, when we find that girl, our man won't be far off."

"Well, you might be right, of course; but I should strongly advise you to get hold of the man first," replied Lord Raymond.

"Very well, my lord," said the detective, who meant to do just whatever he liked about the matter. "How is Lord Northbridge getting on?"

"Slowly, I'm sorry to say. His reason seems to have completely deserted him," was the reply.

"Not well enough to see me, then?" queried the detective.

"Certainly not," said Lord Raymond, emphatically. "By the way, I think you had better offer a reward for that rascal—say a hundred. You have my description of him, haven't you?"

"Yes, my lord;" and the detective took his leave.

"I should imagine there's more truth in the old woman's story than I gave her credit for. My lord seems mighty anxious that the man should be caught. Naturally—and more especially if it should turn out that there's a little bad blood over the girl. Seemed very anxious the girl shouldn't be implicated. H'm!" was the detective's comment upon the interview.

Meantime Lord Raymond was having a little conversation with Hubert Denville.

"I promise you I'll send the cheque along during the next day or two. It's only a question of time; just while I get matters here more into my own hands.

But I say, old chap, there isn't any likelihood of—er—of anything being found out about the girl, is there?"

"Not a bit of it," was Denville's cool reply. "We managed it too well for that."

"Thanks. I won't forget you for it, Denville, my boy," said Raymond, shaking Denville's hand in a somewhat too demonstrative farewell; for the latter had seen very plainly, that he could scarcely have any excuse for staying on at a house which was over-shadowed by the illness of the host. He determined, however, not to lose touch with the game which he intended to win sometime or other.

"By the way," he said, casually, "I forgot to tell you that little Judy Slade wrote asking for news of you. She was rather afraid you'd got smashed up, too, in this rotten business. I think she's more than a little gone in your direction, old chap."

"Think so?" asked Raymond, obviously flattered. "I shall be running up to town in the next week or two. Tell her I'll call, will you? Good-bye."

Lord Northbridge was certainly in a bad way, as Raymond had said. He was suffering from intense weakness, and a strange hallucination which displayed itself perpetually when his son's name was mentioned. It needed all Veronica's efforts to quiet him on these occasions; and Lord Raymond, finding that his father recognized him only too well, visited the sick-room as rarely as possible.

A great change was coming over Raymond. He was just as pale as ever; but his moroseness had settled into a stealthy taciturnity. Already he had begun to assume an insolent authority that his inferiors resented; and the villagers of Northbridge realized it would be a bad day for them when Lord Raymond was their master in good truth.

The subject of the robbery was so terrible a one to Veronica that she did not care about discussing it with anyone; and, as yet, she was in total ignorance of the suspicions which had closed around Tazoni, or that a reward was to be offered for his apprehension. She knew that the gipsies had left the common; for very early on the morning after the robbery one of the men had brought back her horse, and having received the money, told the groom that the encampment was going away. Thinking that it was for her sake he had gone, Veronica determined that she on her side would do her best to follow the path Duty pointed out to her, and try to forget the man she loved with her whole soul.

So the days passed on; and still Lord Northbridge's health did not improve. Her time being fully occupied in the sick-room, it was not immediately that Veronica heard of the black imputations made by Lord Raymond against the man she loved.

While Detective Fraser was looking high and low for a rough-looking gipsy in a brown velveteen coat and knee-breeches, Tazoni was lying ill in London at a place where they did not dream of seeking him.

His first thought had been to go to the Hall and ask for Lord Raymond, in order to try to force the secret of Maya's disappearance from his lips. But reflection warned him that—even should he find him at the Hall—Lord Raymond could easily deny the story, and order his servants to turn him out of the house. He would gain nothing by this means, and only lose time in pursuit of Maya. He therefore spurred his horse to its greatest speed upon the road which he believed Maya's captors to have taken, hoping against hope that he might save her still. But he could find no clue.

He had brought but little money with him from the camp; for it could not be spared. The sale of his horse, however, which, by a stroke of luck, he accomplished on his first day in London, added to his store, and with the money he bought some clothes ready-made. Having paid a visit to a barber, and changed his clothes at the public-house where he had spent the night, he set out to begin his search for Maya; and, tracing him to this point, Detective Fraser utterly lost sight of him.

Tazoni made his way westward, intending to go first of all to the Northbridge town house, for he imagined that Maya might possibly have been conveyed thither.

The busy London thoroughfares greatly bewildered him, and gave him a sense of hopelessness about the accomplishment of his task which made him feel very unhappy. The swiftly-moving motors seemed like so many devils bent upon killing him. Piccadilly was a maze, taking his breath away and making him long for the quiet country roads once more.

Presently, however, he caught sight of green trees and shady paths through iron railings, and, forgetful of all else but the desire to throw himself down upon the verdant grass, he made a sudden rush to cross the wide thoroughfare.

At that very moment a car turned quickly out of a side street; there was a deafening and bewildering "hoot," a shout, a cry, and Tazoni lay upon the ground. From his forehead blood began to flow, for in falling he had struck against the kerb.

From the *tonneau* of the car stepped a well-dressed little woman, who anxiously exclaimed: "Oh, I do hope he isn't hurt," as her chauffeur raised Tazoni's head.

"I must take your name and address, if you please, madam, in case of consequences," said a police constable at her side, busy with his notebook.

She gave her name—Lady Gertrude Plunkett—and her address, stating that it was her intention to take the injured man to her house until he should recover.

"He would be much better at the hospital, madam," put in the practical policeman; "if you will let us take him there in your motor it would save time fetching the ambulance."

So Tazoni was taken to a hospital; and while the hue and cry was out after him, he lay there in delirious unconsciousness. On the third day, however, he fell into a quiet sleep, and at the end of the week Lady Gertrude Plunkett, who had called or sent to enquire after him almost every day, asked to be allowed to see him. Tazoni's face, as he lay silent and still upon the pavement, had scarcely ever left her mind, and she could not but feel that she was responsible for his illness. She was anxious to see him, therefore, in order to relieve her anxiety on his account by making sure that he was actually on the highroad towards recovery.

"Well, and how do you feel to-day?" she asked in a kind, sympathetic voice that won Tazoni's heart.

"Almost well, thank you," he replied, with a bright smile; but as Lady Gertrude scanned the pale face beneath the bandages, she did not feel as sure about the matter as Tazoni might have wished.

When she spoke to the nurse after the very short interview that was allowed her with Tazoni, Lady Gertrude was informed that the patient would be out of hospital the following week.

"You see, we are dreadfully over-crowded just now," explained the nurse, "and so cannot keep our patients any longer than is absolutely necessary. Of course, I don't know what this patient's actual circumstances may be. He hasn't spoken freely of himself to me like most of the others do. I asked if he had any friends or relations with whom he would like to communicate, but he said no."

"Poor, lonely fellow," replied Lady Gertrude. "I must make arrangements for him to come and stay with me until he has recovered."

The nurse opened her eyes a little, but made no reply.

At first Tazoni refused to accept Lady Gertrude Plunkett's generous proposal, for he thought it would delay his further search for Maya. But when on the day he left the hospital he realized how very weak he was, and that he had no home in London, he was only too glad to step into the electric brougham that Lady Gertrude had sent for him, and thus accept the kind invitation she still held out to him.

Both Lady Gertrude and her husband, who was the editor of the leading London weekly, *The Social World*, received Tazoni with a warm welcome, and he was given a bright room on the first floor overlooking a small, but neatly laid-out garden. Here everything was at hand for his comfort—books, flowers and papers—and Lady Gertrude herself would often come and sit with him, though she never asked him anything about his past. Like the nurse, she had remarked his reticence about himself.

When Tazoni had recovered consciousness at the hospital and they had asked him his name, for some reason he could scarcely explain even to himself, he had given the name of Francis, and that was all that Lady Gertrude actually knew of him. However, she felt convinced that he was a gentleman, and she had certainly grown to like him for himself; that was sufficient both for herself and her husband.

It was not until his third week in London, therefore, that Tazoni heard anything about the robbery at Northbridge.

Chancing to look through a copy of *The Social World* his eyes fell upon the following paragraph:

"The gipsy, Tazoni, for news of whom a reward of a hundred pounds is being offered, is still at large," he read. "Lord Northbridge's health is slightly better, but it necessarily will be a long time before he recovers from the shock that he received."

In a tone of subdued excitement, Tazoni asked one of the servants if they had an earlier copy of *The Social World*, and when the two previous numbers were brought to him, Tazoni read as in a dream the full version of the burglary at Northbridge Hall.

One hundred pounds had been offered for his apprehension! What did it all mean? he asked himself. Could it be possible that he was suspected of the burglary at Northbridge Hall and the murderous attack on Lord Northbridge? It was his duty in any case to give himself up to the police, and endeavour to clear himself of the stigma cast upon him.

He could not see his way clearly as yet: the intelligence had come so suddenly, so like a physical shock, that he had not fully realized it. For a long time he thought deeply, and at last a little light came to aid him. Suppose all this should be only a trick to remove him from the pursuit of Maya? Suppose—and it was not unlikely—that the betrayer of Maya had thrown the suspicion upon him to get rid of him, and so secure Maya without further obstacle or danger?

Once the idea had entered his mind, he could not get rid of it. It grew more plausible every moment. If it were true, then it was necessary for him to be as cunning as his enemy, and to this end it would be a thousand times better for him to lie low, and at the same time continue his search.

He took up the paper again, and as he read the description given of himself, he could not repress a bitter smile. Lord Raymond, or whoever had dictated the notice, had, in his malignity, overreached himself. The description was such as an enemy, prejudiced against Tazoni, and thinking him no better than a vagabond gipsy, would have given; and, as it stood, was calculated to mislead in every point.

The papers also published a bulletin to the effect that it was feared that the earl would lose his reason; and that Lord Raymond, during his father's illness, had his hands full with the administration of such a vast estate as that of the Earl of Northbridge.

Tazoni, who believed, in view of Martha's story and his own personal instinct, that it was Lord Raymond who had stolen Maya from her people, was glad to feel that, for the present, he would be too busily occupied at Northbridge to think of Maya. This should give him, Tazoni, a chance of finding out her whereabouts before any harm came to her.

Meantime, the object of Tazoni's anxiety was drinking the bitter dregs of a life of captivity, in a lonely house situated on one of the backwaters of the Thames. It was a beautiful place, and had witnessed many a riotous scene upon occasions when Lord Raymond and his friends had chanced to visit it. He had originally bought it to please one of the stars in a popular musical comedy, who had had it given her by some equally brainless member of the aristocracy, and her object in parting with it had been to "pocket the cash," to use the graceful phrase of the lady who disposed of it.

The house itself and the furniture were all that could be desired, and Maya was allowed to roam where she pleased; but the doors that led into the beloved world outside were guarded night and day, while the windows were impracticable, either from their height, or because they had been secured with nails or bars of iron.

Night and day then she was watched like Danae of old, and her life seemed one long misery. The servants were kind and attentive to her; but she knew that they were her gaolers all the same. One of them, who had been set aside as her maid, at first tried to rouse her to some interest in the luxuries around her; but at length she gave up trying to please her, and Maya was left more than ever to herself.

Sometimes she would sit for hours together at the window of her room, which overlooked the river, with a mad hope in her heart that if Tazoni should be seeking her he might chance to see her. This was the only ray of light that lit up her darkness; and, after a time, even this failed to bring her comfort.

Few people ever brought their boats up that backwater, for it was rather out of the way of the river traffic generally, and as "The Cottage" was the only house in the immediate neighbourhood, there was little reason why anyone should disturb its tranquil waters. One day, however, a boat was rowed up the backwater; and having moored it to the bank, its occupant took out a book and lay at full length reading.

From her window Maya watched his every movement, her heart beating fast. His face looked kind, she thought; suppose she called to him for help? She did not let her maid see that she had noticed the advent of the stranger, and asking, in her usual indifferent tone, for some tea, sent the girl to fetch it for her. Guessing she would in all probability be away some little time, Maya raised the window—for her room was too high up for her to imagine that she could try to escape that way—and in tones just sufficiently loud to reach the stranger, began to sing a gipsy ballad. He started slightly, looked round, and, seeing her, closed his book. With a beating heart Maya beckoned to him; but, to her surprise and anguish, he looked at her and shook his head, then unmoored his boat and rowed away.

With a cry of bitter disappointment Maya turned and found her maid watching her.

"It's no use, miss," she said, kindly. "It isn't likely that the master would let you sit at the window within sight of the river and all that, without taking proper precautions to prevent your escaping."

"What do you mean?" asked Maya.

"Well, miss, if I tell you you mustn't round on me. It's like this. Everybody believes as you're a relation of the master's, and not quite right in your mind."

"That I am mad?"

"Yes, miss," replied the girl, unwillingly. "You see, it's very convenient—it does stop such a lot of gossiping. But if I were you, miss, I shouldn't try and attract people's attention—they won't take any notice of you."

Maya sank into a chair and buried her face in her hands, for despair had blotted out all hope.

CHAPTER XXI

It was well for Maya, that although Lord Raymond did not fear any ill consequences to himself from Detective Fraser, he yet thought it only common precaution to keep a close guard on his own actions for some time to come. Therefore, lest his steps should be dogged, he let the girl alone for the present, and confined himself to playing the still difficult game which was necessary to avert suspicion from himself.

He knew that he could trust his servants at "The Cottage"; for they had been in his service some time, and were bound to him by the strongest tie of all—self-interest. The happy idea that had come to him, of proclaiming Maya insane, relieved him of any fears concerning her rescue; and so, having netted his bird, he decided to leave her in her cage for a time.

Matters progressed at Northbridge without any great change. Lord Northbridge still continued weak, both in mind and body; and, although improved sufficiently to allow of his removal to another part of the house, where a fresh suite of rooms had been prepared for him, Sir John Blake, who had been down to see him more than once, forbade him to leave the house, or to concern himself in any business matters.

The management of the estate had thus devolved upon Lord Raymond; and, to the surprise of all who knew his character, he set about his stewardship seriously. But soon the tenants discovered another trait in his singular and far from prepossessing character. He was avaricious; and whereas his father had always been slow to demand money and quick to bestow it, Lord Raymond not only demanded his due, but enforced its payment. The steward—an old servant as easy-going as the earl himself—soon found that, if he wished to continue in favour with his new master, he must be more exacting with the tenants and raise the revenues of the estate as high as possible.

This fresh development of Lord Raymond's character greatly distressed Lord and Lady Dartworth; but they comforted themselves with the reflection that if he had suddenly become avaricious he had also become sober, for Lord Raymond was now almost an abstainer. In their eyes, he was still an eligible son-in-law; and when Veronica returned to the Manor, they waited anxiously for the girl to show some sign of her liking for him.

But Veronica's mind was full of another. She was learning the bitterest lesson that life holds—to love and to doubt. She loved Tazoni, and yet, to her inexpressible agony, she was almost beginning to doubt him. If he were guiltless of the crime Lord Raymond did not hesitate to lay to his charge, why did he not come forward and prove his innocence? The question was beginning to haunt her with horrible persistence; and the grey shadow of distrust began to deepen every day.

Lord Raymond had taken Luke Smeaton's advice with respect to Veronica; but, as the days passed, he began to see how hopeless it was even to attempt to interest her. He had not by any means forgotten Luke's story; and the knowledge that Marion Smeaton knew so much of his affairs was a continual source of anxiety to him. She was the perpetual thorn in his side; and at last he determined to make an effort to remove her from the house, to some spot, not too far from his supervision, but sufficiently distant to keep her from his sight. For that purpose he had a small cottage in the woods fitted up for her; and one morning, meeting her on the stairs, he said suddenly:

"Oh, Marion, I want you to look after 'Wood Cottage.' I wish it to be occupied, so that the keepers need not come up to the house for everything they want."

Marion made no reply, and Lord Raymond passed on; but a few hours later a distinct feeling of relief came over him when he asked for her, and was told that she had already removed to the cottage in the woods.

He sat down at his writing-table, and opening a drawer, took out a bundle of letters. He frowned as he did so, for they were all of an unpleasant nature. One in particular—from Mr. Levy Jacobs—reminded him very forcibly of his promise, and at this Lord Raymond looked blacker than ever; for as yet Luke Smeaton had not given him his share of the plunder, and he could not tell how long he would be kept before he did so.

"Curse him!" Lord Raymond muttered. "I shall be in a hell of a fix if he doesn't let me have it soon!"

What would happen if he did not get the money he was saved from thinking, for he was interrupted by a respectful knock at the door. Before he answered, he bundled the letters into the drawer again and locked it.

"Well?" he asked, impatiently, as the footman—the second since Lord Northbridge's illness—entered.

"There's a man wanting to see you, my lord," he said; "but he wouldn't tell me his name."

Raymond thought a moment. Then he said, sharply:

"I suppose I'd better see him; show him up."

A few moments later, the footman ushered in Luke Smeaton.

Lord Raymond started; but with a warning look in his eyes, Luke said, for the benefit of the servant who was leaving the room:

"I'm sorry to intrude, my lord; but I've just heard as your lordship requires a keeper, and I've made so bold as to apply for the place."

Lord Raymond looked at him enquiringly; but in a flash he saw that his accomplice had determined to ignore the last occasion upon which they had met, and to act, even when they were alone, as if there had been no former connection, or even casual acquaintanceship, between them.

"Well," said Lord Raymond, at last, after writing nothing particular on his blotting-pad in order to gain time; "I do want a keeper; and I have no objection to you, my man, if you can show a good character."

"My name is Smeaton, my lord. I'm your foster-mother's husband."

"Then you have a claim upon my consideration," said Lord Raymond. "Sit down."

"Thank you, my lord. As to character, I've been serving a nobleman abroad for some time, as a sort of handy man. He's dead now—that's why I've come back to England—but he was kind enough to give me a character afore he died. Perhaps your lordship wouldn't mind reading it?"

There was a faint smile about the corners of Luke Smeaton's mouth, as he laid a bundle of papers upon the writing-table in front of Lord Raymond. With no small amount of astonishment, and wondering why Luke was keeping up the farce so long, Raymond tore off the envelope. The character consisted of a tightly folded packet of bank-notes!

"Is it quite satisfactory, my lord?" asked Smeaton, when he considered that Raymond had had sufficient time to recover from his surprise.

"Quite," said Lord Raymond, huskily. "I—I engage you. You—you may go now."

"What wages may I expect, my lord?" asked Luke, rising.

"Oh—er—two hundred a year."

The man smiled broadly, and moved towards the door.

"And the board, my lord? My wife has gone to live at the cottage, I hear. Perhaps——"

"Yes, yes—you may live at the cottage—wherever you like," interrupted Lord Raymond; "but go now, please, I'm busy."

His face was deathly white; and when Luke had gone, he dropped his head upon his hands and literally shook with fear. He had thought himself so safe, and yet—should Lord Northbridge die after all—there were two people down at the cottage in the woods who had it in their power to bring him to the gallows!

Much astonishment was expressed by everyone, that Luke Smeaton should be taken into the Northbridge service; and not a few people remarked, that it was not so very long ago that Lord Raymond had evinced an intense dislike for gipsies, and had even spoken of Luke Smeaton himself as a rogue and a thief.

At present, however, Luke gave little cause for gossip. He was quiet, taciturn, and stuck to his duties—for the time, at least—with laudable honesty. It was said that there had been a scene when Luke had arrived at the cottage; and Marion was reported to have said that she would not remain in the same house with him; but her fear of him was too great for her to carry out her threat, and in the end Luke conquered.

After a time, Lord Raymond thought he might venture to look after his own private affairs, seeing that Lord Northbridge was improving a little, and that the detective was still busily engaged in his search for Tazoni. Accordingly, one morning, he announced to Veronica, who was still in almost constant attendance upon Lord Northbridge, his intention of going up to town.

"Don't stay away long," she advised. "Your father may miss you."

"Scarcely," replied Raymond, sullenly; "considering he never even asks for me——"

"You really mustn't speak like that," she said, reproachfully. "Remember, that under such an affliction, those whom they love best they desire to see least.

It's a phase of your father's illness. Anyway, will you tell me where to find you, if he should take a turn for the worse?"

"My club will be the best place, I think."

"Won't you go to the house in Grosvenor Square?" she asked.

"No, I shall go to Claridge's; I can't stick a house that's shrouded in holland —gives me the blues."

"Very well," replied Veronica.

As he was being driven to the station, Lord Raymond saw Luke Smeaton leaning against a stile. The man touched his hat so significantly, that Raymond told the chauffeur to stop the car for a moment.

"Do you want to speak to me, Smeaton?" he called out.

Luke Smeaton made his way to the car.

"I heard as ye was going to London, my lord," he said; "and I thought I'd ask ye about them cartridges; they've been ordered some time, but they haven't come down, and we're a-wanting them rather badly. I've wrote the name of the shop on this 'ere bit of paper, if yer lordship wouldn't mind calling to enquire."

He handed up a small piece of paper. Lord Raymond glanced at it casually. The address of the gunmaker's shop was, to say the least, peculiar. It was:

"For goodness' sake mind the detective."

"All right. I'll see to it," said Lord Raymond, briskly.

On arriving in London, he drove straight to Mr. Levy Jacobs' office, and, much to that gentleman's surprise, settled his account. Then he called at a jeweller's in Piccadilly, to pay off a debt that had been owing for some months. The jeweller had intimated a few days previously that unless the account were settled quickly he should be compelled, much against his will, to resort to other measures.

"I think that is all I owe," said Lord Raymond, insolently, as he handed over a cheque for the amount. "I should advise you to be a little less insistent in the future. It is most annoying to be pestered like this. I shall not come here again."

"That sounded as though he meant to be nasty," remarked Mr. Fraser to the jeweller, when Lord Raymond had left the shop. He had called in with respect to a jewel robbery, and was in another part of the shop when Lord Raymond had entered. He had, however, overheard all the conversation. "You might just let me look at that cheque, will you?" he asked affably.

"Certainly," said the jeweller, as he handed it to him.

Mr. Fraser looked at the cheque for a few moments; and after taking due note that it was drawn on Coutts's bank and that it was for a large amount, he handed it back.

"Thanks," he said. "Well, I'll see about that other matter as soon as possible. I'm glad you've got your money all right for Lord Raymond's little account. A bird in the hand, you know—good afternoon."

The detective left the shop, asking himself where in the world Lord Raymond had managed to get so much ready money.

"If he's paid the jeweller's bill," he said to himself, "I'll be bound he's paid the Jew's. But he couldn't have squeezed all that money out of the estate. Then where the dickens did he get it from?" Even Mr. Fraser with all his astuteness could hit upon no solution of the mystery.

CHAPTER XXII

"It is my opinion that there is more behind that young man than we think," observed Mr. Plunkett to his wife one evening. "He does not seem to be well off; yet he has certainly received a very fair education, although he is remarkably secretive as regards himself and his antecedents."

"Is there anything we could do for him, do you think, Robert?" asked Lady Gertrude.

"I don't know. We might try, certainly; though we must be careful not to make our desire too palpable; he is very proud, you know. However, he and I were talking upon various topics last night, and I was quite interested in the way he spoke about Nature study—seemed to know all sorts of queer things no one's ever heard of before. So I thought I'd get him to write me a column for 'The Country Walk' corner, as Strongworth is ill."

"Capital!" replied Lady Gertrude; "if you think he can do it?"

"Oh, he'll probably want polishing as regards style; but I think he could give us some new facts, in a new way, too, that ought to prove good reading."

It was in this way, therefore, that Tazoni wrote his first article for *The Social World*, during his convalescence, and Mr. Plunkett was so pleased with its style and the information it contained, that he asked him to write another for his paper. That meant money in Tazoni's pocket—money that should help him forward in his search for Maya.

When he was practically well again, he suggested leaving the Plunketts' hospitable roof, saying that he had trespassed too long upon their kindness. But they would not hear of it, at any rate for a week or two, reminding him that it was through them he had met with his accident.

As soon as he was able to go about alone, Tazoni haunted the vicinity of the Northbridge house in Grosvenor Square, but was unable to glean any information regarding Maya. He made several covert enquiries; but he could only gather that Lord Raymond was not there; and Tazoni felt that he had reason to believe Maya was not there either.

One day Lady Gertrude Plunkett remarked to her husband that she had heard that Sir Harry Beriford intended standing for the Chestershire division at the next General Election, and that she thought of using her influence with such an old friend to get Tazoni taken on as his secretary.

"But how do you know our guest would care about it?" interposed her husband.

"Well, but he hasn't very much money, I know," Lady Gertrude replied; "and he has no home, and no friends. Besides, Harry is so nice, that they ought to get on well together."

"Ask him to lunch on Sunday and see first," advised Robert Plunkett, laughing.

So it was arranged, and Tazoni, much against his will, consented to meet Sir Harry Beriford at his host's table, not knowing, however, the plans that had been made for his future welfare. Afterwards he thought it was the hand of Providence which directed and helped him when he had almost given up hope of ever finding Maya.

In Sir Harry Beriford he felt he had met with a kindred spirit, and they were half-way through lunch, when the colour suddenly fled from Tazoni's face on hearing Lady Gertrude say:

"By the way, Harry, you went down to Lady Dartworth's ball, didn't you?"

"Yes; why didn't you go too, Gertrude? You were invited, weren't you?"

"Yes; but Robert was very put about by the sudden illness of someone in the office, and I wouldn't go without him."

Sir Harry Beriford smiled; for Lady Gertrude's attachment to her husband was almost a by-word among her friends.

"Did you hear anything of the robbery, Sir Harry?" asked Tazoni, with an assumption of interest.

"Just the fag end of it, you know. I left fairly early, and learned more through the newspapers than anything else. By the way, I can't stand Lord Raymond at any price, Gertrude; of all the—well, if I open my mouth too wide I may put my foot into it."

"That would be a pity," laughed Lady Gertrude, maliciously.

"Oh, yes," was the retort, "I dare say you think it's large enough already. But to return to our muttons—as I heard a young hopeful say the other day—you really must own, Gertrude, that that young cub is far from prepossessing."

"I certainly agree with you there," Lady Gertrude replied; "and yet there are few people in the world I like better than Lord Northbridge."

"Do you know, Plunkett, I heard a very curious story the other day," said Sir Harry Beriford, in a thoughtful tone. "I've been saving it up for you, since I know you like these little tit-bits."

"That's very kind of you, I'm sure," replied Mr. Plunkett, with a laugh.

"Oh, it's nothing funny, I assure you," remarked Sir Harry. "I was spending a few days on the Purbrights' house-boat, and—well, you know what that crew is—glad to get away from them for an hour or two; so I took a book, and found a nice little backwater where I guessed none of the gang would find me, and determined to have an hour or two by myself. They'd pointed out this particular spot, and said it belonged to Lord Raymond; but that he didn't stay there himself, because a relative, who was out of her mind, was living there—sort of private asylum, don't you know."

An exclamation escaped from Tazoni's lips, which he tried to account for by his great interest in the story.

"It certainly is strange," assented Lady Gertrude.

"But that isn't all," continued Sir Harry. "I was naturally a wee bit curious; though I really went down that backwater to get away from the Purbright girls, as I tell you. I had been there some time, and was just getting well into my book, when I heard the sweetest voice in the world singing. I don't know what it was—

sounded rather queer, I own. I looked up and saw a very pretty girl at one of the windows making signs to me; but knowing that she was insane, I just made off."

"Are you sure she is insane?" asked Tazoni suddenly.

"That I can't say," was the reply.

"For my part, I can only reiterate Gertrude's words—it is a very curious story," said Mr. Plunkett, and changed the subject.

When Sir Harry Beriford took his leave Tazoni seized the opportunity to ask if he might walk a little way with him. Sir Harry, having proposed that he should spend an hour at his flat, the two men set out, and Tazoni eagerly launched into his subject.

"Sir Harry, I have every reason to believe that the girl you mentioned during lunch is my adopted sister, for whom I have been searching all over London for some time past, and who, I have cause to think, was stolen away from me by none other than Lord Raymond."

For half a second Sir Harry Beriford stood still with astonishment. Then he said quietly, as he proceeded:

"I didn't know you knew Lord Raymond."

"I have every cause to regret the fact," was the reply.

"If I can help you in any way I shall be most willing to do so," said Sir Harry, in almost the same tone as he would have asked him to dine with him; but Tazoni saw in his face a curious look of dislike, and guessed, from what he had said during lunch, that he would not be sorry to be able to do Lord Raymond a "bad turn."

Tazoni did not know that ever since Sir Harry had heard Maya's voice it had haunted him, as well as her sad, beautiful face. If it were not true that she was mad, then he felt he would like to be beforehand with Tazoni in giving Raymond a thorough good thrashing—a punishment which generally appeals to an Englishman's sense of justice far more than an application to the law.

"We must start at once. Are you ready?" he asked, in the same cool manner.

"I have been ready to save her from that devil ever since the night he stole her from me," answered Tazoni, with a strange smile.

"Very well, then. Come along to my flat, and we'll have some dinner, and trot down in my car as soon as it's dark."

The greater part of their journey was accomplished in silence; for Sir Harry fell in with, and understood, his companion's mood. They put up at an inn, which Sir Harry informed Tazoni was quite near the villa on the backwater, and prowled about in the dusk to discover any means of entering the house, without making Maya's captors aware of their presence.

"There ought to be a ladder of some sort in those stables," said Tazoni, in a low voice, as they peered through the high iron gates.

"We've got to get round to them from the river, then," said Sir Harry; "we shall escape those beastly walls that way. We can get a boat from the inn—they know me there."

From the river they climbed a small fence, and proceeded stealthily, and with the greatest caution, up the garden until they stood beneath Maya's window. Not a single light was to be seen; and having found that it was impossible to climb to the room without a ladder, Tazoni decided to go round to the stables while Sir Harry stood beneath the window to ascertain if Maya were awake, or whether there were signs of anyone else moving in the house.

Tazoni easily succeeded in locating the stables; and creeping silently forward found to his joy that no one was about. His gipsy instinct for quickly detecting the presence of horses, told him that the stables had not been used recently; and he deduced from this fact that no groom would be employed there.

Fortunately the doors were only barred, not locked; and opening them with as little noise as possible, he entered, and then waited to see if he had been heard. Apparently he had not, however; and he was therefore free to pursue his search for some means whereby he could reach Maya's room.

It was a glorious summer night, and the full moon cast a gleam of light through the dirty stable window, thus enabling Tazoni to distinguish a small detachable ladder placed against a loft. It might not prove long enough, he thought; but in any case it would have to serve their purpose. He managed to carry the ladder out into the yard, carefully avoiding striking it against the swinging doors. A few moments sufficed for him to reach the garden, where Sir Harry reported "all serene." The moon, however, was shining full upon them, so that the two men feared they might be seen at any moment from one of the windows.

"We must get the matter over, and be off as soon as possible," whispered Sir Harry. "Anyway, I believe there are only women in the house; and we're two men, so we ought to bring the job off. Now then—up with it!"

The ladder proved to be a few feet too short; but Tazoni was nothing daunted, and managed the distance between the topmost rung and the window-ledge in a manner that earned Sir Harry's highest approval.

They paused in silence to listen. Not a sound could be heard, save the screech of an owl as it flew across the river. Tazoni tried the window, and, as might have been expected, found it fastened. Nothing daunted, he produced a clasp knife from his pocket, and manipulated it in such a fashion that the catch was thrust back, and the window made practicable. He lifted the sash, and entered the room; upon which Sir Harry immediately scaled the ladder, and raised himself to the window-sill, in order to be within call if he should be needed.

Tazoni found himself in a sort of boudoir, and the bright moonlight showed up the luxurious furniture and elegance of the room. Exactly opposite the window was a door, standing a little ajar, while on his left was another which was closed.

Stepping very cautiously, Tazoni crossed the room and peeped through the open door, to find, as he had expected, that this was the bedroom of the suite, with a window facing the front of the house. Breathless with excitement, he pushed the door open, and entered the room. Stealing up to the bed, he whispered, "Maya!" There was no answer. He called her name again, this time in a louder voice, "Maya!" Again there was no reply; and knowing the value of every moment, he determined to rouse her.

He drew aside the long white curtains that hung at the side of the bed; while his eyes, which were accustomed to the twilight of summer nights, immediately told him that the bed was empty.

It had been occupied recently, however; for the clothes were disturbed, and there was a quantity of wearing apparel, in great disorder, about the room, as if it had been worn but lately. Glancing quickly round for some clue that Maya had been there, he came upon another door, which he opened cautiously. This was the dressing-room, and, like the one he had just left, was in confusion. Tazoni's eyes travelled immediately to the window, which was wide open; and, going closer, in order to look into the garden, he found a rope-ladder hanging from the sill.

Then it all flashed upon him. Maya had escaped, had been rescued, perhaps, the very night he had discovered her prison. With a feeling of thankfulness, tinged by bewilderment, he retraced his steps.

"Well," said Sir Harry, "where is she?"

"That I can't tell you," replied Tazoni. "She's gone."

"Whatever do you mean?"

"She's escaped," replied Tazoni. "There's a rope-ladder hanging from the dressing-room window. That explains a lot."

"How extraordinary!" exclaimed Sir Harry. "Have you any idea who helped her; or do you think she managed it herself?"

"I can't imagine. But I must find her. She may be in greater danger, for all I know; and I must keep my promise."

"Ssh!" whispered Sir Harry. "I hear someone moving. The window, quick!"

Apparently the household had been alarmed in some way; and before they could reach the boat, a light shone from Maya's room, and a cry told them that the open window and the ladder had been discovered.

"Let's hope she has got safely away by now," said Sir Harry, as he took up the oars.

"Poor Maya!" murmured Tazoni sadly; for it was brought home to him very forcibly, that it was through his folly in loving Veronica that all this trouble had come to her.

"Maya!" repeated Sir Harry. "Maya! The name suits her, I should think"; and a little smile of interest played about the corners of his mouth, which, however, Tazoni could not see, for it was dark under the trees on the riverbank.

CHAPTER XXIII

The effect of Luke Smeaton's message upon Lord Raymond was to delay his visit to "The Cottage" for some days; though he had determined to go there before he returned to Northbridge.

To compensate himself for the delay, he determined to call upon Judy Slade. Whatever else went wrong, he knew he could always be sure of having a "good time" with her. So, having settled his business with some of his most pressing creditors, he lunched at his club; and having ordered dinner there for eight o'clock, took a cab and drove to her flat in Sloane Street.

A smart maid opened the door, and having ushered him into a small but tastefully-furnished drawing-room, said she would inform her mistress that he was there. Lord Raymond had time to examine his surroundings, which he found eminently to his taste. All the chairs were large, and designed for comfort, while the pink chintzes and curtains gave an air of daintiness to the room which, he thought, made it preferable to any one in the big house in Grosvenor Square.

In a few minutes Miss Slade entered; and, holding out both hands in a manner that Raymond thought rather charming, told him she was so very pleased to see him. Tea was brought in; and as he watched her small hands playing in a dainty manner with the tea-cups, Raymond told himself that he admired her even more as a hostess in her own flat, than he had done at Dartworth. Altogether he was distinctly pleased with himself and her. It was certainly a pity she had not got Vee's money, or he would have married her on the spot. After chatting quite amiably, and having accepted an invitation to dine at Sloane Street the following evening, Lord Raymond took his leave.

He had no sooner gone, than Judy sat down to her writing-table and dispatched the following telegram:

The cub in town. Dines here to-morrow. Shall expect you. JUDY.

Having given it to her maid to send off, she sat for over an hour crouched up in one of the big, chintz-covered chairs, with her pointed face resting in her clasped hands.

The next morning Lord Raymond did not rise in the best of humours; for he had spent a riotous night with some men of his own particular set, and he consequently awoke with a headache. He went down to the telephone of the hotel, deciding to ring up "The Cottage" and ask for news of Maya, thinking it might put him in a better humour, and he could, at the same time, advise the servants of his coming.

A benevolent-looking old gentleman, who chanced to be sitting in the hall near the telephone, could not help overhearing the following conversation:

"I want 245 Post Bramfield—sharp."

"Is that 'The Cottage'? Oh—er—how's your—er—mistress? Lord Raymond speaking."

"What's that? I can't hear—speak up."

"*Gone!*"

An imprecation followed which caused the benevolent-looking old gentleman to jump in his chair.

"What's that?" demanded Lord Raymond. "Last night? Police? No—let the girl go; and be hanged to her!"

The receiver was jammed down upon its rest, and Lord Raymond stalked away with a face as black as night.

When he had gone, the benevolent-looking old gentleman rose to his feet.

"Yes—I was sure that young man had something to do with the disappearance of the gipsy girl," he muttered below his breath; then took up his soft hat and went out.

Going over the "pros" and "cons" of Maya's escape, Raymond began to feel decidedly uncomfortable; for he knew that, should the matter get into the hands of the police, he could be imprisoned for abduction; and he very much feared that other, and more undesirable, matters would come to light if the police once got wind of this delinquency. Anyhow, the thing was done now, and couldn't be helped, he told himself; so he tried to drown his trouble in an additional number of brandy-and-sodas, until at last he betook himself to his room to dress for Miss Slade's little dinner.

Judy was waiting for him in the cosy drawing-room, and welcomed him with a soft emphasis which was peculiarly grateful to him in his present troubled mood. He thought she was prettier even than Veronica, with the soft light of the pink-shaded lamp upon her. But Veronica had money, together with the position that was to safeguard his own—for he fully believed now that Luke Smeaton had told him the truth, though he tried to forget it like a bad dream.

An old lady, very like Miss Slade, but extremely quiet and timid, entered the room, and was introduced to Lord Raymond as Cousin Penelope, who said something about the weather, and asked after Veronica, of whom she seemed inclined to talk, until a frown from Judy made her drop into silence.

Presently, when Lord Raymond's sullenness was beginning to melt into geniality, the servant announced Mr. Hubert Denville; and that gentleman entered the room with his usual bored smile, dressed with his own incomparable good taste.

"My dear Raymond, an unexpected pleasure! I had no idea you were in town."

"Nor I you," answered Raymond, extending his hand without rising, and eyeing him jealously; for his own black thoughts had immediately created an intimacy between Denville and Judy Slade.

The dining-room, for comfort and good taste, matched the drawing-room; and Lord Raymond as he took stock of it, the table, its appointments, and the smart parlour-maid, mentally pronounced the whole to be perfect of its kind. The dinner was excellent, and Denville's cynicisms and Judy's smart repartee kept the sullen, ill-bred guest in a good humour.

"You don't choose your own wine, I bet," he said, addressing Miss Slade with his glass to his lips. "This is too good for a woman."

"Oh, but I did choose it, though," replied Judy, with a smile.

Raymond was not allowed to stay long over his wine; for it was not Denville's intention to lose any time in bringing about the accomplishment of the plan he had discussed with Miss Slade on the night of the Dartworth ball.

"Cousin Penelope" having retired, Judy dispensed delicious coffee in the daintiest of china in such a charming manner that Lord Raymond thought her prettier than ever.

At last Denville proposed that Raymond should go with him to his club; and the two men said good night to their hostess.

"Capital dinner you gave us, and first-rate wine. I wonder where you got it from! It's too good for a woman," was Lord Raymond's amiable comment.

Miss Slade said she hoped he could come again; and Lord Raymond frankly informed her she was "one of the jolliest girls" he knew.

"I say, as it's such a fine night, let's walk," suggested Denville, when the two men left the house. Raymond agreed, and Denville thereupon began his subtle attack upon the base and credulous person who, as he intended, was to be his stepping-stone towards Veronica and her fortune.

"Jolly little place that girl's got, eh?" he drawled.

"Rather," was the retort. "A great deal more comfortable than any of our places. She must be pretty well off to be able to keep up that flat."

"Oh, only so-so," replied Denville; then, not wishing to proceed too fast, he changed the subject for a while. "I say, what about the pretty little gipsy girl, eh?"

"Confound her!" exclaimed Raymond, viciously. "The little cat has run away."

Denville emitted a low whistle, and mentally thanked his "lucky stars" that he had managed to get Lord Raymond's cheque before the girl had made good her escape—for which he could hardly blame her.

"Did she get away on her own?" he asked.

"How do I know? They only told me on the 'phone she had gone—that was enough, wasn't it?"

"Oh, quite," was the answer, beneath which ran a strain of sarcasm that Raymond could scarcely appreciate.

"Perhaps it's as well. You know the old tag about being 'off with the old love, etc., etc.' "

"Who do you mean?" asked Lord Raymond, puzzled.

"Oh, I say, now!" laughed Denville, giving him a dig in the side. "What a sly dog you are! Do you mean to tell me you haven't got your eye on little Judy Slade? Anyway, she's fearfully keen on you."

"D'you think so?" said Raymond, touched in his most susceptible point—his personal vanity.

"Anyone could see that with half an eye, my dear chap," was the reply.

"No; you don't say so!" put in Lord Raymond, eagerly. "Well, now you mention it, I did think she seemed a bit sweet. And she's a jolly nice girl, too. Got good taste, and very pretty. But, of course, I couldn't marry her," he added, quickly, with a side glance at Denville.

"Oh, that's out of the question," was the encouraging answer. "But, I say, my dear fellow, couldn't it be arranged without a marriage?"

"No, thanks," was the emphatic reply. "I've had enough of abductions. One's enough for me in a lifetime; and I don't suppose Judy Slade would be fool enough to have me under any other condition except marriage; she's too 'cute for that, and I admire her for it."

Hubert Denville laughed softly.

"It's a good thing you've got me behind you, Raymond, my boy," he drawled. "Look here—suppose you propose a clandestine marriage. You can give her plenty of plausible reasons, you know."

"But that wouldn't be any better than a public one for me," said Lord Raymond, peevishly.

"You can have a private marriage, that would satisfy her, but not really marry her," replied Denville, insinuatingly, his eyes upon Raymond's face, as they passed a lamp-post, to note the effect of his words. "Get her to consent to marry you on the quiet; have the thing done at a private house—special licence, but a sham one, don't you know—and the parson one of our own providing."

Raymond started; but his base, ignoble nature leapt to the bait.

"The very thing! What a clever chap you are, Denville! Poor little Judy! It's a great shame; but, upon my soul, it's too tempting. A parson of my own providing —that's good!"

Suddenly he looked with sharp suspicion at his companion's face.

"What's your own little game, anyway?" he asked, coarsely.

"Oh, the usual one," replied Denville, with disarming frankness. "I want money. If our little game works, you wouldn't mind a cheque for—say—a thousand, I suppose?"

"No," answered Raymond, completely taken in. "I'll make it a thousand, if it comes off all right."

"Payable on the morning of the marriage. Marriage! Rather a joke, what!"

"Yes," assented Raymond, laughing. "But, I say, who's going to get the chap to do it, and the licence and all that? I should only make a hash of it if I tried to do it myself."

"Oh, you leave it to me," replied Denville. "I'll manufacture the licence all right; and get an unfrocked parson I know to come and do the needful."

"Good!" said Raymond. "I'll leave it all in your hands, Denville, my boy. And you shall be my best man into the bargain."

"So I will; the best you'll ever have," was the truthful answer.

CHAPTER XXIV

During the absence of Tazoni and Maya, old Martha displayed unusual activity and penetration, and took command of the little company in a dogged, determined way which had procured her implicit obedience.

With the promptitude for which their kind are celebrated, the gipsies packed up their belongings, and made their way towards a wild stretch of common not far from London. In a few days they were aware of the stigma which had been cast upon their chief, and that a reward was out for his apprehension. This redoubled their fury against Raymond, whom they had come to look upon as the author of all their troubles; and it was only Martha's iron rule that kept some of the men from going back to Northbridge and lying in wait for him. Had they done so, a deed of violence must have followed which might have ended in imprisonment, if not worse.

No news came to them either from Maya or Tazoni; and a feeling of sullen disappointment began to pervade the men. But Martha's cunning brain was hatching some definite plots, destined to bear fruit in the after days.

Constant exercise and a life spent in the open air had rendered her old age a hardy one. Her memory was acute; and her physical powers far better than those of an ordinary woman of forty. From the Surrey common she would make journeys of two or three days' extent, passing quietly into London, and haunting some of its courts and by-streets where her face was familiar, and extorted a rough respect. In this way, by means only known to herself, she learned many things that should in the end bring about her vengeance upon her son, Luke Smeaton—the man who had been false to his mother, and, what is worse in the eyes of a gipsy, to his tribe. It was no mere excuse that Luke had urged against the capture of Maya; for he knew that henceforth the hand of his brethren would be against him until the day of his death.

Sometimes old Martha made her way into more fashionable quarters, and effecting an entry into the servants' hall, would reveal the future to some superstitious maid in exchange for a small piece of silver and a little gossip. In this last respect the old woman was insatiable, and welcomed every scrap of information that she could obtain.

Hence she obtained an entry into Northbridge House, in Grosvenor Square, and listened to the chatter of the servants; deftly leading them on to talk of their young master, and keenly catching at any little word that might give a clue to his movements. But the servants knew little of Lord Raymond. He was down at Northbridge, they believed—no, he wasn't in town, though he might perhaps be down at his house on the Thames.

Martha pricked up her ears at that.

"And so the young lord has a house on the river, has he? *Oh, yes, my dear, ye're bound to marry money.* Where did ye say the house was?"

But none of the servants could tell her; and it almost seemed that Martha would have to give up her task in despair, although that was the last thing she thought of.

Meantime Maya, little knowing the unwearying efforts that were being made by her kinsfolk for her rescue, had been pining away in her prison, unconscious of any means by which she might regain her freedom.

The servants were kind to her in their way, and really commiserated her; but they were powerless to help her, for they dared not connive at her escape.

During this unhappy period of her life, the gipsy girl felt grateful that Tazoni had led her to cultivate her taste for reading, since books were now her only solace.

One day, as she sat reading, she heard the hum of voices in the hall below; and presently one of the maids, who had treated her with the greatest consideration, ran upstairs to her, and said in an excited voice:

"Oh, miss, here's an old gipsy woman. She wants to tell our fortunes. Would you like to come down? Only you mustn't make a scene and get me into trouble."

The mere word "gipsy" struck a chord of hope in Maya's heart; for she thought it might be a member of another tribe, who would take a message for her, perhaps, to her own people. She was clever enough not to let the maid see her eagerness, and fenced with the demand for a promise of silence.

"I don't think I want my fortune told. The present is too dark; and the future I can only dread."

The maid felt sorry for her, and replied, kindly:

"But the old woman has some little charms, and canvas and silks for fancywork, miss. If you like, I'll teach you how to do it."

Here was Maya's excuse; and she took it without undue eagerness.

"Make haste, then, and come down, miss," admonished the maid, and ran downstairs as she spoke, leaving Maya to follow her. It was as well she came down alone; for what she saw gave her so sudden a shock that she staggered, and was obliged to hold to the stair-rail for support. There, sitting in the hall, with a box of fancy articles on her lap, was old Martha!

For a moment Maya thought she must cry out, or do something equally senseless; but the old gipsy's behaviour was a lesson to her. Martha's eyes were not raised the slightest part of an inch, though she knew that what she had been searching for was found at last. She quietly displayed her wares to the chattering maids, and used all her wiles to entice them to buy, just as though no such creature as Maya even existed.

The girl came slowly down, and stood at the back of the group; and at last her maid suggested that she should buy certain articles for the fancy-work, into the mysteries of which she was to be duly initiated.

"Tell yer fortune, lady dear?" said Martha at last. "Cross the old woman's hand with a bit o' silver, and she'll send ye a duke and four cream horses."

Maya saw from Martha's eyes that she should do as she was told; and having given her the requisite bribe, stretched out her hand with an unbelieving smile.

The maids gathered round, while old Martha began to croon over the hand in words only half intelligible to the maids, although, to Maya, they were full of hidden meaning.

"The pretty lady's life will be a bright one—*Maya, friends are near you.* I see carriages with horses, and carriages without horses—*To-morrow night, wait for the hand that shall save you.* Silks, satins, and flowers, all for the pretty lady—*don't let them suspect.* The lady is sad to-day; but love shall come, and wipe away her tears."

As soon as she had finished, the maids wanted their fortunes told; and by means of the same running under-current, Maya was advised to go upstairs as quickly as she could and stand at the window which was best for her escape; then when the household had retired on the following night, help should come to her. A quick flash of the girl's eyes told Martha that she understood.

The girls made a few more purchases, but Maya did not wait to see them completed, and went slowly upstairs, with Martha's words ringing in her ears like heavenly music.

Her bedroom and dressing-room looked out on the high-walled garden in front of the house through which she knew Martha would have to pass to get to the main road. The dressing-room was farthest from the rooms in which the maids slept, so Maya posted herself at this window, impatiently awaiting her deliverer's appearance.

At last she came, hobbling with feigned slowness along the gravelled path, calling back replies to the laughing maids who still stood in the doorway watching her go. One of them followed her to the gate to lock it carefully after her, and all the while old Martha gave never a glance back at the house.

Once outside the gate, however, she turned to say something to the maid who had accompanied her, and Maya saw her cast a sly glance over the front of the house, noting almost immediately the right window. At that same moment the maid also looked back at the house; but Maya had quickly hidden herself behind the curtains. She knew that old Martha had seen her, and in order to avoid suspicion she went back to the little sitting-room overlooking the river, where she invariably sat.

For the rest of the day she had a hard job to assume her sad, despairing manner; and the next—the last she hoped to spend in that hateful house—was a still greater difficulty. Try as she would to look unhappy, a smile would insist upon chasing the sadness from her face.

She trembled lest some small mishap should occur to spoil Martha's plans, and so prevent her escape. At night she went to her room, her heart beating rapidly. Directly the maid had left her, she redressed herself and stole into the next room, crouching in the darkness, while she waited for the help that was to come to her. But first she had taken care to unfasten the window, and raise the sash.

At last, after what seemed hours, she heard a faint click on the window-ledge; then there flashed a light, and a man leapt into her room. It was Colin! With a bound she caught his arm; but he laid his hand upon her mouth to warn

132

her to silence. Then he lifted her in his arms, and, getting out on to the window-sill, cautiously descended a rope-ladder. A moment later Maya felt that they had reached the ground. In a few more minutes Colin had climbed the wall, lifted her over by means of a noosed rope round her waist, and then she was in Martha's arms!

For a moment Maya fancied it must be another of her dreams, from she would presently awaken, to find she was still a prisoner in the house she had left. But something Colin was saying in a low voice brought to her the reality of her freedom.

"I saw two men prowling round a while ago. Take Maya home, and I'll come behind to see they don't follow."

So the two women hurried away through the country lanes to the spot where the gipsies had encamped; and at dawn they crept into the caravan that had been practically the only home Maya had ever known.

Colin and Zillah, who alone were in the secret, breathed not a word, and it was with great surprise and greater rejoicing that the rest of Maya's friends learned of her return. Martha would not let them question her, however, bidding them trust to an old woman's cunning to bring about, not only the return of their chief, but also the punishment of the man who had brought upon them all their troubles.

It proved, however, that Martha herself wanted some information, and after making Maya comfortable, she said she must know everything that had happened. It did not take the girl long to give a full recital, and while she sat listening, the old woman was a study for an artist.

"It was Lord Raymond's house ye were in, dearie, even though he didn't take ye away," she put in, as Maya tried to describe Denville; "the other one was just doing it for him. But tell me what the devil was like who got ye both away from the camp."

Maya could only give her a vague description of Luke; but when she mentioned the fact that he had used some words of Romany—although with a purposely distorted accent—Martha's shrivelled lips opened, and she snarled like a threatening wolf.

"That's him!" she exclaimed; "that's the black traitor! Oh, but I'll have my hands at his throat; and small mercy he'll get from me."

Suddenly she rose and left the tent; but in a few minutes she returned, and began to pack up the bundle which she usually carried with her on her journeys.

"Dearie," she said, "I be going to Northbridge again. I have work to do there, if the black traitor is to be punished, and Tazoni brought to his own again. Don't fear for yer safety. Every one of the men stands pledged to watch over ye night and day. To-morrow the camp is to follow me. Don't be afraid; no harm can come to ye, but keep close—keep close, dearie."

Maya, who owed her freedom to the sagacity of the old woman, could not but kiss her and promise to obey; and so they parted, Maya clinging to her to the last minute, and watching her bent but active form until it had disappeared.

The strain of assisting to nurse Lord Northbridge had told upon Veronica more than she believed, and her bitter misery at the thought that Tazoni was the thief who had entered the Hall and struck down the gentle old man, had also aided in undermining her health. Deep shadows had come beneath her eyes, and gradually she had lost her own happy manner, except in the sick-room, where she invariably contrived to be brightness itself. But she did not deceive the keen eyes of Doctor Browne.

"Miss Dartworth, I am going to advise you change of scene. I should suggest you went up to town for a few weeks—theatres, and a little amusement generally, is what you want—something to take you out of yourself."

When Lady Dartworth heard what Doctor Browne had advised for Veronica, she suggested that the girl should accept Gertrude Plunkett's invitation to spend a week or two with her in town. Lord Raymond was also in London, and Lady Dartworth was anxious that Veronica should meet him as much as possible, for she still desired that the marriage should be arranged.

"Go up and spend a couple of weeks with Gertrude," she said. "Your father and I may be coming up later; he has business in town, I believe."

So it happened, that a few days later, Veronica found herself in Lady Gertrude's arms, being gently reproved for allowing herself to get run down to such an extent.

"We must have a good time now you are here, Vee darling. Nobody very special is in town, I know; but I have got one or two nice young men who may amuse you."

"Who is the latest *protégé*, Gertrude?" asked Veronica, with a little laugh.

"Of course, if you're going to make fun of my little foibles, I shall pack you off bag and baggage back to your mother; so now you know you've got to behave yourself, my dear."

"But, Gertrude, I'm most interested," laughed Veronica, feeling better already for the tender, bantering tone of her friend. "Is it some nice young man, with long hair and a spiritual face, who writes ununderstandable poetry; or is it a new artist, with long finger-nails and a huge green tie?"

"There you go again; but as it happens you're wrong. This young man has done nothing great so far—only he's promising."

"Oh!" Veronica tried to look serious, but exploded into a peal of merry laughter; and so together the two women descended to the dining-room, where they lunched alone.

"And this young man—when shall I be allowed to worship at his shrine of 'abundant promise'?" asked Veronica, teasingly.

"I rather think he is staying in this very house," said Lady Gertrude, smiling. "We had an accident with the car, and the poor young man got very much hurt. Robert has taken a fancy to him, and has given him some work to do for him at the office. I'll 'phone Robert, and tell him to come home early to-night. We'll dine *en famille*. My young man is poor and very proud, and he usually refuses to dine with us if we have anyone here. But he simply must to-night. I'll say Harry

Beriford is coming—those two get on awfully together, and see a great deal of each other."

"Which, being interpreted, means that Harry hasn't been asked really; but that you'll ask him at once because you know he amuses me. Oh, Gertrude, I know you too well. You're one of the dearest frauds on earth."

Veronica stretched her left hand across the table, and Lady Gertrude gave it a friendly squeeze. She saw that the girl looked sad and worried, and determined that if she could do her any good, she would; while Veronica, looking into her friend's kind eyes, thought that here, at least, was a woman to whom she could confide the secret of her trouble.

Lady Gertrude had been one of three wealthy sisters, and had married beneath her, in the eyes of the world; but she had succeeded in making her friends appreciate the man for whom she had renounced a coronet. She made them recognize, too, that having married for love, she had no regrets, but was the happiest as she was certainly the kindliest of women. She could feel for those in sorrow, and—what is far more difficult—sympathize whole-heartedly with those who have achieved success.

That evening, Veronica was sitting talking to Sir Harry Beriford in Lady Gertrude's drawing-room, when Mr. Richard Francis entered. The hostess went forward to meet him, demanding whether he happened to know what was keeping her husband so long, since he had not returned and would not have time to receive his guests before dinner was announced.

"I can't say, I'm afraid. When I left there seemed to be nothing on hand to be done."

Veronica's heart leapt; then all the colour left her face. Everything seemed whirling about her, and she clasped her hands tightly so as not to lose her senses.

This, then, she told herself, was the way Tazoni had managed to elude the skilful search of the police. He was masquerading in her friend's house—he, who by right should be in a prison cell. But, indeed, he should not be allowed to deceive honest people any longer. She would denounce him herself.

"Mr. Francis, I want to introduce you to a very great friend of mine—Miss Dartworth."

Veronica raised her eyes and met those of Tazoni, the gipsy thief. No, she could not call him that, now she saw him face to face.

When he glanced at her, a great light transfigured his features, which, she was quick to notice, wore a tired, sad expression; but it died away, and he was acknowledging his hostess's introduction for all the world as though he had never seen Veronica before. That fact somehow hardened her heart against him; and she bent her head coldly, and almost immediately afterwards resumed her conversation with Sir Harry Beriford.

"You are wanted on the telephone, my lady," announced one of the servants presently.

With a murmured apology, Lady Gertrude left her guests to themselves; and Veronica could not help noticing upon what friendly terms Sir Harry Beriford appeared to be with the man who, as she believed, had broken into Lord North-bridge's house and nearly murdered him.

Once only, her eyes met Tazoni's; and then her scornful, accusing gaze fell before his look of honest purpose and devotion. After a few moments, Lady Gertrude returned.

"As I thought—it was Robert. He has been unavoidably detained, and hopes his guests will pardon him. He will not be long now, but we won't delay dinner for him all the same. Mr. Francis, will you take in Miss Dartworth? Harry, you must do your best to console me for Robert's absence."

Sir Harry Beriford laughed, and with a merry reply led his hostess to the dining-room. Tazoni's lips tightened as he offered his arm to Veronica, for he knew what she must think of him. His eyes were upon hers; and he saw that it was her intention to ignore him as far as possible.

"You cannot judge," he said, in a low voice.

She started and trembled, and his words angered while they tortured her with hope.

"Would an innocent man accept the hospitality of honourable people like Lady Gertrude, while his name stood before all the world stained and dishonoured?"

"You can only judge from outward appearances—you do not know everything; therefore you cannot judge at all, lady," he replied.

The old form of address sent the crimson colour to Veronica's face, and to hide her confusion she placed the tips of her fingers upon his arm, and they followed Lady Gertrude to the dining-room.

Tazoni talked well, but not much; and Veronica could not help feeling astonished that a man who was, after all, nothing but a gipsy vagabond, should be so self-possessed and well-bred among people who were immeasurably his superiors. Could it be possible that such a one could stoop to midnight robbery—murder almost? She determined to do as he had asked, and defer her judgment until she had heard his own version of the matter.

Lady Gertrude had resolved to have her revenge upon Veronica for her teasing manner over the "promising" young man; so she said, with an air of sweet simplicity—which, however, did not succeed in deceiving her guest, although for reasons Lady Gertrude could not guess, she pretended that it did:

"Veronica, I've been trying to teach Mr. Francis to play billiards. But you are better than I at the game; will you take him in hand?"

Tazoni's eyes were upon the girl's face, supplicating, pleading with her, and Veronica found herself saying, almost unconsciously, she would be pleased if she could be of any use whatever.

The two men left the dining-room with the ladies, and Veronica passed out with Sir Harry Beriford.

"Have you known Mr. Francis long?" she asked, in a low, constrained voice so that Tazoni should not hear.

"No, not long," he answered; "but quite long enough to know him to be the best-hearted and cleverest fellow I've ever met."

"You said once you made very few friends, Harry," she said.

"And I hope I may consider him one of them," was the reply.

"Are you coming to play billiards?" asked Veronica aloud, as they entered the drawing-room.

"No, I'm doomed to hammer away at some songs Gertrude has beguiled me into singing at one of her tea-and-bread-and-butter-with-a-little-music affairs," said Sir Harry, dolefully. "You won't listen to my wretched efforts, will you? Please go to the billiard-room, and 'shut hard' the door to keep the sound from roaming."

Veronica could not help laughing.

"I don't think that I will. I think listening to your efforts would be decidedly amusing. I remember a former occasion, you see, when you rapped Gertrude's fingers with a paper-knife and she threw the music at your head because neither of you could keep in time."

"We have both learnt better manners since then," said Lady Gertrude, demurely.

"Which is a hint to us to run away and play, I suppose," replied Veronica, moving slowly towards the door.

"I will try to show Miss Dartworth that I have had a good teacher, Lady Gertrude—even if I am a bad pupil," said Tazoni, smiling.

"In the circle of literary dullness that passes for wit, Veronica," laughed Lady Gertrude.

"I hope I fully appreciate it," answered Veronica; then she and Tazoni crossed the hall to the billiard-room.

"This is a farce—our playing—isn't it?" she asked, coldly.

"As you please," he replied, his eyes searching her face for a sign that she cared just a little for him still. "Miss Dartworth," he said suddenly, "you have got to hear my story from my own lips. I cannot bear your doubt of me any longer."

"And if I refuse to listen—judging for myself—what then?" His commanding tone had made her obstinate.

"Your duty would require you to give me up to the police," was the quiet reply.

She covered her face with her hands. Yes, he was right. If she would not listen to him, then, thinking what she did of him, she was bound to give him up to the police. That she could never do! And yet, to consent to listen to his story almost amounted to owning, that although she had believed him to be guilty, he had forced her to change her opinion as soon as she was brought face to face with him. That she was too proud to own.

"I will listen," she said, slowly; "but I will form my own opinion as to its truth."

"That is what I should wish," he replied, and his coldness hurt her like a blow.

"I am waiting for you to produce the proofs of your innocence," she said, impatiently.

"And I am almost compelled to admit that I have none," he answered.

Veronica sank into a chair, her face deathly white.

"What am I to understand from that?" she asked.

"I will not ask you of what you suspect me," replied Tazoni. "You believe me guilty of the robbery, and almost the murder, of Lord Northbridge; to which I would answer, that when that cowardly deed was committed I was miles away."

"Yes," she said, in a hard voice, "you ran away—*afterwards*."

"That's not true," he answered; and his voice, though low, rang with vehement truth. "I was searching for Maya, whom I had sworn to love and guard with my own life."

"Oh, the gipsy girl!" said Veronica, flushing.

"My adopted sister," he answered simply. "She was stolen from us that same night."

"But where were you?" asked Veronica, quickly.

"I"—he hesitated—"I had been tricked like a fool. While Maya was being lured away from us, I, her brother, was waiting patiently half a mile away, for one whom I had been led to believe needed my presence."

"Who was it needed you?" she asked, filled with vague surmise.

"I was told you needed me, lady," replied Tazoni, in a low voice.

Veronica rose, her face crimson.

"It is false," she said. "I never sent for you."

"I know," he answered, with bent head. "Listen! The night of the ball at Dartworth Manor a man came to the camp and told a plausible tale, which I, only too willingly, believed. He said that he came from you, that you wished to see me, that I was to do you some service. I was to go at once to the rose-garden where— where I had seen you before. Lady, I would have gone through fire and water to serve you. I listened, and believed. Maya was not so credulous; she doubted both the man and his message. But I was obstinate and went. I waited patiently for your coming, as I would have waited until death, had you commanded it, until I knew you would not come."

His eyes were fixed upon her face, as if he would read her heart; but she said no word; and he continued:

"With a heavy heart I returned to the camp, to find I had been tricked. Maya was gone; my oath to her dead mother had been a bitter mockery! I almost lost my reason, for the weight of my broken trust was upon my soul like a mill-stone. I vowed I would know no peace until she was found. I started off on horseback to fulfil my promise; and at the hour the robbery was committed at Northbridge Hall, I was on my way to London."

"And your proofs?" asked Veronica.

"I have none," he answered.

"That would not plead your case in a court of law," she said, not unkindly.

"I do not plead before the law, but before you," was the reply. "I will place myself in the hands of the law the instant Maya is found. Lady, I would go to prison with a smile upon my lips, if I knew you believed in my innocence."

Veronica's hands pulled nervously at the lace upon her gown.

"You—you have not told me if you have discovered who stole your sister from you," she said, suddenly.

"Forgive me, if I say I may not tell you," he replied, knowing full well that report had said she was to marry Lord Raymond sooner or later.

"How can I believe in you, then?" she asked.

"Lady, I keep silence for your sake," he answered.

A vague suspicion crossed her mind that she knew to whom he referred.

"Can you prove his guilt?" she questioned.

"She has been traced to his house," was the quiet reply.

"Your proof?"

"Sir Harry Beriford."

Question and answer came short and sharp.

"Does he know?" asked Veronica, eagerly.

"But very little," said Tazoni, hastening to silence her. "He is a true friend; one who—like Lady Gertrude and her husband—stretches out a helping hand without questioning 'why' and 'wherefore.' But for him, I should not have traced Maya even so far; with his aid, I hope to find that she has baffled her persecutor and escaped. Lady, I am in your hands."

The simple, direct appeal to her judgment went to Veronica's heart. With a frank confidence she held out her hand to him.

"I *do* believe in you," she said, softly. "I have done so all along, I think; only —only doubts crept in sometimes and tortured me, because of my faith in you."

He bent and kissed the hand he held; and when he raised his head, her eyes were bright with tears.

CHAPTER XXV

After a great deal of persuasion on the part of Lord Raymond, and a pretence of reluctance and suspicion upon that of Judy Slade, the clandestine marriage had been arranged to take place, by special licence, with the shortest possible delay.

At nine o'clock one morning, Miss Slade stood in her drawing-room putting on her gloves, when the door opened and Lord Raymond was shown in.

"Hullo, Judy," he exclaimed, boisterously, "getting nervous, now that the eleventh hour has come?"

"No," she faltered, and her nervousness was not altogether feigned; "I know I can trust myself to you, Geoffrey."

"Oh, of course you can," he said, rallying her.

She submitted to his embrace, and then descended with him in the lift to the street, where an electric brougham was in waiting to take them to Lord Raymond's hotel. When they were seated, he commenced to talk hurriedly and nervously; and Judy, fighting for calm, answered him almost at random. But by the time the car had stopped, she had regained all her old self-possession, and had begun to play her part to the best of her ability.

Hubert Denville received them in Lord Raymond's suite. "It's all right," he said; "you're a little behind your time. Come, Miss Slade, keep up your courage. Anyone would think you were going to be buried instead of married, eh, Raymond?"

He cast a sly glance at Lord Raymond, who replied by a very pronounced wink. So they entered the drawing-room. A man wearing a surplice, and carrying a prayer-book, flanked by another who looked like a City clerk, entered almost immediately.

Once or twice Lord Raymond seemed uneasy, but a glance at Hubert Denville's smiling face, or Judy Slade's nervously suspicious look, calmed his fears.

Then the little man with the clerk-like face produced a book, and said:

"Will you sign here, if you please, madam."

Miss Slade took up the pen and signed her own name for the last time.

"Now you, if you please, sir," said the little man to Lord Raymond.

"I? Er—is that necessary?" he asked, nervously.

"It's all right," whispered Denville; "they're in the know."

The little man was greatly surprised when he saw Lord Raymond wink slyly at him in a manner decidedly ill-bred. With a clumsy, nervous hand Lord Raymond wrote his name, without, however, glancing at the matter which he had attested. Then, the necessary business being over, the clergyman and the registrar were shown out.

"Good-bye, Denville," said Lord Raymond; "we'd better be off now, or we shan't catch that train."

"Yes, you're right. Hope you'll have a good time. Good-bye, Lady Raymond," said Denville, bending over her hand with an ironic smile, which was duly remarked by the newly-made husband. He was turning away with Judy when Denville added: "By the way, Raymond, don't forget that letter you asked me to post."

"Oh, yes," replied Raymond, with a sulky smile. "I had forgotten it. Here it is."

"Thanks. I'll post it for you," said Denville.

After he had seen the bride and bridegroom into their car *en route* for Paris, he returned to the hotel, and drawing from his pocket the envelope Lord Raymond had given him, extracted a cheque for a thousand pounds.

"The mean hound!" he muttered to himself. "He would have shuffled off without paying me. Oh, but I mean to make a nice little bit out of this marriage— one way and another."

Meanwhile Lord Raymond and his wife were speeding away towards Dover, travelling under the name of Westworth, for Raymond had persuaded the woman whom he thought he was deceiving, that it was highly desirable to keep the news of their marriage, secret for the present.

Paris soon palled upon him, however; and they had not been there more than a week when he declared they must return to London.

"Why, Geoffrey, I thought we were going to stay here a month?" said Judy, with a mixture of curiosity and annoyance, though she smiled her compliance.

"Oh, I'm sick of the place," he began, coarsely.

"And of me?" she interrupted, raising her eyebrows.

"I didn't say so," he replied, sullenly. "There, don't let's have any talk about it, but pack up and we'll catch the night-boat."

His wife's eyes were upon him, and he did not see the little smile that played about her lips, otherwise he might have felt far from comfortable concerning his future control over her.

On reaching London, Judy returned to her flat as Judy Slade for a little while longer; and Raymond went back to his hotel, where he found a letter from Lady Dartworth, containing a pressing invitation to dine at Dartworth House as soon as he returned.

"I'll go," he decided. "There's no time to lose. I'm like a man standing on a landslip; I must get on to firm ground as soon as possible. I'll go to-night."

Apparently the sense of insecurity was not merely confined to Lord Raymond, for the dinner at Dartworth House was to prove a great surprise to him, though the earlier part seemed much like other meals of which he had partaken there.

"Where have you been, Geoffrey?" asked Lady Dartworth, as they seated themselves at the dinner-table.

"Biarritz," he replied, without looking up from his soup.

"Oh! that accounts for your not having left your address at the club," said Lord Dartworth, who appeared to have been seeking him during the last day or two.

"I'm glad you got back before we left town," said Lady Dartworth. "Veronica and I go down to Dartworth the day after to-morrow."

"I have my hands tied with business, you see, Geoffrey," put in her husband, with a smile that barely masked the anxious look that lay beneath.

"Why don't you all stay in town, then?" asked Lord Raymond, impulsively. "Vee doesn't want to go back, do you?"

"I don't mind," Veronica answered, indifferently.

"You'll be coming down soon, I suppose?" said Lady Dartworth.

"Perhaps," answered Raymond. "I say, can't you and Vee stay a little while longer? I could take you both about a bit, you know. I'm not so much engaged now."

"That's very nice of you," replied Lady Dartworth, exchanging an intelligent glance with her husband. "I dare say we can manage it."

"That's right; and we'll give Vee the best time she's ever had," said Raymond, smiling across at Veronica in what he meant to be a winning way.

When the ladies left the room, Raymond asked, for the mere sake of conversation:

"How's business going, Lord Dartworth?"

"Bad," was the significant answer, and, for the first time, Lord Raymond noticed the careworn look on his face.

"What's up?" he asked, crudely.

"You remember me telling your father one night at Northbridge about a wonderful copper mine in which I was interested?"

"Yes, I do remember something about it," replied Raymond.

"Well, this wonderful mine, in which everybody believed, has shown itself to be, like everything else—uncertain; but so implicitly did some of us believe in it that we invested our all in it. I am one of the directors, and I have invested what now seems to be an enormous amount, and, what is more, I am liable for a still greater sum should the company fail. News has come to our agent that the water has got into the mine, and that the works are destroyed. So that, unless some almost miraculous relief arrives, we fail. If we do, not only the Dartworth estate goes, but my own money, my wife's, and Veronica's private fortune into the bargain. All the directors are sure that the mine will tide round, if only money can be brought in to stop the gap. Money is what we want, and that we cannot get, for already the bad news has got about, and the shares have fallen."

"How much do you want?" asked Raymond, chuckling inwardly with malicious pleasure.

"Fifty thousand," was the sad reply.

"Phew! That's a large amount."

"Yes, it is, I know. I shall be practically ruined if the mine is lost: but I hope to be able to save it. Indeed, I am sure I can do so if I can get someone to back me up. If your father were well enough, I would confide all to him; but it would be cruelty to trouble him in his present state of health. Geoffrey, you are the only person who can help me."

142

"How can I do that?" asked Raymond, with an assumed sympathy that warmed the elder man's heart towards him.

"I need not say it is bitter for me to ask even you, my boy, for the assistance; but necessity acknowledges no false sentiment. Geoffrey, upon your marriage you receive twenty thousand from the Northbridge estate——"

"Yes, but I'm not married yet," interrupted Lord Raymond with a smile.

"No; but give me a note of hand to the effect that you stand responsible; that is sufficient. With that I can raise the credit of the mine on the Exchange and give the public confidence."

Lord Raymond filled up his glass, and drank slowly and thoughtfully.

"Lord Dartworth," he said, "I think I can see an easy way out of your difficulty, and not an unpleasant one for me. Vee's fortune means a good deal to you, I know; perhaps it's something to me. Vee and I have known each other ever since we were children together; and I dare say we're fond of each other—at least I'm very fond of her, and I suppose she doesn't hate me. It would be a good thing to join Northbridge and Dartworth, eh? Anyway, I shall be very glad to marry Vee, if she'll have me, and you'll give her to me."

Lord Dartworth held out his hand in silence; then he said in a voice, low with feeling:

"If she will be your wife, I shall not wish to withhold my permission. Heaven knows I think it would be for her happiness, or I would not do so, if my life itself depended on it."

"Of course not," replied Raymond, with an ill-concealed sneer. "I'll make her happy right enough, never you fear."

When they reached the drawing-room, they found Lady Dartworth looking very sad over a letter she was reading.

"Geoffrey," she said, "I have bad news for you. Marion Smeaton died last night."

Veronica looked at Lord Raymond, fearing that the death of his foster-mother might affect him. What she saw, however, filled her with astonishment; for into his face had come a look of joy.

CHAPTER XXVI

It was a well-asserted fact at Northbridge, that Luke Smeaton was not only drunk almost every night, but that he also made away with a great deal of the game. Yet no one dared to say anything against him, for he had been placed above those who for years had been faithful to the interests of the Northbridge estate, when Lord Raymond made him keeper.

Luke Smeaton's salary, people said, must be a good one; for he always had plenty of money, and when intoxicated had often boasted that so soon as his present stock of cash ran out he knew where to get some more. He went further than that; for he had several times declared that Lord Raymond was completely under his thumb. The men he associated with at the "Blue Peacock" paid little attention to his bragging; but when a stranger happened to be present, which was very seldom, Luke was silent.

One night he was in a particularly boastful mood, as well as very excited with the quantity of beer he had consumed. Besides the usual frequenters of the "Blue Peacock," there was no one but a sleepy-headed farm-hand, of whom Luke took little or no notice.

"Well, and how be the young master, Mr. Smeaton?" asked one of the men, knowing that he was expected to lead up to Luke's favourite topic, since he had generously ordered drinks for the entire company.

"Oh, he's all right," said Luke, lighting his pipe and looking round with a tipsy wink. "He's all right, and so he'll continue while he keeps friends with me. I know how to manage him, boys. Ah, we've been partners in many a spree, and one as none of ye don't guess on. Lord Raymond—he knows he's got to keep in with me, or the trick's out. Go on, drink up, boys—plenty of money to pay for it all"—and Luke struck his pocket. "What's that chap a-doing in the corner there? Wake him up, Bill, and give him a drink."

The labourer trudged across the room, and shook the sleeping farm-hand by the shoulder.

"Here, wake up, sonny. Don't 'ee hear the gentleman a-askin' ye to have a drink? Why, what a stoopid face the youngster's got!"

The boy lifted his head, and stared round expressionlessly, then drained the tankard held out to him, and dropped into his sleepy attitude again.

"Never mind, sonny; you go to sleep," laughed Luke.

"Say, Luke," said one of his companions, who was jealous of his sudden and unaccountable prosperity, "Steward was a-saying on'y yesterday as how the birds was growing thin, and as he'd have to write and tell the young lord ye was a-makin' away with 'em."

"Let him!" roared Luke, in drunken defiance. "Who cares for the young lord? Not me! I'll do as I like with the birds; and ye may tell him as I says so. Why, I could have the whole blessed show if I liked to open my mouth wide enough. As for the old steward—I'll have him sent about his business. I'll show him I'm as great a man as him—greater'n anyone in Northbridge village."

"How yer tongue do run on, Mr. Smeaton," said Bill, warningly. "S'pose the young lord was to hear of it?"

"Young lord!" roared Luke, setting down a tankard he had just emptied of its contents. "He's no more a lord than I am! Who's afraid of him, the insolent, ungrateful young fool! Am I to run the risk o' being sent to quod without a 'thankee' for it? No, gen'lemen! I s-said, no, gen'lemen! Halves—half the ris-sk an' half the s-swag, see, gen'lemen? S'right, ain't it? Here, fill the gen'lemen's g-glass, can't you?"

"No, you've had too much already, Luke," said the landlord. "Time's up, we've got to close. Here, you chap, wake up!"

Taking the sleeping farm-hand by the shoulders, he shook him until he saw signs of waking in his sleepy customer. Then, with the aid of some of the men, he at length got Luke himself out into the road. The farm-hand followed a few moments later, and the landlord slammed the door and bolted it.

Finding the other men had all disappeared, the sleepy boy transformed himself into a very sharp and active individual, and was about to take a path that ran by the side of the inn when he collided with an old woman. The light that still shone from the window of the inn-parlour enabled him to catch a glimpse of her features.

"Hullo, mother," he muttered, with a dry laugh. "How's the camp?"

"Oh, ye're the detective from Lunnon, ain't ye?" she croaked.

"Mum's the word, if you please, old lady."

"Well, I guess you'll do as well as a parson. Marion Smeaton's a-dying, and wants to confess."

As soon as Tazoni found that Maya had gone from the house on the river, the thought had immediately come to him that some of his own people had been before him and helped her to escape. He thereupon made a secret journey to Northbridge to try and trace them; but they had, of course, left the common, and all their tracks were obliterated.

Nothing daunted, he borrowed a horse from Sir Harry Beriford, and often rode out into the country around London, thinking they might have gone in that direction, since they had at first thought that Maya had been taken there. He had almost given up hope of finding them, when one day he came upon the remains of a camp in Surrey. It might or might not have been theirs; but he managed to trace them some little way by signs which only a gipsy can decipher, and they seemed to be going in the direction of Northbridge. Soon, however, he lost the trail, and was forced to give it up. But he determined to go down there once more on the very first day he could leave London. Then, if he should find the tribe, and Maya with them, he would give himself up to the police, and allow the law to take its course. It might mean the vindication of his character, or it might mean imprisonment for a theft he had never committed; but, anyway, that was the only honourable course open to him.

Moved by his great respect and affection for Sir Harry Beriford, Tazoni had told him everything, and he had promised not only to go down to Northbridge with him, but also to stand by him through thick and thin. One morning, Tazoni took advantage of Sir Harry's offer to motor him down to Northbridge, and as they neared their destination, his keen eyes caught sight of four caravans drawn up on the common.

"They're here!" he exclaimed, excitedly. "Oh, I do hope Maya is with them!"

"So do I," put in Sir Harry. "I—I've got quite fond of Maya, don't you know. But I say, old chap, it won't be so merry and bright for you if she is."

"As long as she's there, safe and well, that's all I care about," replied his companion, springing from the car almost before it stopped.

Sir Harry hastened after him, leaving the car in the hands of the chauffeur, and was soon surrounded by a group of excited gipsies.

Detective Fraser, who happened to be crossing the common towards the encampment, heard enthusiastic shouts of "Tazoni! Tazoni!" and smiled to himself, as he muttered:

"I'd just like to know where that young man's been all this long time, and then I guess there isn't another thing about this case that's worth knowing, that I don't know."

In the camp Tazoni was greeted with wildest enthusiasm, while Maya threw herself into his arms in a way that made Sir Harry envious.

"Maya," said Tazoni at last, "I want to introduce a great friend of mine, who I hope will also be a friend of yours."

"He's ready made," replied Sir Harry, with a smile; "that is, if you'll accept him?"

For the first time Maya noticed his presence, and as her eyes rested on his face her lips quivered as she recognized him, and remembered where she had first seen him.

"Why, you are——!"

"I expect you're right, but I won't be, if you don't wish it?" said Sir Harry, with mock humility; so that she had to laugh away her sad memories on the instant.

"We are glad to have ye back, my son," Martha was mumbling over Tazoni's hand.

"And I'm glad to be with you, Martha," he replied; "but it won't be for long, I fear."

"Why?" she asked, her sharp eyes upon his face.

But he would not answer her, fearing she might try to dissuade him from his purpose.

"Tell us what has been happening to you," exclaimed Maya; "everything—this moment!"

Tazoni told his story, not forgetting Sir Harry's part in the matter; and the latter thought he had never seen such "awfully jolly" eyes—as he put it privately to himself—as those Maya turned upon him, full of sweet, warm gratitude for his friendship to Tazoni.

When the story was finished Tazoni asked Maya eagerly for tidings of Veronica. Martha answered him, and grudgingly told him that Miss Dartworth was to marry Lord Raymond that morning. Tazoni turned white as death, while Sir Harry exclaimed, incredulously:

"Oh, that's impossible! Why, I'm one of the oldest friends of the Dartworths, and I should have heard something about it if it had been true."

"It's been kept almost a secret—private, they calls it," said Martha, adding with a sardonic smile: "It's on account of the earl's illness, the young lord says."

The two men looked at each other.

"Do you think the Dartworths have any idea what a beastly villain they're giving their daughter to?" asked Sir Harry. "My boy, this is where your humble friend steps in and gives them all a piece of his mind."

Without another word, he was striding away from the camp with Tazoni, who had not spoken since he heard the news.

"Er—Mr. Tazoni, I'm afraid I shall have to arrest you."

The two men came to a sudden standstill and stared the detective—for it was he—in the face. Suddenly Sir Harry caught him by the arm.

"Look here, we've got a bit of business on hand; and don't you interrupt us, or I'll call a whole blessed squadron of gipsies out to settle with you. When our little business is done, we'll both come and give ourselves up, and let the law take its course, and 'anything-you-may-say-will-be-brought-against-you-at-the-trial,' and all that nonsense. But, for the present, we're to be let alone—and well alone, mark you!"

With his head high in the air, Sir Harry was marching off, when the detective placed himself before Tazoni, and said:

"Now that your highly humorous friend allows me to put in a word, I'd like to say that I have not arrested you yet, Mr.—er—Tazoni, but I shall be forced to do so if you go up to Dartworth Manor. I couldn't stand that."

"Why not?" asked Sir Harry, peremptorily.

"Because it would probably help a certain person to defeat the ends of justice. My plans are laid, and you must on no account interfere with them."

"But this marriage must not take place," interrupted Sir Harry.

"It probably won't," was the curious answer. "Anyway, I must ask Mr.—er—Tazoni to give me his word not to go up to Dartworth Manor until I send for him."

"We'll both do that," said Sir Harry; but the detective's eyes were upon Tazoni, who answered, quietly:

"I am in your hands. I give you my promise."

CHAPTER XXVII

A few days before his wedding with Veronica, Lord Raymond wrote a some-what curious letter to his friend Hubert Denville, who happened to be spending a few days in Paris.

> "DEAR DENVILLE,—I hope you'll find it convenient to return to town before next Tuesday. The fact is, I want you to come and look af-ter Judy Slade, for I'm afraid I'm going to have a deuce of a trouble in that quarter. I'm marrying Veronica Dartworth on the QT., and want to get the whole thing over before Judy hears about it, though you can never be sure that the papers won't get hold of the affair; and then not the very devil himself would keep Judy from coming down and mak-ing an almighty row. If you'll come and keep her out of my way until after the wedding, I won't forget you, my boy.
> "Yours,
> "RAYMOND."

Hubert Denville was greatly amused by the perusal of this letter. He had al-ready heard from Judy that she had managed to get wind of the marriage.

> "This, I rather think, is the opportunity for which you have been waiting, isn't it?" she wrote. "You step in and put a stop to the mar-riage and show what a villain he is, and thus earn the eternal gratitude of the Dartworths, including the hand, fortune, and affection of the daughter. Isn't that the game? If so, I suppose I can count upon you to back me up in this hour of bitter trial? I rather like the turn of that last sentence.
> "Au revoir,
> "JUDY.
> "P.S.—His lordship is here every day, and seems inclined to keep it up until the very end. I think he is rather fond of me personally, so that when the truth comes out, he may not be so fearfully mad that he has been caught; but for some reason, which I can't quite fathom, I have learnt that he is the prime mover in this marriage with Veronica Dart-worth. Why—do you know?"

But Hubert Denville did not wish to fathom why Lord Raymond wished to marry Veronica. It was enough for him that he believed the prize for which he had been striving was at last within his reach. Accordingly he packed up and left Paris, arriving in London in time to get a fresh bribe from Lord Raymond before he left town for Northbridge.

The day of the wedding broke with a promise of brilliant weather. The sun emerged from a bank of cloud, and filtered through the curtains of Veronica's room, touching with its light her pallid face and white-robed figure as she lay extended wearily upon the bed.

Her maid brought her some breakfast, and then through the open door of her dressing-room, Veronica could see them laying out something filmy white, that glistened here and there in the morning sunshine. Then it all flashed back upon her—it was her wedding morning!

With a moan, she buried her face in the pillows, feeling very like a prisoner on the morning of his execution. And there was no way out of it! If she wished to save those she loved from utter ruin, there was no other course open to her.

"Let me understand what I have to confront," she had said to her father when he had broached the matter to her. "Lord Raymond will lend us the money you require on the condition that I consent to become his wife?"

"You put it harshly—unnecessarily so," Lord Dartworth had replied, deprecatingly. "Geoffrey has promised to lend the money as unconditionally as he can do so. He cannot get the money till he marries."

So she had given her promise to marry Lord Raymond; but neither her father nor her mother had any idea how much that promise cost her.

When Veronica was completely dressed, and her bridal veil and wreath adjusted, she sent her maid away. She locked her door, and, going to her desk, opened a secret drawer and took from it Tazoni's book, on the fly-leaf of which beneath the pencilled poem, she wrote these words:

> "*Here our ways must part for ever. Forgive me.*
> "*Veronica.*"

Then she bound it up in a parcel, which she addressed to Richard Francis, c/o "The Social World."

At this moment Lady Dartworth knocked at the door, to tell her that the bishop had arrived, and to ask her to come down to see her father, who had been anxiously longing to speak to her. Veronica cast a look of sorrowful regret at the room which had been hers since early girlhood; and placing her hand in her mother's, she descended to the drawing-room.

The bishop, a relative, was talking to Veronica's only bridesmaid—for in every way the marriage was to be a quiet one. This was in accordance with the wish of Lord Raymond, who had urged his father's illness as an incontestable excuse.

The ceremony was to take place in the private chapel attached to the Manor, and only the chief tenants of the two estates and the family servants had been allowed to attend, besides a few very intimate relatives of the bride and bridegroom.

As in a dream, Veronica entered the chapel upon her father's arm; and she did not once glance up at Lord Raymond's face as he stood beside her. Out of some far distance the bishop's voice came to her as he began the service; and Veronica wondered if it really had anything to do with her, or whether she was listening to a service that was being read for someone else.

"I require and charge you both, as ye will answer at the dreadful day of judgment . . . that if either of you know any impediment why ye may not be lawfully joined together in Matrimony, ye do now confess it."

A slight noise at the back of the chapel made Lord Raymond turn suddenly pale, and he gave a gasp of horror as the commotion increased, and someone said:

"I forbid this marriage!"

"By what right do you forbid the marriage?" asked the bishop, sternly.

A closely veiled figure stepped forward and confronted him.

"My right to forbid it is unquestionable. I am Lord Raymond's wife."

"Judy Slade!" gasped Lord Dartworth, as the intruder threw back her veil. "Is —is this true?" he demanded of Lord Raymond, in a hoarse voice.

"No," he shouted, "it isn't. It's all a lie. You fool!" he said, coarsely, to Judy. "You're not my wife. The whole thing was a plant."

She took a step towards him, laughing softly.

"It's you who have been fooled," she said. "The marriage was a genuine one; you fell into the pit you thought you had dug for me. You are my lawful husband, as I am your lawful wife."

"Where is your proof?" demanded Lord Dartworth.

"Here is my witness, who has in his possession the certificate of my marriage," replied Judy.

As Hubert Denville stepped forward with his cynical smile, Lord Raymond knew that he had been finely caught. What else might come out, he did not dare to think. He would leave the country at once, having got as much money from Northbridge as he could at a moment's notice. Then he would be freed from Luke Smeaton, and the whole circle of his troublesome friends. A dream of a golden future in some South American city rose suddenly before his mental vision, to be instantly dispelled by a not over gentle hand laid upon his shoulder.

"Lord Raymond, I arrest you for burglary, with violence," said Detective Fraser's hateful voice.

CHAPTER XXVIII

The sun, filtering through the stained-glass windows, the song of the birds that came through an open door leading into the Dartworth grounds, the sanctity of the chapel—all seemed at such variance with the shock that had fallen upon the little congregation like a thunderbolt, that there was hardly one amongst their number who did not believe he would wake up soon to find it nothing but a curious dream.

Veronica alone was fully alive to the significance of the words spoken by the sleepy-looking detective. To her it meant the complete exculpation of the man she loved. It meant that her trust in him had been justified, and she was content.

Since Lord Dartworth was the nearest magistrate, the detective called upon him to act in his official capacity, and, having heard the evidence against the prisoner, give an order for his commitment.

To Lord Dartworth himself, it seemed as if the world had come suddenly to an end. He had looked upon that day as that of the salvation of his house; and, almost in an instant, all his cherished hopes were banished, and he was brought face to face once more with ruin.

He seemed to have grown suddenly into an old man, and Veronica felt full of pity and tender love for him, as she realized the maze of trouble through which he was about to pass. She had been willing to sacrifice her life's happiness to save him from it, but all to no purpose.

Only Veronica, besides the detective, seemed to be perfectly self-possessed; and as she slipped her hand through her father's arm, she took occasion to whisper:

"Courage, father dear; it may not be so bad as you fear."

Veronica's calm in the face of the danger from which she had so narrowly escaped surprised Lord Dartworth, and awakened him to a sense of his responsibilities. In a low voice he asked the detective to bring his prisoner to the dining-room, together with such witnesses as might be necessary.

It was arranged that the proceedings should be conducted as quietly as possible, and although the little congregation was naturally consumed with curiosity, no one not absolutely connected with the case was allowed to enter the room that had been fixed upon as a court of justice.

Lord Raymond looked wildly round for some means of flight; but his arms were immediately held by two stalwart constables. Even if it had not been so, he knew that not one of the crowd, composed mostly of servants and tenants of the joint estates, would help him to escape. They had always looked upon him with feelings of dislike, and it was not likely that their feelings were going to change when he was arrested for committing such a heinous crime as robbery with violence. Where that crime had actually taken place was still a secret; but that did not lessen the ugliness of the charge against him.

Only Lady Dartworth—who had always insisted upon believing nothing but good of him—refused to think there was any foundation for the charge.

"Whatever they may say against you, I don't believe it, Geoffrey," she managed to whisper to him as they made their way out of the chapel. But Lord Raymond's face was decidedly discouraging to anyone who ardently desired to consider him innocent, and his partisan could not help feeling that his case was a poor one.

As for Judy and Hubert Denville, it would be hard to conceive the surprise and chagrin they were experiencing. They knew Lord Raymond's despicable nature, and they had not scrupled to play upon it; but that he should have stooped to such wickedness as the crime of which he was accused had not entered their calculations.

"Pretty fine 'surprise-packet' you've laid hold of," remarked Denville in a low tone of sarcasm.

Judy's face looked hard and bitter.

"But it doesn't make any difference to the fact that I'm the future Countess of Northbridge, does it?"

"Oh, no, no. You may not be received, that's all," was the biting answer. "Anyway, we'll stay and see the game out," Denville added, and offering her his arm, they followed the others to the dining-room.

Lord Dartworth seated himself in a high-backed chair at the top of the table, while the prisoner stood facing him at the foot. It was but natural, as the eyes of the two men met, that they should call to mind how many, many times they had sat together at that same table—the one extending, the other ungraciously accepting, a generous hospitality.

"You have all your witnesses here?" asked Lord Dartworth, in a dull, hopeless voice, of the detective.

"I have sent word that they should be brought here, my lord. If I may say so they are all at hand."

"Proceed at once, then," was the cold answer.

The detective smiled slightly beneath his lank moustache. He had not expected that Lord Dartworth would welcome the news that his intended son-in-law was a common thief. However, Mr. Fraser was very pleased with himself because his task was now well-nigh accomplished; and this same satisfaction made him appear more wide-awake than usual as he opened his case. In that moment Lord Raymond realized what a mistake he had made in thinking that this weak-eyed little man was nothing but a fool.

"My lord," began the detective, "with your permission I would inform you that, by power of a warrant from London, we have this morning arrested Luke Smeaton on the charge of burglary, and by the same warrant we have arrested the prisoner here on a charge of burglary, with violence. The charge also includes the attempt to obtain, under false pretences, the title and estates of Northbridge, and of the wilful personation, by the prisoner, of the heir-at-law."

"It's a lie! I don't know anything about it!" cried Raymond, clinging to a straw.

"The man, Luke Smeaton—the prisoner's father, my lord—has made a deposition in gaol, to the effect that the prisoner was cognisant of the true facts of the case when he committed the burglary at Northbridge Hall."

Lord Dartworth's astonished gaze was turned upon the trembling, white-faced impostor. For the fraction of a second no one spoke; then the woman who had so confidently believed herself to be the future Countess of Northbridge gave a cry of baffled hate. Instantly Hubert Denville's fingers were upon her wrist, compelling her to silence, and save for him, no one else heeded her. She had played high—and lost. But she had faced the risk.

"I would ask that Martha Smeaton be brought, my lord," said the detective, and the constable who guarded the door went out and returned with the gipsy woman. As she caught sight of Raymond, her wrinkled face was wreathed in smiles, and she began to chuckle in a horrible way, until Lord Dartworth called her sternly to order with the command to tell them all she knew.

"I was present when the babies was changed," croaked old Martha, "and I took the other one away in my arms."

"Then you were an accessory," said Lord Dartworth, sternly.

"King's evidence, my lord," put in the detective, in a low voice.

"Where is your next witness?" demanded Lord Dartworth.

"We have a statement here, my lord, made by Marion Smeaton, the prisoner's mother, duly attested by her in the presence of Martha Smeaton and myself, who witnessed her signature. We have also another document, duly signed by her, stating that she saw the prisoner as he left the room where the assault was committed, and recognized him in spite of his disguise."

"Next, my lord," continued the detective, "we have the deposition of Lord Northbridge himself, who states that the man who struck him is no other than the prisoner."

In the pause that followed, Lady Dartworth was heard sobbing quietly, while Veronica strove to comfort her. She was weeping partly out of sympathy for poor Lord Northbridge and his great trouble, partly from pity for herself, and the utter collapse of her radiant dreams for her daughter's future.

As for Lord Raymond, his face was white with fear. He looked more like a trapped rabbit than anything else, as one of the constables remarked. Yet many, as so often happens, pitied the poor craven thing; he was too despicable for resentment, even from those who had most cause to hate him.

"My lord, I would call Tazoni, the gipsy," said the detective, in his business-like way; and then suddenly, to the surprise of all present, Veronica cried out:

"He is innocent, father. He saved my life—he is the most upright man I know."

Lord Dartworth's eyes were upon her face, so pale and beautiful beneath the drapery of her rejected veil; but he said no word, for the thought that he had so nearly sold the daughter he loved into a bondage worse than death almost choked him.

At that moment the constable brought in Tazoni, who was accompanied by his staunch ally, Sir Harry Beriford.

"My lord," continued the detective hurriedly, in order to cover Veronica's interruption, "as you are aware a reward has been offered for the apprehension of this gentleman, and having been arrested, it was necessary that he should be brought before a magistrate. But I may as well intimate that there is not a tittle of evidence against him, other than that which emanated from the fertile brains of the prisoners, Luke and Geoffrey Smeaton, and this has been proved to be a fabrication. They had a powerful motive for wishing to get him out of the way. The gentleman known as Tazoni, the gipsy, and in London by the name of Mr. Richard Francis, is the rightful heir-at-law to the Northbridge estate."

For a moment deep silence followed his words; then, unable to bear the tension any longer, Sir Harry Beriford ejaculated:

"By Jove! How jolly!" and began to shake hands with everyone.

"For Heaven's sake get me out of this," murmured Judy to Hubert Denville, and as the constable closed the door behind them his face broke into a broad grin.

"I guess they've been bit as was going to do all the biting theirselves," he whispered to a comrade.

Meantime Lord Dartworth had grasped Tazoni's hand and shook it warmly.

"This is the only gleam of happiness in the darkest day of my life," he said, and his face was shadowed with deep sadness as he prepared to make out the commitment order for the man whom he had once looked upon as the son of his best friend.

Tazoni turned from her father to Veronica, and with a radiant face took her outstretched hands in his.

"Oh, thank God, thank God!" she murmured.

Then her wonderful self-control gave way at last, and she fell in a senseless heap at the feet of the man she loved, her wedding finery forming a white cloud about her.

CHAPTER XXIX

"God bless you, my son," murmured Lord Northbridge, later on, on that eventful day, as he placed his hand upon Tazoni's head. "God bless you! Veronica has spoken to me about you many times, and I learned first of all to see you with her eyes. So that now I find I am not altogether unacquainted with my long-lost son."

"I have been lonely all my life, I think," said Tazoni in a low voice; "but now I have found home, friends, father, all in a single day, and I don't know how to feel grateful enough for them."

For long hours Lord Northbridge talked with his son, and every moment that passed made each of them more grateful that Providence had ordered that they should meet after so many years in the sweet, tender joy of new-born love.

Tazoni opened his whole heart to his father, and he saw that here, at any rate, he had a son who was worthy of his affection.

"I want to speak to you about Veron—Miss Dartworth," said Tazoni. "I love her, and believe she loves me. I want to marry her, with your permission, sir."

Lord Northbridge smiled as he answered, softly, "I wish you joy with all my heart, my son," and held out his hand to Tazoni, who clasped it in contented silence.

Towards evening, Lord Dartworth called to see his old friend, to congratulate him. He looked very worried and anxious, but endeavoured to cast aside all thought of his troubles while in the sick-room.

Lord Northbridge, who seemed much stronger and better, asked to be left alone with him, and Tazoni left the two old men together for a while.

"Dartworth," said Lord Northbridge, softly, when Tazoni had gone, "you and I have been friends through many a long year, and it has always been our unspoken wish, I know, that that friendship should be yet more surely cemented by the marriage of our children. Dartworth, my son loves your daughter, and I have been led to think that Veronica does not altogether dislike my son—the son that was lost and is found. He has asked my permission; he now asks for yours. May I tell him you will not withhold it?"

The two men's hands clasped, and Lord Dartworth said, brokenly:

"It is my own desire, since Veronica loves him. This day is going to end better than I'd ever dared to hope. Northbridge, I was on the verge of selling my own flesh and blood to a man whom she hated."

Then he poured out the story of the difficulties that had led him to give his consent to Veronica's marriage with the man he had been led to look upon for so long as Lord Raymond. When he had finished, Lord Northbridge said quietly:

"You should have come to me, Dartworth. I am never too ill to help my best friend."

Once more the two men grasped hands; and then Tazoni was sent for, and Lord Dartworth told him, a little brokenly, that he would be proud and pleased to accept him as a son-in-law if Veronica returned his love.

"May I go to her at once?" he pleaded.

"Hasn't she had enough excitement for to-day?" asked Lord Dartworth, smiling.

"Well, I won't say a word to her about love and marriage," said Tazoni, with a happy laugh. "It's just to see her, you know——"

"And talk about the weather, I expect," interrupted his father, laughing too. "I know, I know. I was in love myself once," and he broke off with a sigh as he thought of the sweet young wife he had lost so long ago, and whom he had never ceased to mourn.

"Go, my son," he said softly, "and may you find your happiness, as I, too, found mine when I won your dear mother's love."

So Tazoni went, and taking the old bridle-path through the Northbridge and Dartworth woods, he made his way first of all to the caravans on the common, for he had a mission to perform before he sought Veronica.

In the gipsy camp he was greeted with wild enthusiasm, and it was with his heart full of deep affection for these wandering people that he returned their embraces and thanked them for their congratulations.

Martha was one of the loudest in giving him a welcome to their midst; but she made no allusion to the fact that she had been partly instrumental in bringing about the change of children; nor by word or look did Tazoni himself ever mention it to her, either then, or in the happy after-days.

"Maya," whispered Tazoni, as he bade them all good night, "in the morning I shall come and take you up to the Hall with me. You are my little sister, and so you will always be, I hope."

"But I shall always be a gipsy," she replied, significantly.

Old Martha chanced to overhear her words, and said in a curious, dull voice that held the attention of all the rest:

"Nay, dearie, the day of the gipsies is past now. Soon they will disappear from the face of the earth, and a lost people they'll be; for they'll never, never return. Only now and again will a word of the Romany pass between friend and friend; then they will go away and forget. And the gipsy tongue will die out, at last, and the old songs and stories will be forgotten, too. The little children of the Gentiles will read about us sometimes, and they will be sorry that our caravans are seen no more upon the highways, nor our campfires upon the moors."

The queer Romany words fell from her lips in a prophetic croon, and each one who listened saw the coming of the days of which she spoke when they and their people should be as nothing but a memory.

When Tazoni bade his friends good night, and walked away with his beloved violin under his arm, his thoughts were full of the little company of wanderers over whom he had been master for three years, and whom he had looked upon as his own kinsfolk ever since he could remember. He would do all he could for them, he thought, and perhaps he might be able to persuade them to settle down at Northbridge under his affectionate care.

As he passed out of the woods he put his violin under his chin and began the plaintive melody he had played on the morning when he had first met Veronica. Something told him that she would be waiting for him in the rose-arbour, just where they said good-bye to each other at that same hour years and years ago. So he played on and on, wooing her with music, calling to her soul, and whispering that he loved her.

And Veronica in the old stone arbour sat and listened, her face radiant, her joy complete.

So he found her in the sweet summer dusk, and they knew that the happiness of their mutual love had come home to them at last.

The next morning Tazoni spoke to his father of Maya.

"She is like my own sister," he explained. "I promised faithfully I would look after her always, and with your permission, sir, I should like to do so still. I made one foolish blunder which caused her a great deal of trouble and anxiety; but I hope to make up to her for it to the best of my ability."

"That you shall," replied Lord Northbridge. "Since she is your adopted sister, it necessarily falls out that she is my daughter, doesn't it?"

"That is very generous of you," said Tazoni, greatly moved by his father's kindness to one whom he only knew as the adopted sister of his new-found son.

"You will like her, I know, sir," Tazoni added. "She is not without education, for she showed great ability under the old schoolmaster's teaching. I would like her to go to some good school for a year or so, to mix with girls of her own age. You will be very proud of your adopted daughter, then."

"And my other daughter that is to be?" asked Lord Northbridge, with a happy smile.

"Veronica and I want to be married as soon as possible," said Tazoni, his eyes bright with eagerness. "Then we wish to take you abroad, sir—the doctor says you ought to go at once."

"Oh, come, come!" laughed Lord Northbridge, "that's quick work. And what about the honeymoon? Two's company, and three's none, remember."

"Yes, but a newly found father is only half—and two-and-a-half make very good company indeed, sir."

"Your arithmetic is not very convincing," was the smiling reply, but the old man's face was radiant with happiness.

Lord Northbridge soon became attached to Maya; indeed, he loved her already for her deep affection to the son upon whom his heart was centred.

However, before Lord Northbridge's intentions with regard to Maya were made known, Sir Harry Beriford, who was ostensibly staying at the Hall, but who spent a great deal of his time up on the common near the gipsy caravans, came to Tazoni and said, with a mysterious smile:

"I say, you'll have to resign your position as head of the illustrious order of gipsies, won't you? Really I think you'd better appoint me in your place. I'd fill it most excellently, and—er—I'm very fond of Maya."

When, however, he heard that Lord Northbridge intended adopting her, he remarked:

"Well, I don't suppose she could wish for anything better; and I'm glad it should be so. All the same, I can't say I thank you for interfering with my own little game."

Tazoni's eyes met his, and it was evident they understood each other perfectly, for a moment later their hands met in a grasp of friendship.

After all, Maya did not go to school, as Tazoni had suggested, for Lord Northbridge thought that if she went abroad it would be an education for her. It was necessary for his health that he should travel, and it was impossible for him to accompany Tazoni and Veronica.

It was really remarkable the number of places at which they ran across Sir Harry Beriford; and at last he was audacious enough to suggest he should join them for good and all. As his intentions with regard to Maya were pretty obvious, Lord Northbridge accepted him as a travelling companion, and pretended to be perfectly blind to the possibility that they might be in love with each other, until his consent to their engagement was sought for and gladly given.

The trial, to which all had been looking forward with so much pain, came and passed away. It was a severe sentence; but no one could help feeling that it was deserved.

As for the woman who had once believed herself to be Lady Raymond, she suddenly disappeared, and although Veronica did her utmost to find her, she never succeeded in learning what had really become of her.

One person alone knew of her whereabouts, and from time to time visited her in the little French town where she had hidden herself. The occasions when Hubert Denville visited her were the only bright spots in her miserable life. As for Denville himself, he succeeded in trapping an American heiress, to whose heart he had been laying siege at the same time that he was trying to snare Veronica Dartworth. He had always believed in having more than one iron in the fire, and his theory had worked out well. Anyway, his little American wife adored him, so that they were both well satisfied.

One day, during the course of the happy honeymoon which Tazoni and his wife were spending in Egypt, Veronica broached a subject that lay very near her heart.

"Dearest," she said, raising her husband's hand to her lips, "when Geoffrey Smeaton comes out of prison I want you to do something for me, will you?"

"With all my heart," he replied, knowing full well what her generous nature was prompting her to say. "May I guess, sweetheart?"

"Oh, you thought it yourself, too—I'm so glad," she cried. "It would be so awful when he comes out—no home, no friends, no anything at all—and we—

we have so much."

He took her in his arms and kissed her trembling lips, sealing the promise which in after years he faithfully redeemed.

So it was that when Geoffrey Smeaton came out of prison—a broken, penitent figure—a hand was stretched out to help him, a door was opened to receive him, a welcome generously extended to him at the very hearthside where he had once been a usurper. But it was not for any length of time; he only survived his release from prison for about a year.